I0585972

CHANCE & LACEY

SARAH DELANY

Copyright © 2022 Sarah Delany

All rights reserved. No part of this book may be used, reproduced or stored in a retrieval system, or transmitted in any form or by any means electronic, mechanical, photocopying, recording or otherwise, without express written permission of the publisher except in the case of brief quotations embodied in critical articles or reviews.

The characters and events portrayed in this book are fictitious. Any similarity to real persons, living or dead, businesses, or locales is coincidental and is not intended by the author.

Graphic Design (Cover) - Michael Pati Fuiava

Editing & Proofreading - Rebecca Andrews

ISBN: **978-0648814436**

To all the kids who grew up in the nineties who wish they could go back to a simpler time when life was easy and carefree.
This book is for you.

CONTENTS

Prologue

LACEY 1994

22ND NOVEMBER

These ten seconds are the best part of my day. He's waiting for me so we can climb our tree together like we do most days after school. I silently watch him for a few precious moments unnoticed, before he senses me. He's entranced by the blaring music pumping into his ears through his headphones. His walkman, his most prized possession he is never without, plays one of his favourite songs 'All I Want For Christmas Is You' by Mariah Carey. With his back to me, he uses his goofiest dance moves, the ones you use if no one is watching. He doesn't realise I live to see these moves as they are the highlight of my day.

He begins to sing out loud which is my cue to step out from behind the big weeping willow tree trunk, my hiding place, and pretend I just arrived and haven't been spying on him. Belting out the lyrics, he whips around as the smile spreads across my face. As he realises I'm standing there, his singing quietens and feels more intimate for some reason. It's as if he's singing the words to me and not doing it to make me laugh. He takes a slow, tentative step forward, never breaking eye contact, grabs my shaggy blonde locks off my shoulder, gives it a hard tug while at the top of his lungs screaming out the last line of the song, making me full on belly laugh. The moment is broken, like it never happened and we are back to being friends. The best of friends.

CHANCE

22ND NOVEMBER

She thinks she's so smart and can sneak up on me. Little does she know I can always feel when she's near. I have my very own Lacey detector built in. I can't wait for this moment, it's the favourite part of my day because it's when I get to see her true self shine through. No more pretending or faking. She drops the mask and for a short time, I get to see the real her. The most beautiful girl I have ever seen. My best friend.

Doing my coolest dance moves, which I'm sure she secretly likes, I bob my head in time to the beat. With my best singing voice, I sing along to one of my favourite jams. Pretending I'm oblivious to her presence, which is no easy feat, I pivot around feigning shock like I've been sprung by her. I catch a glimpse of her smile. A rare, magnificent sight because it's a real smile. I know because you can see it in her sparkling blue eyes. Transfixed on those baby blues, I sing softer. At this moment, I'm a boy singing his heart out to a girl. I slowly step forward, yank her hair and belt out the song to break the moment. Tugging out my headphones, I let them dangle towards the ground so I can hear my favourite sound in the whole world. Her perfect, uncensored laugh.

Every day after school we meet at the big, strong tree towering between our backyards, standing guard over our homes. You see Lacey is my neighbour as well as my best friend. She has been since her family moved into the house next door to mine over two years ago.

You know those moments in your life, the ones you feel are going to change your life in some way? Well the day I met Lacey when I was six years old was one of those moments for me. I knew deep in my bones, my life had been changed forever.

CHAPTER 1

CHANCE 1992

7TH MARCH

A black SUV pulls into the driveway next door to my house where we live in a small suburb in Auckland, New Zealand. The front doors open and out climb a man and a woman. They aren't what catch my attention though. My focus is on the back door where a young skinny girl jumps out. She is wearing pink tights, a pink tutu and an even brighter pink t-shirt. She has shaggy blonde hair and the bluest eyes I have ever seen. I know right then my life will never be the same.

"Lacey, sweetheart, come inside and see our new house," the lady calls to her. Lacey. The perfect name for a pretty girl. Peeking out from behind my blue curtains, I watch as she skips up the driveway to the front steps before her pink blurry form disappears behind the door.

The next day, the day I officially meet Lacey, it is raining heavily. The sky is angry and keeps storming, making the thunder crash and the lightning strike. I'm in my room watching the droplets of water race down my window because my mum won't let me play outside. Being stuck inside is the worst because there's never anything to do. My fluffy white dog Bronco, my faithful companion, doesn't like being cooped up inside either.

I've been at school for over a year now but I'm not good at making friends. The kids make fun of me because I have a big scar that runs along the right side of my face. It trails from my eyebrow to the bottom of my jawline. My mum says my scar makes me unique but it doesn't stop the kids making fun of it. Their favourite taunt for me is scarface.

As the rain trickles down my window, a pink blur moves across the neighbour's yard. Squinting through the rain to get a better look, I see her scruffy blonde hair bobbing up and down as she runs. Where is she going in this horrible weather? My eyes follow her as she runs towards the huge weeping willow tree.

The tree is my favourite place to play. The base branches out so I can easily climb to the higher branches. I don't want to be stuck inside when Lacey is outside in the rain so I put on my blue raincoat and matching gumboots to join her.

Sneaking down the hall to the back door, I make my escape out into the icy cold weather before my mum can catch me. My rubber gumboots slip and slide racing towards the tree, all the while being pelted by the harsh rain drops.

Standing at the base of the tree, I catch sight of a pink tutu disappearing into the tree branches so I yell to her, "Hey, what are you doing in my tree?"

"Who are you?" she yells from where she's sitting in the tree.

"I'm Chance Alexander and you're in my tree," I yell back to the pink ball above me. Does she wear anything besides pink? Ugh girls.

"Well this tree is half mine. My daddy said so," she squeals at me.

"If you behave, I'll share it with you."

"No, if you behave then I'll share it with you," she counters. Ugh this girl is already giving me a headache. Are girls always this annoying?

"Fine, we can share the tree then Lacey," I concede, not wanting to fight any more.

"How do you know my name? Have you been stalking me?" she squeals again. Her high pitched voice makes my ears ring, maybe it was a bad idea to come out here.

"No, I saw you arrive yesterday and heard your mum call out to you. I'm not stalking you," I explain.

"Then how did you know I was out here if you weren't stalking me?" she asks. Does she always ask so many questions?

"I was watching the rain and saw your scruffy little head running in the rain. I thought I'd come out and play with you but if you don't want me to then I'll go back inside," I say to the strange girl.

"Fine. Can you climb?" she asks.

"That's a stupid question. This is my tree, isn't it?" I tell her, huffing.

"Half your tree, remember. The other half is mine," she says.

"Fine. Half my tree," I say, as the wind whips around me and a chill crosses my wet face.

"Well, what are you waiting for? Come on," she says, with a hint of a smile in her voice.

Wasting no time at all, I grab hold of the familiar branches and pull myself up. I've climbed this tree a million times and know it like the back of my hand. It doesn't take me long before I'm straddling a branch opposite the strange girl, dressed all in pink. Once I'm sheltered from the rain, I lower my raincoat hood causing her sharp intake of breath as she covers her mouth with her hand.

"What happened to your face?" she asks. The kids at school never asked me what happened; they made fun of me when they saw it.

"My mum said I got it from the car accident that killed my dad but I was too little so I don't remember," I tell her honestly.

"Aww I'm sorry. Since you're sharing your tree with me, how about I share my dad with you. He's the best daddy ever."

"Thanks," I reply.

She stares at me for such a long time after that, I'm worried she is going to react like the other kids but then she says, "Instead of your scar making you sad and thinking of your dad, you should tell people a bear attacked you."

I can't help but smile and say, "What about a shark attack?" making her laugh.

"I know, how about an alligator bit you?" she squeaks in between bouts of laughter.

"Or it could have been a stingray."

"What's with you and sea animals?" she asks.

"I like the ocean and sea creatures," I tell her.

"That's cool," she says, without any amusement in her voice. The other kids at school always laugh at me because of my fondness for sharks and dolphins.

"Do you want to be my friend?" My cheeks blush, waiting for her reply. I've never had a friend so I don't know how it works. She looks at me and tilts her head to the side like she's considering it.

"Okay," she says, and my heart nearly leaps out of my chest. I've finally made a friend, even if she is a bit weird with her unbrushed scraggy hair and her bright pink clothes.

We stay out there talking and laughing until the rain pours harder. Lacey's shivers increase but she doesn't look like she wants to move.

"Let's head home Lacey, I'm getting cold," I tell her, so she thinks I'm the reason we have to go. I don't want her getting sick because then we can't play together until she's feeling better. It's a purely selfish move on my part.

"Okay," she says. Manoeuvering down the wet branches, I take my time so as not to fall.

"Be careful, the tree gets slippery when it's been raining," I inform her. My feet land on the now squishy grass at the base of the tree. Lacey is above me on a branch. She slides her legs over the side and tries to lower herself but the branch is too wet and she loses her grip.

"Lacey!" I scream, watching in slow motion as she falls backwards, hitting the base of the tree then continuing to the ground. I rush to her side as she clutches her arm to her chest.

"It hurts, Chance," she cries, as tears mix with raindrops dripping down her face. I don't know what gets into me but I gather Lacey into my arms and stumble my way back to Lacey's house and wail at the front door for help. The door flings open and a man looks at us. When he sees Lacey his eyes widen.

"Honey, what happened?" he asks, as he takes Lacey out of my arms, taking her warmth with her.

"I fell out of the tree. My arm hurts," she cries into her daddy's chest.

Her daddy looks at me and asks, "Who are you?"

"I'm Chance sir, I live next door," I say, shivering as I point to my house.

"Okay Chance, you can head home now. I've got her," he tells me, holding Lacey tighter.

I step backwards then sprint over to my house and through the front door, forgetting I'd snuck out the back door because my mum forbade me to go outside. Mum's angry face greets me and doesn't disappear until I tell her Lacey got hurt then worry is etched on her face instead. I explain to her who Lacey is. When I tell her she's my new friend, a small smile flashes across Mum's face while she ushers me into the bath to warm up.

LACEY

7TH MARCH
Dear Diary,

I'm currently sitting in a hospital bed with my dad sitting in the chair next to me. I can't help but admire my new cast. It's a pretty shade of pink (my favourite colour ever) and is the coolest thing I've ever gotten. I have my new friend Chance to thank for it. I think he's super special.

I knew the moment I laid eyes on him, he was special. He's like those treasures you find that you don't want anyone else to have so you bury it in your favourite box where you can keep it safe and no one else will ever find it. When you pull it out of your box and hold it in your hand, you know deep in your bones how special it is and it brings a smile to your face because it's yours. It's the exact feeling I got when I truly saw Chance for the first time and he showed me his scar. He was my treasure. I can't lock him in my favourite box but I can do anything in the world to keep him safe and it's what I'm going to do.

Beyond excited,
Lacey

LACEY

8TH MARCH
Dear Diary,

Mum and Dad have fussed over me all day. I wasn't allowed to get out of bed much. You would think the way they were reacting I broke both my legs and not my arm. At least it wasn't my writing arm.

Dad tried to ban me from playing in the tree again but he's already told me it's my tree so he can't stop me. I'll have to wait until my cast comes off before I can climb it. I won't be able to pull myself up without two arms. I wonder if Chance could help me climb it without Dad knowing?

I can't wait to show off my new pretty pink cast to all the kids at my new school. I hope the kids are nice. I'm dying to see Chance again so we can play. I hope he goes to the same school and we are in the same class. I bet he will be excited about my cast. Although I doubt he likes pink. He likes the colour blue, judging by the outfit he was wearing when we met.

I better go. I can hear Dad's heavy steps coming, yet again, to check on me.

Until tomorrow,
Lacey

CHANCE

9TH MARCH

I don't see Lacey for the rest of the weekend so I'm not sure what happened to her. I hope she's okay. I asked Mum if she could go over and check on Lacey but when she knocked on the door, there was no answer. Hopefully Mum will let me go over to check on her after school. Mum gives me a kiss on the head as she ushers me into the classroom.

"Hi Chance," my teacher Mrs Williams says. She's always so cheerful and it's too early for any smiles. Mum says it's because she doesn't think I am a morning person, whatever that means. Plus there is no reason to smile. I hate coming to school since I have no friends and everyone makes fun of my scar. Especially Theodore. He's the worst of the bunch. It's like it's his mission in life to make me more miserable than I already am.

I hang my bag on the cool metal hook with my name above it. Taking a deep breath, I turn and walk over to the reading corner and grab a book to take to my desk. With my back to the door of the classroom, I read like all the other kids and wait patiently for the bell to ring.

"Well hello, you must be Lacey," Mrs Williams says. I whip around in my chair to see if it's my Lacey. Sure enough, there she is with her scraggly hair and a new bright pink cast on her arm.

"Hi," she says in response.

"I'm your teacher, Mrs Williams," she says to Lacey, and my heart pounds loudly in my chest. For once in my life, I'll have a friend at school.

"It's nice to see you both again," Mrs Williams says to Lacey's parents, as she directs her attention to them.

Lacey's eyes wander around the room, glancing at all our art work on the walls. I stare at her, hoping she will finally see me. After what feels like forever, she looks my way and gives me the biggest smile.

She lets go of her dad's hand and comes racing over to me yelling, "Chance, look at my cast. Isn't this like the coolest thing ever?" She turns her cast back and forth, showing me both sides of it. It's so pink it looks like she barfed pink highlighter all over her arm.

The huge smile on her face does something to my chest so instead of telling her what I honestly think, I say, "Yeah Lacey, it's the coolest thing I've ever seen," which makes her smile grow even bigger.

"Come here honey, we are going to hang up your bag." Lacey's attention turns back to her parents and she follows them. They help her hang her bag then her mum and dad both give her a hug before leaving the class.

Mrs Williams brings her back to my desk as I hear Lacey say, "Chance is my next door neighbour."

"Well Chance, since you two know each other, you can be Lacey's buddy today and show her around."

"Sure, I can do that," I tell Mrs Williams, who is smiling at me.

"Great. Lacey, you can take the desk opposite Chance," Mrs Williams says, as the bell rings. I push my chair back and return my book to the reading corner. When I turn around, I see Lacey has followed me.

"Come and sit on the carpet with me. We do this every morning when the bell rings," I inform Lacey. For the first time, I walk side by side with someone and have a friend to sit with on the mat. This is going to be a great day. I can feel it right down to my toes.

Today has been amazing. I don't think I've ever smiled this much. My face is a bit sore from all the smiling to be honest. I showed Lacey around in the first break and she told me all about the hospital and what happened with her arm. The doctor said she has a hairline fracture, whatever that is. She's excited because she gets to wear the cast for six weeks. I would be gutted if I had a cast on my arm because it would mean no climbing my tree for at least forty two days. I haven't known Lacey long but I know her favourite colour is pink. She talks a lot too but it could be because I'm not used to people talking to me at school. She was so excited telling me about her cast, she had to take a big breath in the middle of a sentence. I thought she was going to pass out from not having enough air but she was fine and managed to carry on with her story.

At lunchtime Lacey runs off to the toilet saying she's fine going without me and she will meet me at the sandpit when she is done. A sand castle takes form as I tip the full blue bucket over, tapping on it to release the sand.

"Look who it is. Scarface," Theodore's voice distracts me from my castle building. I usually ignore him and hope he will go away but today he's got a few of the other kids with him. He plays it up for crowds and this means he will carry on calling me names until I cry.

"The new girl must not have seen your face properly or else she wouldn't be playing with you," he taunts, taking a step closer. "That's why you're all alone now because she saw your face and couldn't stand the sight of you." At his last taunt my eyes find his, as the other kids laugh.

I already know Lacey thinks my scar is cool, but for a second doubt creeps in and I wonder if he's right. Did she lie about needing the toilet? Heat builds behind my eyes and I know I'm about to give him what he wants and cry. A big smirk lights Theodore's face as if he can sense the tears I'm about to shed. My attention is focused solely on him and the other kids so I don't notice the ball of scraggly hair racing towards us until she's much closer. My eyes drift to Lacey and boy, she looks so mad. Her face is all red as she stares at me which makes the tears stream down my face. Why is she mad at me?

It isn't until she's right next to me that the kids' laughter filters through my thoughts. Their laughter directed at me. Her anger directed at me. Her eyes leave me and lock onto Theodore who stands proudly with his mouth open wide, laughing loudly. She storms right up to him and I realise she's not mad at me. She's mad for me. The girl with the frizzy hair and the red face surprises me and does something I know she will get in trouble for. She protects me. It's the first time a small part of me falls in love with my new friend Lacey.

LACEY

9TH MARCH
Dear Diary,

I don't care what Dad says but I am not apologising to Theodore, he's a stupid boy. Dad told me I had to go to my room to write an apology letter but I'd rather write in my diary than say sorry. What's the point of saying sorry if I don't mean it? Dad didn't see Theodore teasing Chance and I made the promise to protect Chance last night. What kind of friend would I be if not even twenty four hours go by and I'm already breaking my promise? Like who does that?

Dad didn't see the sad look on Chance's face either but I did. I saw the fresh tears he was trying to hold in because Theodore made the other kids laugh at him. It's not fair. It's not my fault my cast has a mind of its own. I tried to tell Dad I had no control over my cast. It was like magic. It took control of my arm and next thing I knew, my hard pretty pink cast was banging on the top of Theodore's head. I wanted him to stop teasing Chance, I didn't mean to make him cry but now he has had a dose of his own medicine. The kids laughed at him because he got beaten up by a girl. Hopefully this lesson will make him leave Chance alone.

At least it made Chance smile. I saw it. It was a tiny smile reserved for me when no one was looking, after I had been told off by Mum, Dad and the teacher.

Sorry. Dad came in and I got in trouble again because I'm writing to you and not writing the letter I don't want to write. He said if I don't write it then he will ban me from seeing Chance and I can't have that so here it goes.

~~To Theodore,~~

~~I'm sorry you are such a buttface. Why did your parents name you after a singing chipmunk? Is it because you smell like a feral animal?~~

~~Sorry but I'm not sorry,~~

~~Lacey~~

~~To Theodore,~~

~~If you make fun of Chance again, I will do more than hit you over the head with my cast. I will kick you in the butt too.~~

~~Sorry your face looks like a big butt,~~
~~Lacey~~
~~To Theodore,~~
~~My parents are threatening me to write this apology letter to~~
~~you. I don't feel sorry at all. I feel sorry I didn't hit you harder and~~
~~knock some of your meanness out of you.~~
~~You suck,~~
~~Lacey~~
To Theodore,
I'm sorry.
Lacey
~~P.S Stay away from Chance~~

CHANCE

10TH MARCH

Excitement wouldn't let me sleep in this morning. I got dressed in my uniform an hour earlier than usual and Mum didn't have to nag me to find my shoes. Lacey got in big trouble yesterday for hitting Theodore on the head but I'm grateful she stood up for me as I haven't been able to do it myself. I don't need to worry about that now as I know I have a friend in Lacey. Her obsession with the colour pink is quite full on but I think I can let it slide if she's willing to fight bullies for me.

Walking through the school gate today holding Mum's hand, she gives it a big squeeze like she usually does. She didn't realise how bad Theodore was bullying me and she had a sad look on her face when she got called into the office yesterday. She admitted to me she's happy Lacey hit Theo and if anyone bullies me again, I have her permission to hit them back if I feel it's warranted.

As we enter the classroom, I hang my bag on its usual hook and catch sight of Lacey sitting at her desk with her back to me. I know it's her because you can't miss the furball on her head AKA her hair. Mum walks me over to her and as she lifts her head, my eyes slide to the red jagged outline on her face in the same place I have my scar. Her smile lights up her face when she sees me, ignoring whatever she was drawing.

"Good morning Chance," she beams at me.

"What's on your face?" I ask, pointing to the red marker line running the length of her temple and cheek.

Rolling her eyes at me she says, "Duh, can't you see it's a scar? If my best friend has a scar then I have a scar too. Scars are so cool." Dropping her attention back to her paper in front of her, she continues with her drawing. I glance at Mum who looks like she's on the verge of crying as she looks at Lacey. I hope she's not upset with Lacey but then she smiles at me, confusing me.

She leans forward and kisses me on the head whispering, "I'll leave you with your best friend. It sounds like she will take good care of you." She leaves us to go to the office for her meeting with the principal and Theodore's mother. I take my seat at my desk and I'm about to say something to Lacey but then Theodore walks over to us with Mrs Williams by his side.

"Chance and Lacey, Theodore has something he wants to say to you," Mrs Williams says, as she places a hand on Theodore's shoulder. It must give him strength because he raises his eyes and locks onto us when before he couldn't stop staring at the carpet.

"I want to say I'm sorry for yesterday and I'm sorry for bullying you Chance. I won't do it again. Please can you forgive me?"

I stare at my bully. I'm speechless.

I never expected an apology from anyone, least of all him. I don't know what to say so I nod and give a small smile, hoping it's the right thing to do.

"Now I don't want to see any more bullying or fighting between you three, you hear?" Mrs Williams tells us, taking her time looking us each in the eye.

In unison we reply, "Yes, Mrs Williams."

"Great, I'm glad we've settled that. Theodore, I'd like you to move your things to the desk next to Lacey so I can make sure you three are making an effort to get along." Out of the corner of my eye, Lacey's nose wrinkles but she keeps her eyes on her drawing, not saying a word. Theodore collects his things and empties them into his new desk as Mrs Williams walks to the front of the room to address the class for the day.

As she is talking, Lacey whispers to Theodore, "If I hear of you bullying Chance again, I will kick you in the goolies and I promise you, it will hurt a lot more than when I hit you on your head."

Theodore scrunches his own nose in confusion and way too loudly, he asks, "What the heck is a goolie?" His words have Mrs Williams turning our way and her face turning bright red.

"Lacey and Theodore, I think you can both head to the principal's office," she sternly tells them.

Huffing, they both stand and push their chairs in. As they are walking out of the door, Theodore asks Lacey, "Why did you doodle all over your face?" which has Lacey stopping in her tracks and turning to face him with her hands on her hips.

"It's a scar like Chance's because scars are cool. If you don't watch it, I'll kick you in the goolies right now."

"Lacey!" Mrs Williams yells. "Class, continue with your drawing or reading while I escort these two to the office," she tells us, and she strides towards the door. The last thing I see is Lacey staring daggers into Theodore's head as they walk out the door and disappear from view. I think she's gone but then her head pops back in the door frame and she winks at me, offering a smile I can't help but return.

When they return to class Lacey tells me the principal made her and Theodore call a truce and shake hands afterwards. She was not happy about it because according to her, he's got cooties. They both had to promise to get along with each other or else their parents will get called to the office again. By the looks on their sulking faces, I don't think either of them want that. Lacey keeps wiping her hand on her skirt, as if she can wipe away Theodore's touch. I hope she doesn't think I have cooties too.

LACEY

10TH MARCH
Dear Diary,

I'm furious. Mrs Williams has seated Theodore right next to me. Now I have to put up with his stinky butt next to me for the rest of the year. It's the worst punishment ever.

Who doesn't know what goolies are? And did he have to practically yell it so the whole class could hear? You try to threaten someone and they open their mouth and get you into trouble. Stinky butt indeed!

Mum was not impressed. I've been at school for two days and she's already been called into the principal's office twice. Dad thought it was hilarious when I told him what I said about Theodore's goolies. He also said that's my baby girl with so much pride I couldn't help but smile but then Mum saw me smiling and told Dad off for encouraging me. I had to call a truce with Theodore but if I see the slightest inkling he's about to hurt Chance, our truce will be null and void.

Now I've got to write another letter apologising to Theodore. I don't want to keep apologising to this kid when it's him who started it in the first place. Mum was mad this time and threatened to ban me from seeing Chance again. I don't think she's serious, she's trying to manipulate me because she knows I can't stand not seeing Chance now we are friends. I saw Mum and Chance's mum laughing so I think they are becoming friends. If they become friends then there will be nothing keeping me and Chance from seeing each other.

My cast is making my arm itch. It's deep inside and I can't quite scratch it. I wonder if it will help if I poke a pencil or a ruler inside my cast. I'll try after I write my dumb apology letter. Well, here we go again.

~~To Theodore,~~

~~I should say this letter is for any future apologies I have to make for the remainder of the year because you are such a butt hole and are probably going to keep getting me into trouble. Leave me and Chance alone.~~

~~I'll never be sorry,~~

~~Lacey~~

~~To Theodore,~~

~~Seriously, who doesn't know what goolies are? They are connected to your weiner and my Dad said if a boy (you) is being a butthead then I can kick them in the goolies and it's okay. You better protect them goolies because I'll be practising my kicks.~~

~~From super kicker,~~

~~Lacey~~

~~To Theodore,~~

~~Why are you so mean? Why can't you be nice? Don't make fun of Chance's and my scars or else I'll whack your head again with my cast and kick you in the goolies.~~

~~I'm not sorry,~~

~~Lacey~~

To Theodore,

I'm sorry. Again.

From,

Lacey

CHANCE

15TH MARCH

Lacey and I are having a playdate today. Her mum and my mum are having a coffee to get to know each other better. I hope they become good friends because then I will get to spend more time with Lacey. We are on strict instructions not to play in the weeping willow tree since Lacey can't climb with one arm. They don't want any more accidents so here we are in my room, lying on my carpet trying to decide what to do.

"Do you want to draw on my cast or write your name?" Lacey asks, holding her pink cast out for me to examine.

"Yeah okay," I say. I walk over to my desk in the corner and open the top drawer. Moving the knick knacks I keep in there, my fingers wrap around my thick black marker. "This should work," I tell her, holding it for her to see. She sits and crosses her legs so I sit next to her and do the same. Lifting her arm, she holds it in front of me to grab.

"What should I draw?" I ask.

Shrugging her shoulders she says, "I don't know. Anything." Racking my brain for a minute, the capped end of the marker taps against my lips. I've never written or drawn on a cast before so I'm not sure what most people do. Plus Lacey's hasn't gotten any drawings on it yet and I don't want to wreck her cast. It's got to be good as she is going to be stuck with it for weeks. Gripping the cold cast in my hand, I pull her forearm closer to me and run the thick tip across the hard plaster. It's bumpy under the black marker but I manage to get my name written.

I attempt to draw a superman 'S' like I have seen lots of kids draw at school. I draw three lines then three lines under them and join them with diagonal lines. Connecting the two lines on each end, I draw a semi circle on the top and then again on the bottom. Lacey inspects my completed artwork and a wide smile slowly spreads across her face, her eyes crinkling in the process.

"It looks so good Chance," she says, beaming at me. A blush heats my cheeks at her words.

"I'm glad you like it."

"Why did your mum name you Chance?" she asks, tilting her head to the side, staring at her cast.

"She said something about me being her second chance, whatever that means," I tell her. Mum always tells me the same thing whenever I've asked the same question.

"Well if I ever upset you, you'll have to give me a second chance because it's what your name stands for," she says, her smile lighting up her face.

"You're my best friend so you can have unlimited chances," I tell her, which has us both clutching our stomachs laughing.

Once the giggles subside, she asks, "Do you wanna play *Knucklebones?*"

"You'll have to teach me. I don't know how to play," I tell her honestly. Her eyes light up at the prospect of teaching me. She wriggles her hand into the pocket of her pink, yes always pink, shorts, retrieving five silver funny shaped pieces resembling bones.

"You hold them all in one hand then you throw them and try to catch them on the back of your hand. Once they are on the back of your hand, you throw them again and catch them in your palm. It will be easier if I show you," she says, then she goes ahead and demonstrates. She's a bit clumsy with her cast but manages to catch them all. She must be a pro at this game. "Here, you can practice for a bit if you like so you can get used to them," she offers. Taking them in my hand I throw them and try to catch them on the back of my hand like she did but I struggle to get more than one on my hand.

"It's so hard," I tell her, scrunching my nose.

"You need to practice more, that's all," she tells me, as we take turns throwing them and catching them. Once I can manage to catch more than one at a time, she shows me some different moves. One is called overhands where you have to throw them all but only catch one. If you catch more than one you have to wriggle the others off. You throw that one in the air while picking the others individually off the ground. You repeat the same steps with two then three and then four. Lacey makes it look so easy even with her cast on. When I try it is extremely hard.

"Let's go see if there's anything for lunch. I'm getting hungry," I say, feeling a bit over *Knucklebones* as I'm not good at it. Lacey leaves the pieces on the carpet as we open the door and head down the hallway to the kitchen. Our mums' laughter can be heard as we get closer to the kitchen. They are sitting at the kitchen table drinking from their white china mugs. Bronco is curled up nearby, waiting for any scraps to fall off the table. I pull Lacey over and introduce Bronco to her. I have to introduce my new best friend to my old best friend. Lacey laughs as Bronco licks her hand.

"Hey kids," Mum says, drawing our attention away from Bronco.

"We're hungry," I tell her, so she stands, leaving her cup on the saucer in front of her. She walks into the kitchen and fixes us something to eat.

"There you go. Fairy bread," she says, smiling as she hands us each a plate with bread, butter and coloured sprinkles covering it. Our eyes light up as we carefully carry our plates to the table and quickly demolish the colourful treat. With our fairy bread gone, we place our plates on the bench and go back to my room to play.

"Do you like to read?" I ask Lacey.

"I'm not good at reading big words yet," she tells me, her cheeks turning a shade of pink that match her shorts.

"I can read to you if you like," I offer.

"Okay," she says. I hop onto my bed and lie on the duvet like I usually do when reading as I find it the most comfortable. I place one of my pillows next to me for Lacey. I shuffle over so I'm closest to the wall and she can get on the bed easily next to me, without having to struggle with her arm in the cast.

"Can you pass me my book?" I ask, pointing to the copy of Paul Jennings' *Unmentionable Book of Short Stories* I got out of the library recently. The pages flip through my fingers until my bookmark is found. Luckily it's at the beginning of one of the short stories. Lacey follows along with her eyes as I read out loud, causing us both to giggle at the funny parts.

"Aww, they look so cute together," Mum says, waking me from my sleep.

"I'm glad they have each other. I guess we were lucky moving next door to you," Lacey's mum whispers back.

"Yeah, Chance has had trouble making friends so I'm thankful he has Lacey now," Mum says, causing me to sit and rub the sleep from my eyes.

"Mum?" I ask.

"Hey sweetheart, you two fell asleep," she says, as they come closer. Looking at my bed, Lacey is lying on my pillow with her frizzy hair spread around her as her soft snores fill the air.

"We must have fallen asleep while I was reading to her," I tell them, which makes them smile even more.

"Come on Lacey. Time to go," her mum says, gently shaking her shoulder to wake her without scaring her.

"What is it?" Lacey groggily says, as she wakes.

"You fell asleep Lacey and it's time to go home now. Say bye to Chance."

"Bye Chance," she says, as she takes her mum's hand and walks out of the room.

"Bye Lacey," I say to her retreating figure, as I smile at my mum whose big smile reflects back at me.

LACEY

15TH MARCH
Dear Diary,

I had the best day today. Chance and I played Knucklebones and he drew on my cast. I've been practicing the cool 'S' design since I got home. I think I've gotten pretty good at it now.

Chance is so lucky. He has the cutest dog ever. His name is Bronco. I asked my parents for a pet ages ago but my dad said he is allergic to cats. I don't know what that means but hopefully when I'm a bit older they will change their minds. If I ask, hopefully Chance will let me play with and walk Bronco and it will feel like he belongs to me too.

His mum made us fairy bread which was super yummy. I usually don't get fairy bread unless it's at a party. Chance read to me, he's so good at reading. He knows a lot of big words. I tried to keep up and read along with him in my head but he reads a lot faster than me so I ended up listening to him instead. His voice was so magical, it made me fall asleep in the middle of the day. I never nap now as I'm too old for naps but there was something about Chance's voice. It was mesmerising and made me drift off to dreamland.

Mum said I'm allowed to go over to Chance's tomorrow if I want. I think she likes talking to Chance's mum as much as I like talking to Chance. If they become best friends like me and Chance, it would be so cool.

If I go over to Chance's tomorrow, I think I'll take my pack of cards and we can play Go Fish instead of Knucklebones. I don't think Chance liked playing it as he kept huffing and puffing when they fell off his hand and he had to try again. I can play anytime by myself so it's not a big deal.

I can't wait until I get this cast off so then we can go climbing in our tree again. It is getting super itchy now and Mum told me off when she caught me trying to put a ruler inside to scratch the itch. She was worried it would get stuck and then I'd have to go back to the hospital. I don't want that to happen now since I've got Chance's art work on my cast.

I better go. I can hear Mum calling me to wash my hands as dinner is ready.

See ya later alligator,
Lacey

CHAPTER 2

CHANCE

23RD SEPTEMBER

Lacey and I are outside on the pavement after school, chalk at the ready, all set to make the biggest hopscotch we can when Theodore walks past with his brother Anthony.

"Where are you two going?" Lacey asks, standing with her hands on her hips.

"We're going over to Rutherford Park. You wanna come with us?" he asks, as he throws his rugby ball in the air and catches it. I look to Lacey to see what she says and she gives me the slightest nod in agreement.

"Let me run in and tell my mum," I say, abandoning my chalk as I race into the house informing my mum Lacey and I are off to the park and we'll be home before dark. Racing back out to join them, we walk to the park along the footpath. Theodore passes the ball to me and I pass it the best I can to Lacey. She's as awkward as I am passing it to Theodore's brother. We continue throwing the ball around to pass the time as we make our way to the park. Lacey and I don't usually come out here. It's a big sports field so it's not much fun with two people.

The time passes fast with us laughing and throwing the ball. When the park comes into view, Theodore and his brother race ahead, zig zagging through the empty car park as their laughter reaches me and Lacey.

"Check this out," Theodore says, as he stands at the edge then bends down. We look out at the view and see a giant grass covered hill. At the bottom of the steep slope is a huge rugby field with a goal post at either end. The whole field is empty so we've got the whole space to play on uninterrupted. We watch as Theodore lies sideways and then rolls down the grassy hill. It's so steep he picks up momentum fast and his laughter fills the air. We notice Anthony lying down and rolling as fast as he can to catch up with Theodore. Theodore makes it to the bottom, raising his hands above his head with the biggest smile on his face as he looks at us.

"Come on," he yells, as his brother joins him at the bottom.

"Let's go," I say to Lacey, and she nods as she lies down. We lie facing each other and count together.

"One, two, three," we yell in unison, pushing off then laughing the whole way as we tumble down the hill. We turn faster once we get half way, feeling the wind whip against our skin. My smile grows as Lacey's little yelps ring out as she hits bumps on her way down.

"That was awesome," I say, as we make it to the bottom. Standing, my hands dust the dirt and grass off my knees and shirt before helping Lacey stand by giving her a hand.

"Last one to the top is a rotten egg," Theodore yells, already a couple metres ahead of us. We sprint up the hill, trying to catch him. As we come to the top, out of breath, we all lie in a row and roll down together. We continue going up and down until we run out of steam. On our last turn, Theodore kicks his rugby ball which goes sailing into the air and lands at the bottom of the hill. We all line up again and laugh as we make our way down. We're all covered in grass stains now and Lacey's hair has turned into a true birds' nest complete with twigs and grass.

"Let's kick the ball around," Anthony says.

"We'll take this side and you two go on the other side," Theodore tells us, as he and his brother race each other to one end of the field. Lacey and I take our time walking to the other side. Turning around we get ready to catch whatever kicks they send us our way. Their kicks don't make it far so Lacey and I move closer to the middle of the field. We watch as Theodore and his brother whisper to each other behind their hands.

"They're planning something," Lacey whispers to me, and I glance to the brothers with my brows furrowed. I have no idea what they could be contemplating and I turn to tell Lacey she's being paranoid when the whizzing noise grabs my attention, a second before a jet of water hits me in the face.

"Aahhhh," Lacey squeals, as she gets hit by a stream of water from the sprinklers. Soaking wet, I look to where Theodore and Anthony were but they are gone. I spot them running off the field laughing. They make it to safety before the sprinklers on their side of the field turn on so they are nice and dry. Taking hold of Lacey's dripping hand, I pull her through the streams of water that keep attacking us as we run to the edge of the field. Lacey's head and face drip with water so she wipes it out of her eyes.

"Theodore!" she yells at the top of her lungs, as she clenches her jaw. Theodore and his brother continue to laugh at us from the top of the hill.

"You look like a drowned rat Lacey," Theodore yells to us, and I can't help the giggle that escapes my lips. Lacey's head whips around to me but I school my features before she sees.

"Let's get them," I tell her. The glint in her eyes shines as we race up the hill in pursuit. We chase them all the way home and catch up to them two houses before we get to my house. Lacey jumps on Theodore's back.

"Get his front," Lacey squeals, as Theodore tries to shake her off him but she holds on for dear life. My arms wrap around the front of him, giving him a bear hug. "Theodore sandwich," Lacey sings, as we swing in a circle, while Theodore tries to squirm his way out. Anthony stands there laughing at us, as he's still nice and dry. I let go of Theodore and take a step back, then grab Lacey around the waist and pry her off his back. Theodore looks at himself and now his shirt and shorts are soaked like ours. Not as much as us but enough to make him wet. Lacey and I crack up laughing as he inspects his shirt then he looks at us and joins in laughing too.

"Okay I deserved that."

"Too right you did," Lacey says, folding her arms across her chest.

"Okay we better go. It's getting dark," Theodore says, as he turns to his brother. Turning back to us he says, "You guys wanna go again tomorrow?" I look at Lacey and her smile grows. She's not really mad now.

"Hell yeah," I say, which causes Theodore to chuckle as his brother and him wave goodbye.

"We'll get them back tomorrow," Lacey says, looking at her wet clothes as I pull a twig out of her hair. She needs to brush this monstrosity before it turns into an actual bird's nest. She smiles softly at me as she pulls a stick from my hair then drops it on the grass.

"Better go inside. Mum's gonna kill me for getting wet," I tell her.

"Night Chance," Lacey yells, as she takes off to her own house. I head inside planning ways to get Theodore back and I can't wipe the smile off my face until I hear Mum's voice.

"Chance Alexander. What in the world," she yells, and the smile instantly drops from my face.

LACEY

23RD SEPTEMBER

Dear Diary,

I'm going to kill Theodore, Anthony too. I know Theodore was the instigator. Their prank was so not cool. My pink sneakers are brand new and they got all wet so now Dad is not happy with me. Plus Mum made me wash my hair and then spent an hour getting all the tangles out so I got in trouble for not brushing my hair. Again.

Chance and I are going to have to think of something epic to get Theodore back. I must say it was fun rolling down the hill. We haven't done it in so long. A lot of the hills near our houses have prickles but this one was prickle free and perfect. I can't wait to get back to it tomorrow.

I wonder if Chance got in trouble for being wet when he got home. I wonder if instead of egging Theodore's house he'd want to egg Theodore to teach him a lesson.

I wonder if Theodore will ever stop being a butt head.

I better go to bed as my head is all sore from the pulling Mum did when brushing it.

Until tomorrow,
Lacey

CHAPTER 3

CHANCE 1993

12TH JANUARY

Marbles. Marbles are what our lives revolve around now. We both were given a set from Santa for Christmas and we've spent the whole summer holidays playing against each other. We have a similar number of marbles in our collections but some days one person has more marbles until the other wins them back the next day. We've spent most of the holidays finding different holes to play as it got boring playing with the same groove in the footpath between our houses. We moved on from the groove when we found a small hole in the concrete past Lacey's house. She was way too good at sinking the marbles into the hole. Luckily I realised pretty fast because if I kept playing her at the same hole, I would have lost all my marbles to her.

Today we are walking around the neighbourhood trying to find another hole we can fit the marbles into. As we are walking with our heads down searching for holes, we don't notice Theodore and his brother Anthony until they step into our view. Their shadows fall across our path. Both glancing up at the same time, I greet them while Lacey goes back to hunting for holes.

"What are you guys doing?" Theodore asks, curious to know what we are looking at.

"Trying to find a good hole to play marbles in," I tell him, as my eyes scan along the footpath, still searching for the right hole.

"I saw a decent sized hole I bet would be good for marbles," he says.

"Really? Where?" I ask.

"It'll cost you four marbles if I show you," he bargains. His comment stops Lacey in her tracks, as she crosses her arms across her chest.

"We aren't giving you our marbles. What if it's no good?" she argues.

Twisting his mouth while he thinks, he says, "How about I show you first and if it's any good then you give me two marbles each? And if it's not good, then you give me nothing."

I look to Lacey to see what she thinks. Her lips twist to the side of her face so I can tell she's thinking. I keep watching her, waiting for her to make a decision then she nods at me.

"Okay. It's a deal. Lead the way," I tell Theodore, and he high fives his brother as they turn back the way they have come. We end up in front of the dairy and right by the rubbish bin near the road is the perfect hole.

"Let's assess it first," Lacey says, always the stubborn one. We both crouch in front of it to get a closer view of how big it is inside and how many marbles we estimate it will hold at once. "This looks pretty good, don't you think?" Lacey whispers to me, as Theodore and Anthony stand near the dairy entrance.

"Should we pay them?" I ask her.

"Yeah, we should pay them and then play them and try to win the marbles back," she tells me, and we both conspiratorially giggle before standing up with straight faces.

"It's decent," I tell Theodore, and dig into my pocket pulling out my mesh drawstring bag that holds my marbles. Lacey does the same and then we hand them over to Theodore. He takes them and gives Anthony two and they high five each other again as they examine their haul.

"Want to play with us?" I ask.

"Yeah," they both say in unison. I play first against Theodore losing another marble to him while Lacey wins against Anthony. We take turns going back and forth and it isn't until the sun fades we have to stop. If we still had light, I don't think anything could have stopped us from playing as we were having too much fun.

"Wanna meet tomorrow?" Theodore asks, as he juggles his four marbles in his hand while Anthony juggles his two.

"Yeah, we will be here after lunch," Lacey says, as we wave goodbye. Lacey and I go one way and the brothers go the other. Once she is sure they won't hear, Lacey says, "That was fun," and I can't help but agree with her.

"Try to practice in your room tonight so we can win our marbles back tomorrow," I tell her.

"Deal," she says, as I drop her at her house and then run the few steps to mine.

Stepping into the house, Mum has finished cooking dinner judging by the delicious aromas wafting from the kitchen. I go and wash my hands before taking a seat at the table. We are having roast chicken with peas and potatoes. Any leftovers will serve as chicken sandwiches tomorrow for lunch. I devour the food on my plate, having built up an appetite from playing marbles all day. When I finish eating, I fill Mum in on all the fun Lacey and I had with Theodore and Anthony and my plans for tomorrow.

LACEY

12TH JANUARY
Dear Diary,

I surprisingly had a lot of fun today. Theodore and Anthony weren't too bad to hang out with. Plus they showed us the coolest hole outside the dairy. Chance and I hadn't even thought to wander that far in our search.

We lost a few marbles to them in payment for the hole but it was worth it so I can't even be mad. I didn't lose any of my extra special galaxy marbles either. I kept my cat's eye marbles safe in my bag because I wouldn't dare risk them, they are way too pretty.

I need to get some practice in so I have to cut this short. I want to win those marbles back that I lost to stinky Theodore.

Goodnight,

Lacey

CHANCE

24TH FEBRUARY

It turns out marbles were an obsession for all of our classmates over the holidays. Everyone comes to school now bringing their whole collection with them. Some kids carry them in pencil cases or old ice cream containers. Miles has a Christmas cookie container full of marbles. I had to upgrade from my mesh bag to an ice cream container as it had a small hole in it and I was scared to lose my marbles. Plus Mum gave me a lecture and said if Bronco swallowed any marbles I would be in big trouble.

Theodore has increased his stash, he's managed to win more since he got those first two from me. He has half an ice cream container full now. He also has these cool silver ones he calls steelies his older brother gave him. They are heavy and if you play a normal marble against them, you can crack your marble. Lacey was able to win one off him and she showed her dad. The next day she had ten steelies and she gave me five. She said her dad told her they are ball bearings and he was able to get a bunch from work. I don't care what they are, they are cool and pretty rare to have.

At lunch time everyone gathers out near the long patch of grass by the front fence line of the school. There's a large concrete path running alongside it which makes it perfect for marbles. Some of the other kids use the heel of their shoe to dig into the grass then spin around, making the perfect hole. I wish Lacey and I had known about this trick while it was still holidays instead of wasting so much time trying to hunt for holes. There are so many different ways you can play marbles too. Some play by seeing who can get closest to the wall, others play by being the first to hit your opponent's marble five times. We prefer to play the normal way by hitting it into a hole.

The bell for lunch rings and everyone rushes from their desks, grabbing their marble containers before they leave. Squishing our way out the door past everyone, I feel a tug on my shirt which has me turning around.

"You good Lace?" I ask, noticing it was her who was tugging on my sleeve. As everyone rushes out of the hallway, thundering shoes hitting the polished floor, everyone heads in the same direction, racing to see who can claim the best holes first. Tugging Lacey along behind me, we race to the far side of the grass to a hole we find the easiest to win at. We worked out if you can hit the marble at the right angle, it rolls down the hill and straight into the hole. We beat the other kids there and wait for someone to come play against us. It doesn't take long before Theodore comes to challenge me.

"Have you got any pearlies in your collection?" he asks me.

"Yeah, I've got a couple. I'll challenge you with one if you play a galaxy," I bargain, as I'm in desperate need of more galaxies.

"Yeah, okay," he says, as he places his ice cream container on the grass. Peeling off the plastic lid he searches through, finding one he probably likes the least. I do the same with my pearlies finding one that has a chip from when I challenged Lacey with her steelies. Theodore starts a game with me while Miles comes over and challenges Lacey to a game.

"Sure, let's make a new hole," Lacey says, so Miles spins his heel in the grass a few steps away from us.

"I heard you've got a good collection of steelies," Miles says to Lacey.

"Yeah, my dad gave me a bunch of them," she tells him. Miles places his red cookie container on the grass, peels off his own lid and pulls something out for Lacey to see.

"What is that?" She squeals, which has me standing over the hole and shooting my marble backwards between my legs, quickly ending the game so I can see what she's so excited about. I pick up the galaxy I won and my pearlie and Theodore and I walk over to Miles and Lacey.

"It's called a bonker," Miles tells us, holding a huge marble, twice the size of a normal marble.

"Wow," Lacey and I say in unison. The look on Theodore's face shows he's thinking the same thing as us. We all want a bonker now we have seen it.

"Where did you get it?" Theodore asks Miles.

"My cousins came over on the weekend and I won two of them. They had even bigger ones too they call grand daddies," he explains.

"I want a bonker now," Lacey says.

"I can trade you three steelies for one if you want or ten cat's eyes if you don't want to give away your steelies," Miles offers her. She looks at me in a silent question, asking if it sounds like a good deal.

"Who told you what it's worth?" Theodore asks him.

"That's what my cousins said. They did say you can bargain with people. It depends on what you want for it."

"Trade the cat's eyes," I tell Lacey, not wanting her to give away her steelies when they are a hot commodity at the moment. Everyone has cat's eyes so they'll be easy enough to win back.

"I'll take the deal," Lacey tells Miles. Miles hands over his bonker and Lacey counts out ten of her cat's eye marbles into his open hands. "It's so cool," Lacey says, holding the bonker so we can both examine it. Theodore and Miles take over playing at the hole where Theodore and I were playing.

"You want to play a friendly game with me and we can see how good the bonker is?" I ask her, and she nods, her eyes lighting up. It's best to test out new marbles first as you don't want to lose them to someone because you didn't know how to play with them. Lacey and I spend the rest of our lunch break, taking turns playing with the bonker until we think we've perfected how hard we need to hit it to get it a decent distance.

The bell signalling the end of lunchtime rings and everyone rushes to finish their games, pack up their marbles and make their way back to class before we get in trouble for being late. Lacey puts her bonker in her pencil case and we walk back to class. As we enter the classroom, our teacher Mrs Dunn has everyone leave their marble collections on a desk by the doorway.

"What's going on Miss?" I ask, taking in the sad faces of the other kids.

"Everyone is to leave their marbles on this desk. Some of the other classes have had marbles being pulled out and swapped during class time. You can play with your marbles on your time but not when it's learning time. Everyone needs to write their name on their containers and leave them on this desk every time they enter the classroom," she informs us, holding out several markers in her hand for us to take and label our stash.

"It's not fair," Lacey protests.

"The teachers and I have decided if you kids can't keep the marbles to break time then we will have to ban them from school altogether." I turn to Lacey, and her own widened eyes stare back at mine. She nods, giving in so we both take a marker and quickly label our containers. We take our seats, sulking with the rest of the class as no one wants to leave their marbles unguarded.

It's our class's turn to go to the library to borrow books. We get our book bags and walk ten minutes to the public library where we can borrow a few books for the week. This is always my favourite part of school as I get to walk and talk with Lacey plus I get to exchange my books for new ones. I love reading and there's a new Goosebumps out I haven't read yet.

Once we get to the library, I veer off in search of the books I'm after and manage to find *The Curse of the Mummy's Tomb* before anyone else can snatch it. I grab a couple others I think I will like then meet up with Lacey on the bean bags in the corner. She's currently looking through a *Where's Wally* book.

"Did you find the Goosebumps book you wanted?" she asks, without taking her eyes off the book in her hands. She loves to hunt for the hidden man with the red and white stripes.

"Yeah, I did. You find anything good?" I ask her.

"I got *The Rainbow Fish*. The librarian suggested it. She said it's a new one they got in recently."

"Cool," I say, looking over her shoulder at the open pages. My eyes scan through the cluttered picture until I spot Wally hiding behind a beach shed and point him out to Lacey with my finger. "There he is."

"Ugh finally. I've been searching for him on this page forever," she tells me, smiling in thanks for helping her.

"Class, it's time to check out your books and head back to school," Mrs Dunn tells us. Lacey grabs my hand to pull her out of the squishy seat.

Walking back to school, Lacey tells me how we should practice some more with the bonker when we get home so the other kids don't see us and learn our tricks. When we get back to school, it's a few minutes until the end of school so we are allowed to get our school bags, collect our marbles and wait patiently for the bell. The bell rings and again it's a mad rush out the door as some of the kids try to play a few games of marbles before they have to head home.

Lacey and I make our way to the front gate and Lacey unzips her pencil case, searching through her marbles to pull out her bonker.

"Chance, my bonker's not here," she squeaks.

"What?" I ask, stopping to look at her.

"It's not here," she says again, her voice panicking.

"Come over here. Let's tip them out and double check," I tell her, pulling her over to a patch of grass no one is playing on. We crouch as she tips her pencil case upside down and she's right, her newly acquired bonker is missing.

"Someone must have stolen it," she cries. Looking into her eyes, the tears she's trying to hold in are visible.

"Lacey! Chance!" Theodore yells, as he comes running over to us in a hurry. Lacey wipes at her eyes, not wanting Theodore to see she was about to cry and picks up all her scattered marbles while I help.

"Hey Theodore," I say, my eyes fixed on gathering Lacey's marbles and placing them back in her pink pencil case.

"I saw Carson and Julie playing and Carson has your bonker Lacey," he puffs out, having run all the way to tell us. Rage builds inside me as I realise Carson must have stolen it when we were at the library as he's not in our class.

"Where are they?" I ask.

Theodore says, "Around the side of room four."

"Hold my marbles Lacey," I say, handing her my ice cream container which she takes. Theodore and her follow me to where Carson and Julie are playing, unaware of what's about to happen.

"Carson you thief, give back Lacey's bonker," I demand, which has him glancing our way, assessing the three of us.

"It's not yours, it's mine," he tells us, crossing his arms over his chest.

"Where did you get it from?" I ask angrily.

"I won it off Miles this morning," he says.

"No you didn't. I showed you my bonkers this morning but I never played you," Miles says, coming around the other side of the building which has Carson visibly gulping. "It's the bonker I traded with Lacey," Miles finishes, pointing to where it sits on the grass. Theodore quickly picks up the bonker and hands it to Lacey who I can hear sniffling behind me. Knowing she's upset makes me even angrier and before I know it, I'm walking up to Carson and pushing him in the chest so hard he falls back onto the grass, landing hard on his butt.

"Keep your hands off our marbles or else," I warn him, as I stand there glaring at him. He nods, with his own tears forming on his eyelids. I turn, grab Lacey's hand and pull her away so we can walk home.

"Thanks Chancey," she whispers, squeezing my hand in appreciation for sticking up for her. I stuck up for her like she did for me when Theo was bullying me because it's what friends do.

We walk hand in hand all the way home, letting the anger settle as we fall into step beside each other. Theodore and Miles walk with us and we vow to keep an eye out, in case Carson or anyone else tries to steal marbles from us again. Arriving at our houses, we say goodbye to Miles and Theodore as they continue on to their houses. Lacey and I race into our houses to get changed out of our uniforms and agree to meet back on the grass between our houses with our marbles in ten minutes. We spend the rest of the afternoon practicing with Lacey's bonker.

"I think it's best if I keep the bonker at home," she says, while she shoots it at one of my galaxy marbles.

"It sounds like a good idea," I tell her, as I line up my marble, flicking it at her bonker and winning. We aren't playing for keeps so she takes her bonker back and places it in her pencil case.

"Goodnight Chance. I'll see you in the morning," she says, walking away as I do the same. When I smell the dinner Mum cooked and my stomach grumbles in appreciation, I realise we were so busy playing marbles at lunch I forgot to eat.

LACEY

24TH FEBRUARY
Dear Diary,

Carson is a butthead. I DO NOT LIKE HIM. I can't believe he had the nerve to steal my bonker. Especially when I hadn't had it for a whole day yet. Luckily Chance stood up for me and got it back. Theodore telling us he had seen Carson with it in the first place surprised me.

Ugh so I guess Theodore isn't all bad. I will keep an eye on him and see if he keeps doing good deeds or else he will be back to bad in my books in no time.

I think Miles and Theodore will make pretty good friends if Chance and I ever want to play with anyone else. I wonder if Miles can win some more bonkers off his cousins. Those grand daddy marbles sound so cool. You must be able to buy them from the shops. I'll ask Dad if he can buy me some.

I put my bonker on my shelf behind my music box to keep it safe in case anyone else was thinking of stealing it. I don't want to lose my whole collection so I'm going to take my stinky marbles to school and leave my best ones at home for safe keeping.

I can't believe Chance pushed Carson. I've never seen Chance mad before. I hope he doesn't feel bad for pushing him. I don't feel bad. I'm glad he pushed him. Hopefully it'll make Carson think twice about stealing my stuff or anyone else's for that matter.

I'm going to hunt through my marbles now and find the worst ones and hide all my good ones. I'll write to you later.

I HATE CARSON THE STINKY THIEF!!
Lacey

CHAPTER 4

CHANCE

1ST MAY

Mum came home with a new skateboard for me yesterday. She said she found it on her way home in someone's inorganic rubbish. She said one man's trash is another man's treasure. I didn't care what she was saying because all I could think about was how I have a new skateboard. I am currently waiting for Lacey, like I do every Saturday, to go to the dairy. We usually take Bronco with us to the dairy but I had to leave him at home today. I have my board under my arm and my pocket money safely in my jeans pocket. I spin the wheels with my fingers while I wait. It isn't long until Lacey comes racing over. Her face drops when she sees Bronco isn't with me but when she spies what's under my arm, the smile returns to her face.

"It's so cool. Is it yours?" she shrieks, her excitement obvious.

"Yeah, Mum found it in someone's inorganic," I tell her, handing it over for her to examine.

"It looks pretty new," she observes, flipping it back and forth.

"I thought we could ride it to the dairy and test it out. It's why I had to leave Bronco at home," I tell her, which has the biggest smile spreading across her face.

"Yes," she squeals, running over to the grey footpath and putting it down.

"You sit in the front and I'll sit behind you," I tell her, as we both squat on the dark grey board. "Pop your feet on top and hold on tight. I'll steer us with my hands," I instruct, waiting for her to follow my instructions. She bends her knees, placing her feet flat against the front of the board and holds onto the middle of the board in front of her butt.

"You ready?" I ask, as I scoot myself close to her back so we are balanced. I try to push us forward but we don't move fast at all.

"Chance, I don't think this is working," Lacey says.

"Yeah I can't move with my legs out but I can't fit them on with you. We could do one at a time and take turns?" I suggest.

"Hmmm," she says, thinking as she hops off the board to look at it. "I know. Place your legs out straight and then I'll sit on your legs with my knees bent." I follow her instructions and place my legs out straight on the board. Lacey dumps herself on my lap and tucks her legs in again. She puts her hands under my legs to hold onto the board as my hands push off against the rough gravel. My chin drops on top of her shoulder. Our giggles fill the air as I manage to get us moving along at a nice pace.

"Faster Chance," she squeals loudly into my ear. I feed off her exhilaration, doing as she requests and pushing us faster. In our excitement, we've both forgotten about the giant hill between our houses and the dairy. Before we can stop ourselves, we are quickly picking up speed.

"Lacey," I shriek, as my grip tightens under the board, trying to steer us. Both of us laugh at the thrill of the wind blowing against us as we zoom down the hill. My heart rate picks up speed as I realise I don't know how to stop and panic sets in. Steering us out of a driveway, we end up on the road, zig zagging the rest of the way down the hill. Luckily there are no cars around. Lacey's laughter rings in my ears as we travel along the bumpy gravel road, slowing us down. As we slow to a crawl, I direct us towards the kerb and we hit it with a soft thud and stop dead in our tracks.

"This is so much fun," Lacey squeaks, as she jumps off my lap so I can get up. Quickly I pick up the board and we both get back onto the footpath in case any cars come. "Let's do it again," she pants, out of breath from her laughing.

"Let's grab some lollies first," I tell her, seeing as we made it all the way to the dairy.

"Okay," she tells me, skipping the last few steps to the dairy. We enter and I'm about to get her usual ka blueys but before I can, she says, "Can I have the smoke lollies instead?"

"Sure," I say, grabbing the blue packet with the spaceman on it. I ask the dairy owner for two dollar bags of mixed lollies as well. Handing Lacey her smoke lollies we exit the dairy and she opens her packet, handing me one. We both hold a smoke between our index and middle fingers and pretend to smoke like we've seen people do in the movies.

"Do you think you'll smoke for real when you're older?" she asks, pretending to blow smoke out of her mouth with her lips in the shape of an O.

"I don't know. Do you?" I reply, as I bite the end off of my white stick, leaving the little bit of red on the end until last.

"I think I'll try it and see if I like it. You gotta try everything once. It's what living life is about," she tells me, matter of factly while taking a bite of her own stick. "We should make a pact to always try everything at least once," she says, popping the last of her stick into her mouth and holding out her pinky finger to me.

"Ugh okay," I give in, linking my pinky finger with hers.

"Lock it Chance. You always forget the lock," she tells me, holding her thumb out.

"Well I don't need to remember because you're always here to remind me," I inform her.

"What happens if you want to make a pinky promise with some-one else?" she asks, tilting her head to the side.

"Don't be dumb. I only pinky promise with you silly," I tell her, rolling my eyes which has her cheeks turning pink while she smiles back at me.

"I'll race you to the top," she squeals, racing off to get a head start. I snatch the skateboard from the ground and race with all my might to try and catch up with her.

At the top she yells, "I win," as she bends over with her hands on her knees to catch her breath. I drop the skateboard and we hop back on in the positions we had before and get ready to go again. A car driving by has us pausing before checking there are no more cars coming. When the coast is clear, I push off down the bumpy hill, a thrill filling our veins. Laughing the whole way, we take the same route we did the first time. We spend our Saturday afternoon racing to the top of the hill then rolling down with the wind in our hair, feeling like we will burst from living life on the edge.

LACEY

1ST MAY
Dear Diary,

Today was a great day. Chance's mum found him a skateboard and it is the best thing ever. We spent hours racing down the hill. We had one near miss but luckily the car beeped at us when it saw us and waited patiently for us to pass.

I told Mum and Dad all about how much fun I had and Mum told me to stick to the footpath. Dad wasn't worried, he said we need to make sure we keep an eye out for cars. He doesn't want to have to make another trip to the hospital.

I asked Chance if he wants to skateboard again tomorrow and he said yes, so we are going to meet at our tree after breakfast and do some climbing then skateboard for the rest of the day.

Chance said he isn't going to make a pinky promise with anyone else. I wonder if I should get him to make a pinky promise so it's made law then he will have to stick to it. Especially if we lock it.

Anyway, I can't wait for tomorrow. I'm so excited.

Lacey

CHAPTER 5

CHANCE

10TH JULY

Waking from my night's rest, the big red numbers on my alarm clock read five-fifty. Slinging my duvet back I jump out of bed and stagger to the bathroom. The minty toothpaste on my toothbrush runs along my teeth, cleaning them. Knowing Mum she will stop me leaving the house if I haven't done it. Racing back to my room, I grab the blank cassette tape Mum bought for me when she was at the shops yesterday. I'd been asking for more cassettes for a while as Lacey and I have been dying to record some of the newest songs we'd heard on the radio.

"I'm going to Lacey's," I yell out to Mum. My feet thunder down the hall in my rush to get to the front door.

"Chance, it's so early," she calls back, as I open the door and close it gently behind me. Running barefoot down my driveway, I get to Lacey's front door within seconds. Turning the brass knob on her door, I push the door open and enter. I never knock anymore. It's super quiet as I enter so I try not to make too much noise.

Sneaking down the hall, I turn right into Lacey's room and push her door open. Spotting her fluffy hair sticking out from under her pink duvet, I creep closer until her face comes into view. She looks like a sleeping angel, apart from the poofy hair. Her face is peaceful in sleep. Well her peaceful sleep can wait as I want to record songs now. Before she wakes I pounce on her causing her screams to fill the air.

"Chance, you dumb butt, what are you doing?" she yells, as I laugh, looking at her.

"Waking you up. Rick Dee's is nearly on and look what Mum got me," I tell her, shaking the new black cassette in front of her. As her eyes widen, she sits and pushes my chest so I fall backwards onto the bed laughing. She wipes the sleep from her eyes, flings the duvet off her and we make our way to the living room where her boombox is kept.

"What's all this ruckus about so early this morning?" Lacey's dad says, as he walks into the living room, rubbing the sleep from his own eyes. When he sees me, he says, "Oh it's you Chance. I should have known." He ruffles my hair as he leans down, kissing Lacey on top of her head. "Do you two want some pancakes?" he asks.

"Yes please Daddy," Lacey says.

"Yes please sir."

"Two plates of pancakes, coming right up," he tells us, as he leaves us to get to work in the kitchen.

I quickly unwrap the plastic from the tape and hand it to Lacey. She flicks the case open and pops it in the tape deck while I race to the kitchen to put the wrapper in the bin. Racing back, I find her turning the power on, sitting cross legged in front of the boombox. Turning the dial, she finds the right station and we hear Rick Dee announce the top forty playlist is kicking off. We haven't had a new cassette in ages to record new songs. The tape has sixty minutes of space so we have to be selective about what songs we want to record. Rick Dee announces the title and we have to be lightning fast to press record if we want that particular song. It's a life and death situation as you don't want to miss the beginning. You have to time it perfectly to make sure you don't catch any of the host talking at the end either.

Rick Dee announces, "Coming up is Colour me Badd with 'All 4 Love.'"

"Do you want it?" I ask Lacey.

"I'm not sure what song it is," she says, thinking.

"We don't have time, Lace. Hurry and decide. Record or not?" I anxiously say, worried the beginning will get cut off if she doesn't hurry. I know she will turn it around and I'll be to blame for not being fast enough.

"I don't know. I don't want to waste the space if I don't like it," she whines.

"I'm recording it. We can always rewind back and record over it if you don't like it," I say, quickly pressing record with a second to spare. The song's upbeat tempo plays and a smile tips her lips up.

"Oh yes, I love this song," she declares, as she sings along to the words. I roll my eyes at her as it's typical Lacey. She loves so many songs but never knows the titles of them. She sings the whole song, nearly word for word too so you would think she would know the title and artist by now. The song comes to an end so I hover my finger over the stop button waiting for the exact moment to hit stop so Rick Dee's voice doesn't get recorded. I press the button a few seconds before his voice comes back on air.

"You could have waited a few more seconds," Lacey whines. I roll my eyes again.

"The singing had stopped so it's fine," I tell her, defending myself.

"Ugh," she huffs.

"Gosh, you're extra grumpy this morning," I tell her, half listening to the radio to hear what the next song will be. She ignores me, crossing her arms over her chest. "Write Colour Me Badd on the list before you forget." She sticks her tongue out of the corner of her mouth while she focuses on her tiny writing, trying to make it small but legible so everything can fit on the small piece of cardboard that comes in the cassette case.

"Chance!," she screams, making me jump. I was distracted watching her write. "You missed Michael Jackson's 'Black or White'," she whines.

Rolling my eyes for like the millionth time today, I say, "Michael's always in the top forty, we can get him next week. I'll ask Mum to get me another tape." Before she can complain, her dad comes in telling us the pancakes are ready.

"Can we eat here Daddy? We don't want to miss any songs," she pleads, looking at the tall man she has wrapped around her little finger.

"Okay, just this once," he softly tells her, kissing her again on the head. He comes back a minute later with two plates of pancakes covered in maple syrup. We dig in straight away. This song recording has built up an appetite and who can say no to pancakes.

"Oh record, record," Lacey squeals. I drop my fork and quickly press the record button as Shanice's song 'I Love Your Smile' plays. I was so distracted by my delicious syrupy pancakes, I'd forgotten we were recording songs for a minute. Luckily Lacey was listening as this is one of her favourite songs and I wouldn't have heard the end of it if I had missed it. She sings along at the top of her lungs, syrup covering her mouth and I can't help but think the song title is right because I sure do love her smile. When her smile is directed at me, like it is now, it makes my heart flutter and I can't help but feel happy.

I tune back into the song on the radio, listening for the exact moment to press stop. I concentrate extra hard because I don't want to get Lacey mad again if I cut off a few seconds. It isn't long before the tape is full on side A and we have to take it out, flip it over and push it back in to record on side B. We fight over recording Paula Abdul's song because Lacey wants it but I don't. Since it's my cassette, I have final say but it doesn't stop Lacey from screwing her face up at me while the song plays without recording.

Rick Dee announces the next song and I don't make a move to record it. Lacey at the last second flings herself at the boombox, pressing record before I can stop her.

"Lacey!" I scream at her, because she knows damn well I don't like the song. Her rolling around on the carpet in hysterics has me pouncing at her and tickling her sides, while I pin her down so she can't escape. "Do you think it's funny?" I ask, torturing her with my tickling.

"Yes I do," she squeals, as she continues to laugh uncontrollably. Her loud laughter brings her dad into the room.

"What's going on with you two?" he asks, staring at us with his hands on his hips.

"She recorded a song she knows I hate," I defend, continuing to tickle her sides while she squirms under me. Her dad laughs along with her then places his hands under my underarms and lifts me off his daughter. She sits with a huge grin on her face.

"Now every time you listen to it, you can think of me," she says, fluttering her lashes at me.

Folding my arms over my chest I huff, "I can rewind and record over it and not think of you at all." She stares at me, her smile growing because she knows I won't do it. Her dad isn't the only one she has wrapped around her little finger. She leans forward and presses stop in perfect timing to cut the announcer off, her smile widening. I sit there simmering in my anger at her recording the song. Her dad leaves us to it. I don't talk to her as I press record on the next song. Lacey doesn't like when I'm mad at her so she comes over and wraps her tiny arms around my neck, squeezing and pressing her cheek to my cheek.

"I'm sorry Chancey, forgive me?" she asks, and like every time before and probably every time after, I wrap my arms around my best friend and let out a sigh.

"You're forgiven. No more wasting the tape on stink songs," I tell her.

"Okie dokie," she sings, while squeezing my neck tighter. She lets go and lies on the carpet, pulling the book and cardboard sheet closer to her. Writing the name of the stupid song she recorded, her legs wave in the air behind her while she softly sings along to the song currently playing. We continue on until the second side of the tape is complete.

"What number tape are we up to now?" she asks, flattening the top of the cardboard out so she can write the title of the tape along the top so we can see it when it's in its case.

"This is number eleven," I tell her, and she quickly writes the title of our cassette. Taking the tape out of the boombox, I put the cardboard and cassette back into the plastic cover while Lacey runs to her room to get changed out of her nightie. We take our newly completed tape with us as we walk over to my house. Entering the house, Lacey talks with my mum while I get changed out of my own pyjamas and grab my walkman. Walking into the kitchen, we tell my mum we are going to the tree to hang out. Bronco barks at us for ignoring him so we both bend and give him a good scratch behind the ears before we walk outside. I make a mental note to take him for an extra long walk tomorrow.

Opening the back door, Lacey squeals, "Race you," as she runs off. It's always the same with her, she's forever trying to get a head start. If we had an even race I would win eight out of ten times. I'm nice and let her win sometimes because it's what good friends do. We laugh as we race to our tree and climb the lower branches. We both straddle one of the stronger branches close to the bottom of the weeping willow, knowing it will easily hold us both. I unwrap my headphones from my walkman and hand one to her and push the other into my ear. Pulling the new mixed tape from my pocket, I open the case and pop it into the walkman.

Lacey sings along to the first song and I can't help but join in with her. We spend the rest of the day laughing, singing and replaying the tape over and over until we know the order of the songs off by heart. It's a magical day. I don't want it to end so when it's time for bed I slip my walkman under the duvet and pop my headphones in. The new recorded songs play in my ears while I drift off to sleep, letting today's memories replay over and over in my head. I fall asleep with a huge smile on my face, thinking of Lacey.

LACEY

10TH JULY

Dear Diary,

I have the perfect idea for Chance's birthday present. I'm going to make him a mixed tape of his favourite songs. Most of the mixtapes are songs for both of us but I think he should have a special one, just for him. I feel bad since I messed up his tape today by adding the song he hates.

I'll have to ask Daddy to get me a new tape some time as I don't want to record over any of the ones I have already. Yes, I think a mixed tape is the perfect present.

I'm sleepy from all the laughing Chance and I did today so I better go to bed.

Sweet dreams,

Lacey

CHAPTER 6

CHANCE

7TH NOVEMBER

Today is my birthday. I can't believe I'm eight years old. I'm practically a grown man now. I race into Mum's room and jump on her bed to wake her so I can open my presents. She hands me a perfectly wrapped bundle of presents. The wrapping paper tears and flings everywhere in pursuit of uncovering my gifts. She bought me some new clothes, a new pair of shoes, two new Goosebumps books, *The Haunted Mask* and *The Werewolf of Fever Swamp*. I can't wait to read them. She also gives me the cassingle of 'Dreamlover' by Mariah Carey. The cassingle alone would have made my birthday the best, I love Mariah.

After breakfast with Mum, I rush to my room, carrying my haul of gifts and dumping them on my bed. I search through the pile, picking up the cassette tape and grabbing my walkman from my desk. Taking out the old cassette in my walkman, my mind is filled with excitement to hear 'Dreamlover' play. It clicks in place as I pop my headphones in and press play. I have the biggest smile on my face as the music plays. I sing and dance around my room, feeling so happy. I rewind the tape to play it for the fourth time in a row when I hear something behind me. Looking over my shoulder, Lacey leans against my door frame with her hand covering her mouth, her eyes alight with glee. I roll my eyes and turn around to face her as heat fills my face.

"You've got moves, Chance," she giggles, as she walks into my room.

"How long have you been standing there?" I demand.

"Long enough for my ears to bleed from you trying to hit the high notes," she jokes.

"You'll regret your comment one day. When I'm a famous singer and they ask me who my best friend is, it won't be your name I'll say because I will have forgotten all about you," I defend, as I lash out from embarrassment. I see the moment my words hurt her. Her face drops, the smile disappears from her face, and we stand there in stone cold silence, staring at each other. It isn't until a minute later when I've watched her think it over and the pit in my stomach has grown from my harsh words, her eyes light up again.

"Don't be silly, Chance. We both know I'm always gonna be your best friend. You can't get rid of me that easily," she states, as she holds her head high and sits on my bed, getting comfortable. "Now silly butt, I have your birthday present but if you're going to be mean, I can give it to someone else," she tells me, her head tilted to the side.

"I'm sorry. You know I didn't mean it," I sigh, as I take a seat next to her.

"I'm sorry too. Your voice isn't bad."

"Thanks," I say.

"Let's start again. Happy birthday Chancey," she squeals with feigned excitement, but it has my lips smiling at her anyway. She holds out the present for me to take.

"Thanks," I say, ripping off the brown paper she wrapped it in. I pull out the mixed tape she made me and look at the title she's written: Chance's Mix One.

"It has all your favourite songs on it. It's taken me weeks to make," she tells me, as she nudges her shoulder against mine.

"Let's listen to it," I tell her, taking my dreamlover tape out of the walkman to replace it with the mixed tape.

"Wait. Look at the book," she tells me, handing me the other part of my present.

"*Magic Eye*," I say, as I read the cover.

"They're 3D illusions. Let's try it out and see if we can see them," she tells me. We scoot onto the floor, our backs leaning against my bed frame as I open the book. I read the instructions and follow them. Holding the hardcover book to my face, I stare at my nose and then slowly pull the book away. It takes a few tries but then finally the image pops out from the pages.

"Wow. This is so cool," I tell Lacey, as I keep my eyes crossed so the illusion doesn't disappear.

"Can I have a turn?" she pleads, bouncing next to me.

"Here," I say, handing her the book and directing her on what to do. I glance at Laceys' crossed eyes and hold in my laugh because she looks so funny.

"I see it, Chance. I see it," she squeals, her joy filling the air. We take turns passing the book back and forth, trying to see what the hidden illusion is on each page. There's some we struggle to see and decide to skip and come back to them later. Once we get to the last page, I remember the mixtape so I grab my walkman and give Lacey a earbud while I have the other. We sit side by side, listening to the songs Lacey chose specifically for me. She was telling the truth because they are all songs I love.

Mum knocks on my open door, breaking up our singing party and tells us it's time to head to Georgie Pie for lunch. She told me this year I could have a birthday party and invite some friends from school but I only wanted Lacey there. The kids are no longer mean to me and Lacey and I play with them sometimes but for my birthday I wanted my best friend there and nobody else. Everything's better when it is just the two of us anyway. At Georgie Pie, Mum asks us what flavour pie we want and we both choose mince and cheese. She tells us we can play on the playground until our food is ready so we race to the top of the plastic stairs and play on the slide until Mum calls us over to eat. We bite into the delicious, soft pastry to taste the hot mince and tangy cheese. We gobble the food up so fast Mum worries we will burn our tongues. We don't tell her we scoff our food because we want more time to play on the playground before she drags us home.

Bouncing with birthday energy, Mum calls for us a few times before we give in and hop off the playground. She drives us home and we all take a seat at the kitchen table. She surprises me by pulling out a chocolate cake covered in sprinkles sporting eight colourful candles, burning brightly on top of it. She places it carefully on the wooden table as her and Lacey sing 'Happy Birthday' to me.

"Make a wish," she tells me, smiling at me over the candle flames. I close my eyes tight and wish everyday can be this fun. Popping my eyes open, I blow out my candles knowing my wish will come true because as long as I have Mum and Lacey with me, the days will always be good. After we fill our faces with the sweet dessert, licking the chocolate icing from our fingers, we race out the back door. Running barefoot with the soft grass under our feet, we sprint to our destination. When the huge tree looms into view we waste no time climbing the thick branches, enjoying the rest of the sunny day. We continue climbing the tree and laughing until the sun sets and Lacey and I have to part ways.

"Thanks Mum. Today was the best birthday ever," I tell her, as I kiss her cheek and bound off to bed.

"You're welcome," she calls after me. Lying in bed, I drift off listening to my new favourite mixed tape and wishing for all my days to be this fun.

LACEY

7TH NOVEMBER
Dear Diary,

Today was Chance's birthday. He loved the Magic Eye book Mum suggested I get for him since it was something different from the usual books he has. I had wanted to get him more Goosebumps books but luckily I didn't as his mum got him some of those. The Magic Eye book was pretty cool. I want one of my own now.

I'm so glad I took the time to make the mixed tape. He looked so happy singing along to all his favourite songs. I nearly threw the stupid thing at the wall a couple times as I wasn't as good as Chance at recording songs at the right time. There were a few songs I had to record a few times before I got it right. It was worth it as it made Chance happy. The cake his mum made was so yummy. I want one of those cakes for my birthday next year. I wonder if I can convince her to make me one with pink icing.

In all the excitement of Chance's birthday, I nearly forgot to tell you I got a new diary today. The other one was full so I had to beg Mum to get me a new one so I could keep writing. When we grabbed Chance's Magic Eye book at the shop, Mum bought me my new diary. It's a bright yellow colour with purple butterflies all over. I think it's pretty and I can't wait to fill the pages.

Goodnight,
Lacey

CHAPTER 7

CHANCE 1994

16TH MARCH

"Stop scratching," Mum tells me, as she catches me scratching my arm again for the millionth time.

"Mum, it's so itchy," I whine, needing some relief from the itch. Chicken pox is making the rounds at my school and I've finally come down with it. The ringing of the telephone drags Mum away from me as she races to the kitchen to answer it. I rub the palm of my hand against my arm trying to get some relief but Mum must have a sixth sense. She drags the curly phone cord all the way down the hall to keep an eye on me while she talks on the phone.

"Chance!" she sternly says, which has me rolling my eyes at her while she talks into the receiver. "Yes, he won't stop scratching," she says to whoever is on the other end. Her laugh has me paying attention and trying to guess who she is talking to on the phone. She listens to whatever the mystery caller is saying then laughs again. I don't think laughing at my itchy situation is helpful but I don't dare tell her.

"You wouldn't happen to have a spare pair for Chance, would you?" she asks, laughing again. "Perfect, I'll see you both soon," she says, before going back to the kitchen and hanging up the phone.

"Who has got a spare pair of what for me?" I call out, trying to keep my mind on something else other than this torturous itch.

"You'll see," she tells me, with a secretive smile on her face. I screw up my face because I know she won't tell me anything. Cuddling under the blanket, I try to get comfortable on my makeshift bed Mum made on the couch for me so I could watch TV instead of being bored in my room.

Ten minutes later, a knock at the door has Mum getting up from her seat and going to open it. Voices filter into the house as Mum welcomes the guests in. When they step back into the living room, I look to see who it is. Staring at my best friend, the red spots on her face and arms are obvious as she hugs her favourite cabbage patch doll to her chest. Her hands are covered with a pair of pink gloves. We both screw up our noses staring at the other.

"You gave me chicken pox," Lacey huffs, as she steps closer to me.

"These are for you Chance," Lacey's mum says, as she steps in behind her daughter holding out a pair of pink gloves which has my face screwing up even more.

"Ugh, do I have to Mum? They're pink," I scowl. It's bad enough pink has invaded my life as a by-product of being Lacey's friend but I don't want to personally wear it. I have to draw the line somewhere.

"Yes you do. It'll help you stop scratching and no one but Lacey is going to see them."

"Fine," I say, taking the gloves and wriggling my hands into the woollen material.

"I have other gifts too," Lacey's mum says, swinging the plastic bag she's holding.

"My dad went to the video store and picked out some movies for us to watch," Lacey tells me, which has my mood improving significantly. I was worried I was going to be stuck lying on the couch watching Days of Our Lives for the next two weeks.

"Cool, what did he get?" I ask, sitting and leaning against my pillow on the couch. Lacey grabs the bag from her mum and walks over to me.

"Have you got time for a coffee?" Mum says to Lacey's mum.

Twisting her wrist, she checks her watch before saying, "Sure." They disappear down the hallway and head towards the kitchen. Lacey places the plastic bag on my lap so I can look through it. I pull the cases out and read the titles out loud.

"*Hocus Pocus*, *Homeward Bound*, and *The Secret Garden*. Cool, I haven't seen any of these yet. What do you want to watch first?" I ask Lacey.

"Lets watch *Homeward Bound*," she says, pointing to the cover.

"Do you want to top and tail?" I ask. She looks at me on the couch, assessing the size of the couch and whether she can fit.

"Sure," she finally says, grabbing one of the couch cushions and placing it at the other end of the couch for her head.

"What's this?" I ask, finding a bottle of pink lotion in the same bag as the movies.

"It's calamine lotion," Mum says from behind me. My head tilts backwards to look at her upside down. "We need to put it on all your spots because it'll help with the itching. Stand up," she tells me. I do as she says and Lacey's mum gets Lacey to do the same. We stand next to each other as our mums check our bodies and generously lather the pink lotion on every spot they find. At one point Lacey and I stand facing each other and we can't help but laugh at each other's faces. She looks like a pink mud monster with all the pink goop splattered on it so I imagine I look bad too if not worse.

"Okay, on the couch kids and I'll pop the movie in for you," Mum tells us, as the kettle whistles from the kitchen letting her know the water is boiled.

"I'll sort the coffee," Lacey's mum says, walking off to deal with the screeching sound.

Lacey and I squeeze onto the ends of the couch and lay our legs side by side. Our pink gloved hands lay on top of the blanket and Lacey's cabbage patch doll is settled under the blanket next to her. Mum pushes the VHS tape into the slot and presses play. We both snuggle under the blankets and get comfortable while we watch the movie.

"Bye sweetie," Lacey's mum says, as she walks to Lacey and places a kiss on her head.

"Bye Mum," she replies, eyes still zoned in on the TV screen. Both our mums talk by the front door before she leaves.

"Well you kids are stuck with each other for the next two weeks. You're spending this week here and then next week, you'll be at Lacey's house with her dad while I work."

"So no school for two weeks. Yay," I squeal in excitement.

"No. You can't go back until your spots are healed and you aren't infectious anymore."

"Yes!" Both Lacey and I shout, which sends us into a fit of giggles.

Mum shakes her head, smiling at us, "Let me know when you two get hungry. I'll be in the kitchen."

"Okay Mum," I yell to her retreating back. We snuggle back down, get comfortable and watch our movie. When the movie comes to an end, I get off the couch to put *Hocus Pocus* in at Lacey's request.

"Don't forget to rewind it before you take the tape out. Dad said we had to so he doesn't get fined. He can get us some new movies when we get sick of these ones," Lacey informs me. I press the rewind button and when it's finished, I take it out and pop the next tape in.

Mum must hear us making noise as she comes in a few minutes later asking if we want some popcorn. She also wants to apply more calamine lotion so we take turns while she covers our spots again. The lotion feels soothing on the skin and is helping a lot with the itching but boy does it stink. I must share these thoughts out loud without realising because Mum offers an alternative to using the lotion. After hearing her new idea, Lacey and I both beg and plead with Mum to keep using the calamine lotion. It took two words to scare us. Oatmeal bath. No way in hell am I letting it happen. I am not bathing with a girl, even if she is my best friend. Who knows what cooties I might catch from her, she already gave me chicken pox though she wouldn't dare admit it.

LACEY

16TH MARCH
Dear Diary,

Ugh I am so blimmin itchy and it's all Chance's fault. I don't even know if I can get through this diary entry without scratching. It never stops. Those gloves we had on today weren't much help. Chance and I soon realised if we gently slid the gloves against our skin we could relieve some of the itch without looking like we were scratching.

Chance's mum caught me scratching the big one between my eyebrows and she told me to stop or else it would leave a scar. You know what? It is so itchy, I don't even care if it scars. I'm going to scratch it tonight because I can't stand it any longer. If it scars then I've won the lottery because then I'll have a scar on my face like Chance. His one is way cooler because it's bigger but at least we will have something else in common.

His scar isn't as easy to see as it once was. I asked him about it once and he told me his mum said it would probably fade as he aged and blend more into his skin. I hope it doesn't disappear completely as it would be the worst thing ever. I agree with his mum, it gives him character and makes him unique.

Hold on, I can't take it. I need to scratch for a minute. Ahh, so much better. Mum and Dad will be so mad if they know I'm scratching but I need the relief. A girls gotta do what a girls gotta do. I stood against the wall and bent my knees while rubbing my back against it. It was awkward but I needed something that would give me maximum effect. My hands were free to scratch my stomach and arms so it was a bonus.

I may have to do another round of scratching before I try to sleep tonight. I'm so happy I get to spend two weeks with Chance without going to school. I wish I wasn't itching constantly. Dad said he would take the movies back to the video store tomorrow and change them for me. I'm going to ask him if he can get more because three movies don't last long. I'm going to tell him to get more action ones because Chance likes those. He suffers through the princess and romance ones because I like them.

Argh I gotta go, Mum's calling out. It's time to rub the stinky calamine lotion on me again. At least I can't complain about the colour.

Itch ya later,
Lacey

CHAPTER 8

CHANCE

25TH JUNE

Mum arrives home with a new phone as the old one died. The clerk who sold it to her told her the new phone can make three way calls. I don't talk on the phone much and I didn't understand much of what my mum was saying but she explained it to me anyway. I race over to Lacey's house as soon as Mum finishes talking as it sounds like something Lacey would want to know about.

"Hey Mr Connelly, Mrs Connelly," I yell, as I race through their house to Lacey's room and throw her door open. Lacey's sitting on her bed playing with the few trolls she has in her collection. I find it funny she will sit for hours brushing their fluffy coloured hair with her little plastic brush but she refuses to brush her own hair. Their hair isn't even real. She's currently brushing her pink haired troll and her eyes widen as she whips around when she hears the door bang against the wall.

"Chance, did you have to scare me?" she squeaks, continuing to brush the pink hair.

"Sorry, I have something exciting to tell you about."

"Well spit it out."

"Mum said our new phone has three way calling," I tell her, which makes a smile grow on her face.

"Really?" her high pitched voice squeaks up an octave.

"Yeah, she just told me. Do you know what it is?"

"It's the best thing ever. I heard Julie telling Marley she has it and she uses it to prank her cousins. I heard her explain how she does it too. Come on." She jumps off her bed, grabs me by the hand and drags me out of her house.

"Bye Mr Connelly, Mrs Connelly," I yell to her parents, as we pass them and I see her dad shake his head at us, smiling as we go. Opening my front door I tell Mum I'm back with Lacey and we are going to try out the three way calling.

"Don't rack up my phone bill Chance," she warns, before heading back to the kitchen where she is baking some yummy chocolate afghans.

"We won't," I tell her. I grab the handset from the hallway and luckily the new phone cord is long enough to stretch all the way into the lounge. "How do we do it?" I ask Lacey.

"Do you know anyone's phone number apart from mine?" she asks.

"No, I don't think so. We could look in the phone book," I suggest, which has her nodding. I push myself up from where I'm lying on the floor and head to the little cupboard in our hallway. I grab the phone book and heave it back towards where Lacey is. "Whose number should we look for?" I ask Lacey, and watch as an evil glint takes over her eyes.

"Let's prank Theodore," she squeals. I laugh at the prospect of pranking him.

"Okay. Let's see if his number is in here," I say, as I flick through the pages finding the section with W. Scanning the list with my finger, I run it along until I come to Waters. There's several in the list but I find one with an address a few streets away from here. It must be Theodore's house.

"I think I've got it," I say, as my finger taps at the number to show Lacey.

"Okay, to ring you gotta dial me first and I'll answer then press this button quickly. Wait for the dial tone then you dial Theodore. Once he answers, you gotta click this button again to let me join the conversation. Julie said part of the prank was for one person to be on mute so the third person doesn't know they're there."

"So I gotta pretend it's just Theodore and me talking?" I clarify.

"Yeah and get him to confess all his juicy secrets," she cackles, and I can't help but feel this three way power has gone to her head.

"Head home now and I'll ring you. Don't forget to stay on mute," I tell her.

She runs out of my house screaming, "This is the best day ever," which has me laughing. I drum my fingers on the beige carpet while I give her a few minutes to get home and make it to her phone. After what I think is a decent amount of time, I dial her phone number. Holding the receiver to my ear, it rings once before she answers.

"Chance?"

"You're supposed to say hello first. What if it wasn't me?" I tease.

"Chance, you butt head, I knew it was you. You said less than two minutes ago you were going to call," she grunts at me through the phone line, which makes me laugh.

"I'm teasing you, don't get your undies in a twist."

"My undies are perfectly untwisted. Thank you very much," she defends, making me laugh harder. "Hurry up Chance," she whines.

"Fine. I'm ringing now. Remember to press mute," I tell her.

"Got it." I do exactly as she told me and press the button, wait for the dial tone then I dial the number in the phone book we think is Theodore's.

After a few rings, a ladies' voice says, "Hello?"

"Hi, is Theodore there please?" my shaky voice asks, hoping we have the right number.

"He's right here. Can I ask who's calling?"

"It's Chance," I tell her, before I hear a shuffling sound as she gives him the receiver. I quickly click the button Lacey said I had to and hope she has joined the conversation and is on mute.

"Hello?" Theodore's voice comes over the receiver.

"Hi, it's Chance," I tell him.

"How did you get my number?"

"I looked it up in the phone book. What are you doing?"

"Anthony and I are watching cartoons. What are you doing?"

"Not much. Mum got a new phone so I thought I'd try it out."

"Cool. You want to head over to Rutherford Park later? We could kick my new soccer ball around."

"Yeah, it sounds like fun. Can Lacey come?" I ask.

"Ugh Lacey. Does she have to?" he whines.

"Of course, she's my best friend. I do everything with her," I tell him.

"Don't you want some boy time sometimes? You know, without girls?" he asks. My brows furrow because I've never felt like having boy time. All my plans include Lacey.

"Not really. I always want to play with Lacey."

"Do you like her?" he asks.

"Of course I like her, she's my best friend."

"No, I mean like her, like her. Do you want her to be your girlfriend?" he asks, as my eyes bulge out of my friend.

"No. She's my friend," I tell him.

"You sure? Everyone thinks you two like each other and it's why you are always together and holding hands. They think you kiss like parents do," he confesses.

"Whaaaaat?" I squeal.

"Yeah. Have you kissed her?"

"No. She's my best friend."

"You should kiss her because Leo said he likes her and wants to kiss her," he tells me.

"Whaaaaaat?" I squeal again.

"Yeah, he has a huge crush on Lacey. I don't know why. She doesn't even brush her hair."

I'm about to defend her when her own squeaking voice comes on the line, "Theodore you're a butthead, at least I can brush my hair if I want. You will forever be a butthead."

"Lacey? Where did you come from?" Theodore stammers.

"Okay, come over later Theodore and we'll go to the park. Bye," I blurt out, cutting off Lacey before she says anything else. I hang up the receiver and end the call. A minute passes before Lacey bursts through my door.

"Chance, what were you doing? You were supposed to be getting his secrets out of him," she demands, with her hands on her hips.

"He asked me so many questions and I didn't know how to turn it back around on him," I confess. His words linger in my head and my eyes flicker to Lacey's lips.

"What?" she asks.

"Have you ever thought about kissing me?" I blurt, my cheeks heating.

"Chance don't be dumb. You're my best friend," she says, but then her own eyes drift to my lips. "Why? Have you thought about kissing me?"

"No, but we should. Otherwise Leo will be your first kiss. Do you want him to be your first kiss?" I ask.

"Eww gross. No way," she sticks her finger in her mouth in a vomiting action which makes me laugh. "Kiss me Chance, let's get this over with," she says, causing my laughter to stop.

"We don't have to kiss. You should save it for someone special," I tell her, as my cheeks redden.

She rolls her eyes at me, "You're a dumb butt Chance. You're my best friend and the most special person to me. Pucker up," she says, as she steps forward so fast I don't have time to register what's happening. She leans in, closing her eyes as her lips quickly but roughly touch mine. It's over before I realise what happened. My lips tingle and we both stare at each other with wide eyes.

"My lips tingle," I confess.

"Mine too. I think it means we are good kissers," she says, looking at my lips again.

"Does this mean you have to be my girlfriend now?" I ask, unsure what the protocol for this type of situation is.

"No, I think best friend trumps girlfriend," she tells me, matter of factly.

"Are you sure? What about when we are older? Won't girlfriend trump best friend then?" I ask, as my nose scrunches in thought. Her lips twist to the side while she thinks to herself.

Her eyes light up as she focuses back on me, before she says, "Don't worry, no one will ever trump me because now I am forever your first kiss. If you ever have a girlfriend, I'll tell her I was your first kiss and she'll know she doesn't come before me in your life," she rants.

"Lacey, are you sure?"

"Of course. Trust me."

"Okay," I say, because I always trust Lacey and she wouldn't steer me wrong.

"Let's go climb our tree," she says, grabbing my hand and linking our fingers. We've held hands a million times before but never before have my fingertips tingled at the touch of Lacey's. Our kiss has set off the tingles. Racing outside to our tree to play, all thoughts about kisses and tingles are forgotten as we climb higher into the foliage, laughing at each other as we do.

LACEY

25TH JUNE

Dear Diary,

Today was a magical day. I had my first kiss. I didn't wake up thinking today would be the day but it was. Let me tell you, it was great. It was great because it was with Chance.

When Theodore asked Chance about us, I was worried Theodore was going to say he liked me or something. Thank the heavens he didn't confess that because no way do I want his butt head liking me. I'm sorry Leo but I don't like you either. Every time I look at Leo now I'm going to wonder if he's thinking about kissing me.

Anyway, back to my first kiss. I've wanted Chance to be my first kiss for a while now when I heard the girls in my class talking in the toilets about the boys they liked. Julie said she wanted to kiss Chance because she thought he was cute but no way was she stealing my best friend's first kiss. I had to get in there first. Today I saw my chance.

It made my lips tingle. I hope Chance liked it. I'm sure he would have told me if he didn't. Now he will always be my first kiss.

I have a confession to make. I don't think a first kiss or best friend trumps a girlfriend but I didn't want someone to be able to trump me in the future. I hope Chance isn't mad at my lie when he eventually finds out the truth.

I hope Chance is always my best friend. We will have to get Theodore's secrets out of him another day in some other way.

Goodnight secret keeper,

Lacey

CHAPTER 9

CHANCE

11TH SEPTEMBER

Bronco and I are playing outside, testing out his new toy frisbee and playing fetch. He loves chasing after it. A wobbly throw causes the frisbee to ricochet off the fence and bounce onto the road. I try to stop Bronco from running after it but he doesn't listen as he's obsessed with his new toy.

"Bronco!! No!!!" I yell, as a car pulls out of nowhere. Bronco is so little the driver can't see him over their dashboard and they hit him with one of their tyres. Not thinking about anything but getting to Bronco, I run onto the road where the car is and gather Bronco into my arms. The driver tries talking to me but his words are ignored as I rush into my house to my mum.

"Mum!!" I yell, as I get inside. She comes rushing to help when she sees Bronco in my arms, not moving. Laying him down on the kitchen table, Mum feels around his chest and tummy. She looks at him then at me and the expression on her face is one I never want to see again.

"Chance, can you sit down please?" she asks gently. The chair feels cold as I wait for her to continue. "I'm sorry honey but Bronco isn't breathing. The impact must have put too much stress on his small body. He's passed away." I leap out of my chair, tears streaming down my face and run to Lacey for comfort. It doesn't feel real, we were playing outside minutes ago and now he's gone. When Lacey and her parents see me, they fear the worst. I can not speak or voice to them what has happened so Lacey's mum rushes over to my house to speak to my mum. When she comes back, she gives me a big hug before filling in Lacey and Mr Connelly about Bronco.

Lacey and I are sitting under our weeping willow tree while her dad is digging with his big shovel to make a grave for Bronco. Lacey said it's a good idea he'll be under the tree then he will be with us all the time since we spend so much time out here. I watch through my blurry vision as Mr Connelly digs the hole deeper and deeper. Lacey squeezes my hand every once in a while, her signal to let me know she's still there.

"It's time. Chance, do you want to place him in or do you want me to do it for you?" Mr Connelly asks me.

"I'll do it. He was my dog so it's best if it's me who puts him in his final resting place," I tell him, taking a deep breath and controlling my tears while I walk forward. Mum wrapped Bronco in his favourite blanket and she said we could bury him with it because it's like he's having a long sleep. I also grabbed his favourite tennis ball he loved to chew and chase so in doggie heaven he has it to play with.

I lean down, pick up my furry friend and walk the few steps to the fresh hole. I bend down and place him in as gently as I can. Lacey stays by my side the whole time and links her arm with mine when I stand back up. Mr Connelly shovels the dirt back into the hole, covering him until we can't see him anymore. I stare into the dirt hole until it's filled and let my tears flow while Lacey cries and sniffles beside me. She loved Bronco as much as I did so I know she's going to miss him too.

"Here you go honey," I hear Mum say beside me, so I turn and look at her. She's holding a couple of red roses. "I picked these from my garden out the front. I thought you might like one each to lay on top of his grave," she suggests, holding one in each hand.

One for me and one for Lacey. We take the sweet smelling flowers and step forward, carefully placing the pretty flowers on top of the dirt.

"You were a great friend and the best dog ever. I hope you are running and having fun wherever you are now," I say, while looking at his new grave.

"Don't worry Bronco, I'll take extra good care of our Chance. I won't let anything bad happen to him. I promise you," Lacey says softly. She squeezes my hand again and I lead her back to where we were sitting. Dropping down, I sit cross legged and lacey sits beside me. We sit in silence as my eyes lock in on his grave, letting myself feel sad and grieving for the loss of my first friend in this world.

When the sun sets, Lacey walks me home, hugging me goodbye and telling me she will see me in the morning for school. I don't know if I want to go to school tomorrow because I'm so sad. Mum helps me get ready for bed since it was such a hard day. She tucks me in, reads me two bedtime stories and lies with me until I fall asleep.

LACEY

11TH SEPTEMBER
Dear Diary,

Today sucked. Poor Chance, he lost Bronco today. I've never seen Chance so sad before. I loved Bronco but he was Chance's first friend so I know he's going to miss him.

I'll have to try extra hard to make sure he's okay for the next little while. I can't imagine the pain he must feel at losing a pet or a friend as good as Bronco was. He was such a good dog. He would come when you called and he would stay and sit when you told him too. He was extremely friendly and accepted me the first time I met him.

I meant what I said today. I will look after Chance and take care of him because he doesn't have Bronco to watch over him now. I'm not going to mess it up. It's too important to mess up.

I'm sad too so I might go to sleep. It's hard to write tonight being this upset and on the verge of crying because every memory I think of has Bronco in it.

I hope Chance isn't as sad tomorrow as he was today.

Rest In Peace Bronco (the best dog in the world),

Lacey

CHAPTER 10

CHANCE 1995

30TH JANUARY

Lacey and I walk hand in hand, all the way to school. We are excited to be back at school after the summer holidays. We had so much fun these holidays playing by the riverbank in the middle of town. We swung on the old tyre swing there and jumped in the water to cool off after getting hot and sweaty from running around. We even saw Theodore and Anthony there a few times and played with them. We tried to three way call Theodore again but he didn't divulge any secrets. I think he doesn't have any interesting secrets to spill anyway. Lacey thinks we need to keep trying so we ring him at least once a week. He's proving a tough nut to crack. Swinging our joined hands as we head through the school gate, we follow other students to the main courtyard. Walking to room seven where Theodore is, he turns to face us when he sees us approach.

"What's going on?" I ask, nodding my head to the gathered crowd in front of Theodore.

"They've put the class lists up for this year so you can check to see which class you are in," he tells us. Some of the kids move out of the way not finding their name so we move to get a better view of the list.

"Come on Lace, I bet we are in this class," I tell her, pulling her behind me as we squeeze in.

"I'm in here and the teacher is Miss Fernando. She's so cool," Theodore says, which has me smiling because she is known around school as being a friendly and cool teacher. My finger scans the list finding my name at the top because my last name starts with an A.

"We're in here too Lace," I tell her, beaming her way. Her eyes are glued on the white piece of paper taped to the green door. Her brows furrow and her lips droop as I watch her.

"What's wrong?" I whisper to her.

"My name isn't on the list Chance," her voice shakes in reply.

"What?" I say, turning and scanning the list again. There's my name at the top so Lacey's has to be here. I run my finger down slower this time so I can be sure not to miss it. I scan over the C names several times before carrying on with the rest of the list ending with Theodore's name at the bottom. Lacey is right, her name isn't on the list.

"You could be in room eight," Theodore says quietly to us, his eyes focused on Lacey.

"Come on Lace, let's check the list," I tell her, dragging her behind me as we walk through the corridor joining the two classrooms where we also hang our bags. Waiting our turn to read the list on the door of room eight takes forever. Lacey's palm gets sweaty in mine but I'm not sure whose hand it's coming from as we are both nervous.

When it's our turn, my finger slides down the list and we both gasp when I stop on Connelly. Lacey is in room eight. I twist around to see her face and the tears she's holding back glisten in her eyes. I quickly pull her out of the corridor and down the path to the concrete wall with the secret hiding space I discovered last year. I step into it and pull Lacey in with me.

"It's gonna be okay Lacey. I think they made a mistake," I tell her, hoping it's the case.

"I don't think they did Chance," she sniffles, letting one tear fall before she swipes at her face, brushing it roughly away.

"Why would they split us up?" I ask, thinking out loud.

"They are trying to break us apart. They don't want us to be best friends anymore," her small voice shakes.

"Look at me Lace," I tell her, lifting her chin so I can stare into her eyes. Her wet lashes shine at me and my heart cracks because my best friend is hurting. I'm upset too but I hide it because Lacey needs me to be strong right now. "We are best friends and something as silly as being in separate classes isn't going to break us apart. Do you hear me?" I ask her, sternly.

"Ours is an epic friendship they cannot sever," she adds, a smile forming on her lips as her eyes dry.

"A friendship so great one day they'll write stories about us," I tell her, which has her giggling. I pull her into my arms for a quick hug, which she returns, wrapping her arms around my waist.

"They can never break us apart," she whispers.

"Never, ever," I whisper back.

She releases me before saying, "Pinky promise," holding her pinky out.

"Pinky promise and lock it," I say, holding out my thumb which has her smiling as she holds out her own thumb, pushing it to mine. It's the first time I've remembered to lock it and it was perfect timing, as it's what Lacey needed from me. The bell rings and the smiles drop off both our faces as we know it's time to go our separate ways.

I take a deep breath and say, "Epic friendship, remember?" which makes Lacey's smile return. She holds out her hand for me to take and we walk back the way we came. In the corridor, we find two brass bag hooks free next to each other and hang our bags. If we can't be together in class, at least our bags can be together in the hallway.

The other students all push and laugh as they rush to find hooks and make their way into their new classrooms. The earlier excitement we both felt when walking to school has clearly gone and been replaced with a sadness neither of us saw coming. Lacey gives me one last sad smile as I watch her walk into her class and I turn my back to head into mine.

"Chance?" I hear her call. I turn with a raised brow.

"I'll see you at break?" she asks, unsure.

"Every break, every lunchtime and every day after school," I tell her, which makes her smile grow. She nods her head towards me then disappears into the class so I disappear into mine.

At lunch time, we have to sit and eat our lunch on the concrete courtyard at the back of our classrooms. I'm not allowed to mingle with Lacey yet as I've already tried but Miss Fernando called me back. As I'm making my way back to my class, a hard rock under my shoe has me stumbling. After righting myself and doing a quick skim of the ground, a light pink stone is in the place where the rock should have been. Bending down, I pick it up and turn it over in my hand. It's rough all over and has a couple of pointy corners but the colour has me placing it in my pocket.

I shovel my peanut butter sandwiches and banana into my mouth, before our teacher releases us to play. I chuck my ice cream container lunch box in my bag and race to find Lacey. Her smile warms my insides when she sees me.

"Close your eyes and open your hand," I tell her. She stops in her tracks and obeys. I pull the pink stone from my pocket and drop it into her hand. Her eyes fly open at the weight in her hand and she gasps.

"Chance, it's so pretty," she squeals, as she turns it around, inspecting it like I did.

"I found it and thought you might like it," I tell her.

"I love it. Thanks Chancey," she says, giving me a quick embrace before staring back at her new stone.

"Make sure you zip up your pocket when you put it in there, so you don't lose it," I tell her.

"I will," she replies, never taking her eyes off the stone.

"Come on, let's go play," I say, grabbing her hand. She lets go of my hand to hastily put the stone in her pocket and I watch as she zips it up so as not to lose it. She grabs my hand again and we run off to the tennis courts together to join in a game of sting the other kids are already playing. Lacey loves this game but she hates getting hit with the tennis ball, so while we are running around trying to avoid the ball, I leap in front of her if I think she needs protecting. I don't mind. It doe sting; some places hurt more than others, but it doesn't stop us from playing it, day after day.

At the end of the day, I meet Lacey by our bags and we walk home together. Since we are separated for most of the day, we have lots to talk about so we talk non stop the whole walk home.

"I'll meet you at the tree?" I ask Lacey, as we arrive at our houses.

"Yep," she replies, as we both race inside our front doors to get changed. I grab two apples on my way out the back door as I run to meet her. She arrives at our tree a minute after I do and I throw her an apple. She catches it then shows me a sharp knife she's holding in her other hand. "I have an idea," she says.

"We're not gonna cut our hands and become blood brothers or something, are we?" I ask, because it's something crazy Lacey would think of.

"No silly. I thought we could carve our names into our tree as a way to remind people about our epic friendship," she says, moving closer to the tree. I smile because her suggestion sounds like a great idea.

"Let's do it," I say, as I bite into my apple to hold it in my mouth so my hands are free and I can climb. I climb a few branches up and then Lacey follows as she tucks the knife into her shorts' pocket. We sit in branches close together and she hands me the knife, telling me to carve it. We spend the rest of the afternoon chipping away at the bark, carving a L and C into it. I make it as deep as I can in the hope it will last forever.

LACEY

30TH JANUARY
Dear Diary,

Today was an emotional day. I was excited to go to school and then the feeling got washed away as soon as I realised Chance and I aren't in the same class this year. I think the teachers are jealous of our friendship. I know the other kids are. They always mock Chance and I about holding hands and are constantly singing 'Chance and Lacey sitting in a tree K.I.S.S.I.N.G.' It doesn't bother us. We feel sorry for them because they don't have a friendship as awesome as ours.

My class is okay I guess. Miss Lam is nice. She's new to the school so no one knows what to expect. She's seated me next to Miles which I'm not particularly happy about now I know he has a crush on me or he did last year. I hope he's over it now.

Chance gave me the coolest present today. I showed my mum and she said it's a rose quartz and it's supposed to attract love energy or give off love energy or something about love. She said to put it on my shelf so I did. It's so pretty and it reminds me of Chance so everytime I look at it, I think of him. Receiving the stone was the highlight of my day.

It majorly sucks Chance and I aren't in the same class. A year apart is going to be so long but I have to remember a friendship as epic as ours will endure and come out stronger at the other end. Let's hope this year flies by because I hate waiting.

Sweet dreams,
Lacey

CHAPTER 11

CHANCE

8TH APRIL

The nights are feeling cooler as we move into autumn so yesterday at school I suggested to Theodore we should play *Go Home, Stay Home* before it gets too cold and winter arrives. He was excited about the suggestion and said he would get some other kids to play who live close by in the neighbourhood. I told him to meet at my house so Lacey and I are playing at the front of my house on the strip of grass, waiting for the other kids to arrive. Lacey practices her handstands and cartwheels so I join in to pass the time.

I can hold my handstand for a few seconds now so Lacey suggests I practice walking on my hands. Swinging my arms, I kick my legs into the air while my hands are on the ground to take my weight. Keeping my eyes on the ground, I balance myself.

"Now try and move your hands Chance," Lacey encourages, which has me lifting one hand and then the other. I get thrown off balance so before I fall, I lower my legs back to the ground then stand.

"It's hard," I admit.

"You'll get better. You just need to practice some more," she beams at me, making my heart swell with pride.

"Hey Chance," I hear someone call out to me, so I look over my shoulder to find Theodore and his brother Anthony walking towards us.

"Hey," I greet them.

"I told a few kids from school to meet us here so hopefully they arrive soon," Theodore tells us, as Anthony joins Lacey doing handstands. I sit on the grass next to Theodore while we wait. We laugh about Darren letting out a huge fart in class the other day and hold our stomachs when we can't stop laughing about it. We are still cackling about it when Miles and his cousin Zac, Julie, Leo and his younger sister Mary arrive.

"Okay, we will make home base the big weeping willow tree at the back of our yards. If you make it back to home base, touch the tree and yell, "Go home stay home one, two, three," before you are caught which means you've made it home safely. You have to stay there until the last person is caught. You can venture out between Lacey's house and my house and out to the edge of the road but anywhere else is out of bounds. First to get caught takes over catching in the next round. Sound good?" I ask, as I lay out the rules.

"Yep," I hear some say, while others nod.

"I'll be the catcher for the first game. I'll count to a hundred while you all hide. Let's go," I yell, sending them scattering with their laughter filling the cool evening air. The sun is setting in the sky and soon it'll be dark out, which makes the game even more fun. Closing my eyes I count to give them time to hide but by the time I get to seventy I'm over having my eyes closed, so I open them and finish off my counting. I scan the area from the road to where the weeping willow is but can't see any bodies in the dim lighting.

"Ready or not, here I come," I yell into the air. I jog towards the weeping willow. One strategy is to check home base first as someone is always tricky and hangs close to it and sure enough I hear someone close by.

As I get closer, I hear, "Go home, stay home, one, two, three," yelled out by Theodore, before I even catch sight of him.

"You'll get caught next time," I yell back, turning away from him, looking for the next person to catch. The dim lighting helps to hide people so my eyes strain to catch sight of any movement.

At the same time, I catch sight of Lacey's poofy hair creeping along the fence line as well as someone crawling through the grass near my house. I pretend not to see the crawler and tip toe towards Lacey. She sees me coming and lets out a squeal which makes me smile as she races to our tree. I slow my pace to let her win the race and I turn my attention back to the crawler who is still wriggling in the grass, thinking they are unseen.

"Uh oh," I hear Miles say, as he realises I've caught him crawling in the grass. Sprinting his way I manage to tag him before he can get away.

"You're it next." My smile grows with each deep inhale of breath from the exertion of catching him.

"I thought you didn't see me," he confesses, chuckling about his misfortune.

"When it's darker, you probably won't be able to see people lying down," I tell him quietly, and he nods. Busy talking to Miles, I've forgotten about the others who ambush me and all take their chance sprinting towards the tree. It's a frenzy as I don't know which way to run so they all make it home as my indecision catches me out.

"This is so much fun," Julie exclaims from her spot, leaning against the tree and they all agree, smiles directed at me from all angles.

"Miles, you're it," I tell him, which has us racing away while he counts. We continue playing several games until it's pitch black. The wind picks up and it sends a chill in the air. Julie is the catcher this time, having been caught first by Anthony. While she counts, I grab Lacey's hand and pull her behind me. Her hair whips around her face as I tug her to the side of my house, furthest away from hers and where we can bend down and hide, but still have a clear view of the tree.

We catch sight of Theodore as he grabs hold of the middle pole of our washing line. He flings his legs over the other poles then lets go, dangling upside down. I must say it's a pretty cool hiding place and I wish I'd thought of it. Beside me, Lacey shakes as she rubs her arms to warm herself.

"Do you want me to sneak inside and get you a jumper?" I whisper, not wanting to give our hiding spot away.

"No, I'll warm up once we are running. It's cold because we are sitting still," she whispers back.

"Come here," I whisper, holding my arms out for her to snuggle into. She scoots closer, wrapping her arms around me and I do the same, trying to give her some of my warmth. We hear laughter come from the direction of the tree before a voice sings out they've made it home safely.

"When should we make a run for it?" she whispers, as she tilts her face to look at me. I stare into the deep blue of her eyes and they look like the ocean with the night sky shining down on us.

"Not yet," I reply, staring into her eyes, not able to break whatever trance she's captured me in.

"Chance?" she whispers, and I hear the uncertainty in her voice but all my mind is thinking about is wanting to feel those long forgotten tingles again. Without thinking it through, I softly press my lips to hers and hold them there, while I count in my head to three. Releasing her lips, the tingles return and her wide eyes stare at me.

"What was that for?" she whispers.

"To make your lips warm because they were shivering," I quickly lie.

"The tingles warmed them up so thanks," she confesses, and I smile at her which she returns.

"I'm gonna get you," we hear Julie scream, which has us jumping apart, ready to run. She spots Theodore hanging upside down and we watch as he tries to untangle himself before Julie can catch him.

"Let's go while she's distracted," I say, which encourages Lacey to sprint into the darkness and I follow behind her. We make it to the tree yelling out the safe code before Julie even realises we were making a run for it. She caught Theodore so his hiding spot wasn't as good as I thought.

"One more game and then home time kids," Lacey's dad yells from her back door. We play the last round with Theodore as the catcher and it isn't long before the game is over.

"Goodnight," we all yell to each other, as the others all split off into different directions, making their way home.

"Night Chance," Lacey screams from her back door, as she disappears behind it while I wave to her. My sneaky kiss forgotten.

LACEY

8TH APRIL
Dear Diary,

Tonight was so much fun. We haven't played Go Home, Stay Home in so long. Usually it's Chance and I which isn't as fun but with heaps of kids it was so much better. Theodore came through so I'll give him credit for that.

I have a secret to spill. Chance kissed me. It was like one of those fairy tale kisses where the prince kisses the princess and time stands still. He was right about it warming my lips because it made those fantastic tingles return. If I could kiss Chance all the time I would because those tingles are amazing. They don't last forever and I don't think best friends are supposed to kiss each other all the time.

It was magical and I'll forever keep the memory safe. It made my heart race when he looked into my eyes. I wonder if he felt it too.

I hope I can sleep because the excitement from playing tonight and the kiss has happiness spreading throughout me and I think it's going to keep me awake for a while.

Tingles for the win,

Lacey

CHAPTER 12

CHANCE

15TH AUGUST

Stormy rain has pelted down all day long so I haven't gotten to spend much time with Lacey. Her mum dropped us to school and then picked us up again in the afternoon so we wouldn't get drenched walking, which meant we didn't get to hang out after school.

I've eaten all my dinner and now I'm lying in my room, bored out of my mind. I want to play with Lacey like we always do. I'm not going to let the weather stop me from seeing my best friend. I open my closet door and get out my blue raincoat and gumboots. I pull the hood on then race to Mum where she's sitting in her rocking chair, watching the big brown television.

"Mum, I'm gonna head to Lacey's to play. I won't be too long," I tell her, in a pleading voice. She looks at me, examining my wet weather gear.

"If the weather gets worse, come straight home Chance. You are to play in Lacey's house. I don't want you playing outside and catching a cold," she tells me.

"Thanks Mum," I yell, racing to the front door. Opening it, I'm blasted by the wet wind as it stings my face. My gumboots splash in the puddles as I stamp my way across the footpath to Lacey's. I avoid the grass as I don't want to trek mud into her house. At

Lacey's front door, I turn the handle to enter but it won't budge. It's locked which is surprising as it's hardly ever locked. I bang my fist against the wooden frame as I hear muffled yelling coming from inside. It's strange, no one ever yells in Lacey's house. I wonder what's going on. I bang my fist again, hoping someone will hear me. Finally I hear feet thundering down the hallway towards the door. The door is yanked open and I'm greeted by Mrs Connelly.

"Oh hi Chance. I'm sorry, now isn't a good time. How about you come back tomorrow to see Lacey," she says, as she runs her hand through her dishevelled hair.

"Who is knocking on the door in this weather?" I hear Mr Connelly's voice as it thunders through the house. I've never heard his voice loud before and it makes me take a step back.

Mrs Connelly sees my retreat then says softly, "It's okay Chance. Head home now. I'll tell Lacey you stopped by." I nod, letting her gently close the door before I hear her yell to her husband, "It was Chance. Would you stop the yelling, you're scaring the kids."

I can hear his muffled reply but not what he says. My lip wobbles before my thoughts run to Lacey. If I'm upset then I hate to think what she's feeling being in the house with him yelling. Instead of going home, I sneak along the fence line towards Lacey's window. Her light is on so I tap my fingers against the wet glass. It isn't long before her fluffy head is peering out of the window to see who's making the noise. Waving my hand to get her attention, she pushes her window open, enough to talk but not enough so the rain can enter.

"What are you doing Chance?" she asks, as her upper lip wobbles.

"I came to play with you but your mum wouldn't let me in. Are your parents fighting?" She opens her mouth to talk but the sound of loud banging has her eyes widening. We don't dare make a sound while we wait in silence. The lashing of the rain hitting the house surrounds us.

"Hold on," she tells me, once she's sure the banging has stopped. She walks away from the window and I stand on my tiptoes to peek in and see her pulling on pants under her nightgown. She throws on her pink jacket and matching Barbie gumboots then comes back to the window. "Let's go," she says, lifting the window higher so she can climb out. She flicks her legs over the side and I grab her around the waist, helping her down. She grabs my hand and we dash towards the tree. We realise this isn't the best idea as we forgot the tree has shed its leaves for winter so we don't have much shelter. We manage to find a spot near the base under one of the thicker low hanging branches which covers us mostly from the rain. Huddled closely together, we are silent for a minute as we wipe the rain from our faces.

"Are you okay?" I ask.

"Dad lost his job," she says.

"Is that what they are fighting about?"

"Yeah. Mum wasn't happy and said Dad shouldn't be drinking, he should be out looking for another job and then it turned into a big fight. They've never fought like this. I got scared so it's lucky you came to my window. I was about to hide under my blankets," she confides, as a tear escapes from her face, mingling with the raindrops on her skin.

"Do you want to come to my house?" I ask, shivering from the cold wind and rain.

"No, my mum might come looking for me. I needed a minute out of the house. Thanks for coming over Chancey," she softly says.

"Come on then. I'll give you a boost back in your window before they realise you're missing. I don't want them yelling at you because of me," I say, as I grab her hand, pulling her up. We trudge through the now muddy grass, back the way we came to her window. She steps into my locked hands and I hoist her onto the windowsill, where she pulls herself through. Turning back around to me, she drops her hood.

"Thanks Chancey, you always know how to make me feel better," she smiles at me.

"I didn't do anything," I tell her.

"You're you and it's enough," she says, making my face heat.

"You never know, your dad could have a new job by tomorrow," I offer, trying to help by being positive.

"Yeah, you're right. He probably will. Go get out of the rain now. It's freezing," she says, unzipping her raincoat and shaking it off.

"Night Lace. I'll meet you at the tree tomorrow for our weekly dairy shop," I smile at her, which she returns before she closes her window. I race through the deluge to my front door, swinging it open.

"Chance?" Mum calls.

"Yes Mum." I hear her footsteps coming, as I kick my now muddy gumboots off by the door.

"How did I know you were gonna come back soaked?" she huffs, more to herself than me. "In the shower and warm up before bed," she says, ushering me into the bathroom where she places my muddy boots in the bath so they don't get dirt anywhere else.

The warm shower spray thaws my skin and I'm thankful Mum suggested it when I'm lying in bed all cosy and ready for sleep. I read some of my new book *The Golden Compass* by Philip Pullman. I wish I had a daemon like Lyra, I miss Bronco and daemons live as long as you do so they wouldn't die and make me sad. My daemon could help me fight any bullies. If I had a daemon then so would Lacey and hers could help protect her from her parent's fighting. I fall asleep to the rain hitting the rooftop, hoping tomorrow is a better day for Lacey and praying her dad finds a new job.

LACEY

15TH AUGUST
Dear Diary,

I've never heard Dad yell like this. I would have snuck Chance into my room but I didn't want him to hear more of the yelling. It was scary enough I had to hear it. I didn't want him to be scared too. I can hear Dad walking back and forth down the hallway and he won't stop yelling about his boss. He's not happy with the man by the sounds of it.

I hope Dad finds a new job soon. Mum said something about struggling to pay the house if he isn't working. I don't know if it means we would have to move but I can't have that. I can't move away from Chance. Moving would make me even more upset.

I had to change out of my nightgown as it got a bit wet running in the rain with Chance. I would have liked to have a nice hot bath like Mum usually runs for me after I've been out in the rain but I couldn't tell her I'd be out in the rain because she'd be mad. I've put my warm flannel pyjamas on instead and my extra woolly socks. Luckily my hood kept most of my hair dry. I'm still shivering a bit but I'm hoping once I get under the blankets it will warm me up.

My gumboots are muddy so I'm going to have to sneak those out of the house tomorrow and hose them down so Mum and Dad don't see. I'm going to bed because I need to warm up some more. It's not easy writing when my fingers are shaking from the cold.

Goodnight,
Lacey

CHAPTER 13

LACEY 1996

9TH APRIL

Dear Diary,

Mum and Dad are fighting a lot more now. Most nights I cuddle under my mink blanket with my fluffy pillow squished against my ears, trying to drown out the sounds of their shouting. The name calling is the worst and I don't like it when they swear at each other.

Dad smells a lot more lately. It's like a stale musty smell. It makes my nose tickle and not in a good way. I've never thought my dad stunk before. I asked Mum about it today and she let out a big huff and said it's because he lost his job. I don't understand how losing your job relates to the way you smell but if that's the case, when I'm older I never want to lose my job. I don't want to reek like Dad.

I miss the way Dad was before he lost his job. He used to be fun and take me to the park. He'd wrap me in his arms when I was scared. I would feel so safe because nothing could stop my dad from protecting me, not even the monsters in my closet. I don't know what it is about Dad now but I don't feel so safe around him. He would never yell at Mum and now it's all I hear these days.

Mum sent me to bed but I'm huddled under my blanket with my torch so I can keep writing. I'm scared of the yelling. I want it to stop. I don't know if my parents know I can hear them every night or if they think I'm fast asleep but I can't sleep until they stop. It began as hushed whispers but has evolved into full on shouting matches. It's like they don't care who hears them and every night is the same.

Dang it, some glass smashed. Oh no, not glass. Mum's yelling at Dad because it was her mother's old vase he broke. Sorry my writing is a bit wobbly but the crashing of it against the wall scared me. I want to escape here for a bit. I'm so tired and want to sleep as I haven't slept properly for weeks now.

Stuff it, I'm going to knock on Chance's window. I'm sure he will let me in.

Later,
Lacey

CHANCE

9TH APRIL

Tap, tap, tap. What's that noise? I place my Goosebumps book on my bedside table next to my lamp and try to locate where the tapping is coming from. My senses direct me to the window so I push open my Spider-man curtains to peek outside into the darkness. I jump back before I realise it's Lacey's face squished against the glass in a funny face. I swear this girl will be the death of me.

Unlocking the window I slide it open, whispering so my mum doesn't hear, "Lace, what are you doing?" Her arms are wrapped around her waist and she's giggling at the shock on my face but something is off, I can tell.

"Can you help me climb in?" she asks, stretching out her hands for me to pull her up. Without hesitation I lean over the windowsill and grasp her hands. She pushes her bare feet against the side of my house and I tug her through the window. I pull her into my room and once her feet hit the carpeted floor, I release her hands but she wraps them around my waist, giving me a tight squeeze. Naturally my hands drop around her back, squeezing her in return.

"What's wrong Lace?" I can feel her teeny body shaking. I don't know if it's because she's run from her house to mine in her nightgown and it's freezing out or if it's something else.

"Can I stay here for a bit please?" she pleads, her chin tilting up the smallest amount to look into my eyes since I'm taller than her. The thing about Lacey is I can never say no to her. Even if she didn't look so scared, I would have said yes. She has that effect on me. Squeezing her tighter, I nod which makes a smile grace her lips.

"Come, you're shivering. Let's get under the blankets," I tell her. I close the window and pull the curtains back in place. I grasp her hand, tugging her so she follows me to my bed. I flip my camo duvet further back and scoot in while pulling her with me. We lie side by side facing each other on my single bed and I throw the duvet over our heads, encasing us in a safe bubble. I can still make out her face with my lamp shining behind her. "Tell me what's wrong," I say, grabbing her hand and squeezing so she knows I'm listening. Staring into my eyes she takes a deep breath then releases it and her warm breath blows against my face.

"Mum and Dad have been fighting since Dad lost his job." My back straightens with the information because her dad lost his job well over six months ago.

"Since the first day he lost it and I came over in the rain?" I ask, needing to know if it's been going on for ages. Her small nod confirms it. "Why didn't you tell me earlier?"

"I thought they would stop eventually. I didn't want to say something and then they stopped and I told you for nothing."

"Never worry about that. You're supposed to tell your best friend everything, even things you don't think are important," I tell her, making her body relax.

"Okay."

"Okay," I reply.

"I think Dad smashed my nana's ugly vase mum had in the hallway," she softly whispers.

Lacey's dad has always been a hero in her eyes. If you look at Lacey when she's looking at her dad, I swear you feel like the sun is shining on you, even if it's raining. It's one of my favourite smiles of hers because even though the smile is reserved for her dad, it makes me warm inside whenever I see it. The way she's looking now isn't making me feel warm. It scares me but I won't admit it to her. I want to give her some of the warmth she's always given me, so I make a joke instead.

"He could have thrown it because he got sick of looking at the butt ugly thing. Remember, he's the one who pointed out to us how ugly it is in the first place," I remind her.

"That's probably it," she says, with more warmth behind her eyes. For the first time, one of her special smiles is directed at me and it makes me feel great. After a few minutes her eyes begin drooping and I know she'll be fast asleep in a minute so I pull the duvet from over our heads.

"Can you turn the lamp off?" I ask her. Nodding, she turns and presses the switch, cloaking us in darkness as she lies back on my pillow. "Night Lace," I say, as I fumble under the blanket, find her hand and lace our fingers together.

"Night Chancey," she replies, squeezing my hand in return. I listen to her breaths even out before I let myself drift off to sleep as well.

Coming out of my sleep, I yawn and try to move my hand to cover my mouth like I usually do but I feel the tight grip around my fingers which forces me to open my eyes. Lacey's ball of fluff on her head looks worse than usual. My lip tugs up at the thought. All the times I have seen her before were tamed, brushed versions of her hair. Yikes, she looks like roadkill died on top of her head. Her soft hand still grips my finger tips. We must have slept the whole night in this position. A Thump, thump, thump bangs against my door.

"Time to get up, Chance," my mum yells, from the other side of the wooden frame.

"I'm up," I yell back, knowing I need to respond so she won't enter my room. My loud voice causes Lacey to jerk, her eyes flying open. On instinct I quickly place my hand over her mouth, hoping she doesn't make a sound. I place a finger against my lips whispering "Sshhh," before I remove my hand from her face.

"Do you think I'll make it home without getting busted?" she whispers, her big eyes still holding traces of the spooked emotions she showed when she arrived last night.

I want her to give her hope so with a big smile I say, "No doubt. Jump out the window and race across the yard as fast as you can."

"I'm not sure I can climb in my window by myself. I needed your help getting in here last night," she says, fear leaking into her voice.

"I'll stand watch from here then. If you need a boost, send me a signal and I will come running over."

"Okay," she says, as she takes a visible gulp. "Here goes nothing." She quietly steps to the window, pushes the curtains apart and slides the window open. Luckily it doesn't squeak. The bright morning sun hits us in the eyes. She turns back to me, giving me a nervous smile before she moves forward to jump.

"You've got this Lace. I believe in you," I whisper, as her feet touch the grass and she takes off sprinting across the patch of lawn between our houses. As she runs behind her fence, I see the top of her fluffy hair bouncing along the fence line until she gets to her window. The window remains open from last night when she escaped I'm assuming.

I watch as she tries to pull herself up but I can tell she's panicking as her hands wave around frantically. She turns to me and from this far, I can see the worry written on her face.

I point to her and then do a thumbs up mouthing, 'You got this.' I admire the way the worry slips off her face, replaced with determination as she turns back to her window and tries again. She places her hand on her windowsill and using all the strength she can muster, she manages to pull her body through the window and into her room. Her boofy head pops back through her parted curtains and the brightest smile shines my way as she gives me her own thumbs up. I return the smile, proud of her managing to get into her room all by herself. I push my window back into place as my mum barges into my room with one knock as a warning.

"You better be up Chance," she says, glancing at my bed but not seeing my body. Relief washes over me as she misses me closing my window by seconds. "Get a wriggle on or we'll be late for your hair cut," she says, her eyes finding me by the window. It must look like I was opening my curtains like I do each morning so we haven't been caught yet. I do an impression of a wiggly worm, wriggling towards her which has her laughing at my antics and luckily none the wiser about my late night visitor.

CHAPTER 14

LACEY

14TH SEPTEMBER

Dear Diary,

I hate Chance Alexander. Well not really, who am I kidding? I just hate him for today. He's left me with a deep purple bruise along most of my upper arm. Mum and Dad had a fight over it. Mum was worried I needed to go to the ER to get checked out because it was the same arm I broke when I was younger. Dad wasn't worried.

I had to have the longest shower in history to get the gunk off me. Plus it got in my hair which was a nightmare to get out. FYI butter is not just for cooking. If you're ever in need of something slippery don't try moisturiser or oil, go straight for the butter.

My ribs hurt too and if I push anywhere on the dark indigo patch on my arm it feels tender. Note to self, stop poking it.

I did win the bet so now Chance owes me $2. He better pay me. I wish he had more money because I would have taken him for all he's worth but he spent his other $2 at the dairy on lollies. I can't hold it against him as he did share the lollies with me and he bought me a ka bluey lolly which are the best. The blue raspberry flavour is so yum and it paints your tongue blue. Chance and I can spend hours sticking out our tongues at each other, laughing at how blue they are. My mum on the other hand hates them *as it takes ages to get rid of the blue colour and I use heaps of toothpaste.*

I still hate Chance because he got me grounded. I didn't get my $2 off him before his mum walked the pair of us over to my house. I hope she doesn't expect me to replace the butter we had to use. I'm pretty sure butter is more than $2 and then I would have done the stupid bet for nothing. I deserve something for all this pain I am in. I'm not suffering for nothing.

Mum and Dad have stopped fighting for now so I better get to sleep while I can. Here's hoping tomorrow is a better day. I'm pretty sure I won't hate Chance any more. I can never stay angry at the doofus for long.

Goodnight,
Lacey

CHANCE

14TH SEPTEMBER

Mum slipped my pocket money into my hand before she ruffled my hair, telling me what a good son I've been this week. My chores consist of taking out the rubbish bins and washing the dishes three times a week. She did say once I turn thirteen I'll be able to mow the lawns and earn the big bucks. I shove the coins into my pocket and stroll next door to Lacey's house, banging on the front door so she knows I'm here. We always meet at this time every Saturday afternoon so we can walk to the dairy together to spend my pocket money. Slinging the door back, she skips out in her pink bike shorts and a fuschia care bears t-shirt. I wonder if she will ever not like pink.

Closing the door behind her, she continues to skip as we make our way to the dairy. We laugh about all the funny stuff that happened at school during the week.. I tell her about the new chatter ring my mum bought me and her eyes light up. We've seen other kids with them at school and we've both wanted one for ages. I guess with all the pleading I've been doing, Mum finally gave in.

"Eeehhh, let's race to the shop and then back to your house so we can play with it," she squeals with excitement, and I can't help but feed off it.

"Let's go then," I yell out, as I sprint away from her, knowing she will let me cheat this one time as she's too excited about the chatter ring.

"Not fair," her voice squeaks, close behind as she tries to catch me. I can hear her laughter drifting on the breeze behind me.

As I catch sight of the dairy in front of me I slow my pace, letting her join me in our final strides so we get to the corner shop at the same time. Calling it a draw. We walk through the doorway and head straight to the counter where all the lolly bags are set out. Greeting the familiar owner, we grab a bag of lollies each. She loves ka blueys, so I grab four of them for us to split. Shoving our haul in our pockets we wave goodbye to the owner and sprint back down the road to my house. I keep pace with Lacey on the run back even though we both know I'm faster than her. We both slow our steps as we get to my house. Lacey sits on my front steps while I head inside to grab the chatter ring. Her eyes light up as she catches sight of it when I return, her greedy hands snatch it out of my grip as soon as she can.

"Let's go to our tree and play with it," she suggests, so I follow her while I open my bag of lollies and fish through it, eating my favourite ones first. "Do you know any tricks?" she asks, as she holds the stainless steel ring in one hand and flicks the brass beads with her other thumb. It takes her a few tries before she manages to get all the beads spinning at once then she's quickly moving her hands, one in front of the other to keep them spinning around the ring.

"So far I know around the world and how to toss and catch it," I tell her, as I watch her continue to spin the ring. Her tongue sticks out the side of her mouth in concentration as the rattling noise fills the air.

"Can you teach me?" she says, breaking her concentration and glancing at me, which has the rings stopping.

"Sure," I tell her, taking the ring from her hand. I flick the beads and show her the around the world trick as slowly as I can, giving her instructions as I go. After a few minutes of me showing her, she asks for it back so she can try it.

"That's it," I encourage, as she manages to keep the beads spinning as she turns the ring on its side the first time. Her face lights up with a beautiful smile as she keeps her eyes laser focused on her task. We lose track of time, taking turns and eating our lollies in between. Plus after our ka blueys we take turns laughing and admiring each other's blue tongues.

While sitting with our backs against the scratchy bark of the weeping willow, I say, "I bet you can't fit this over you." Lacey eyes the metal ring, calculating if it's possible in her head.

"What do I get if I do it?" she asks. I pull out the last $2 of pocket money from my pocket, opening my palm to show her. She tries to grab it but I quickly shove it back into my pocket before she can steal it.

"You've gotta do the bet first," I tell her, lifting the chatter ring and holding it out to her.

"Easy peasy," she titters, taking the chatter ring. She examines it again for a minute before she puts it over her head and then manoeuvres one arm through. Squeezing the other arm through, she manages to get it around her waist and yells proudly, "I won, you owe me two bucks."

"Fine," I say, defeated. I can't believe she managed to get it over herself and I lost my $2. "Take it off and let's head back home."

With a smug look on her face, she grasps the metal ring in her hands and pushes it down on her hips but it won't budge. The smugness drops from her face as sheer panic takes over.

"Chance, I can't get it off."

"Try taking it off the way you put it on?" I suggest, as I move closer to help her try and wriggle it off. We pull and squeeze but it won't come off. I'm wondering how she managed to get it on her in the first place even though I saw it with my own eyes. "Let's go ask my mum for help, she'll know what to do," I tell her. She's on the verge of tears so I take her hand in mine, dragging her along the trail leading to my house.

"Mum!" I yell, once we walk through the back door.

"Yeah honey," comes her reply from the kitchen, where she's cooking dinner. As she turns to face us, her smile fades as she takes in our predicament.

"Oh no, what have you two done now?" her worried voice shakes, as she wipes her hands on the tea towel and moves closer to inspect Lacey.

"It's stuck," I state the obvious. My mum tries to pull it off using all her strength but it doesn't work.

"We need oil or something," she mumbles, then turns and searches the cupboards for something. Pulling the cooking oil from the cupboard, she pours it into her hands and then rubs it on the ring. Tugging on it, it still doesn't budge. "Chance, run to my room and grab my body moisturiser. Let's give it a go," she says, smiling at Lacey but I notice the panic wrapped around her eyes. I race to Mum's room, grab the blue bottle off her dresser and I'm back in the kitchen in record time. She squirts the thick white cream onto her hands and again tries pulling the ring up but to no avail.

"Do you think butter might work?" I ask, trying to think of oily ingredients we have in our kitchen that may do the trick. She nods at me so I move to the fridge where I find it and pull out our big block of butter.

"Okay Lacey dear, this is the last thing I have that may work, so let's give it our best go." She grabs a sharp knife and cuts the block of butter in half, handing me one half while she holds the other. "Rub it all over her back there Chance where it needs to slide up. I can't be sending you home with this around you Lacey. What will your parents think?" she says, more to herself than us.

Mum and I get to work, spending the next few minutes rubbing the slimy butter all over Lacey. If it wasn't for the worried looks on Mum and Lacey's faces, I'd make a joke but I don't think now is the right time. When our butter pieces are depleted, we pull and slide the steel ring again and this time it moves upwards. It presses in against Lacey's arm and she squeals out in pain, but Mum tells her it's nearly there and with one more tug it's over her head and she's free. Glancing at Lacey from head to toe I think it's safe to say she won't be able to hide this from her parents. She's covered in oil, thick white moisturiser and yellow butter and there is no missing it.

I think Mum arrives at the same conclusion because she shakes her head at us before saying, "Come on you two, time to face the music. Let's get you home Lacey." Together we drag our feet across the yard to Lacey's, knowing we are about to get an earful. It isn't new to us as we always get into trouble when we are together.

"You and your stupid bet," she whispers to me, as her feet stomp towards her house. I know she's not really mad at me. She's mad because she knows we're about to get into trouble and it's exactly what happens next. Once we get told off by both of Lacey's parents, they usher her into the house to get clean and Mum and I walk the short distance home.

"I don't want to see the chatter ring for at least a month," Mum tells me. As soon as we walk into the house, I collect the toy from the table and take it into my room to find a suitable hiding place. Hopefully I'll be able to sneak it out to play with when Mum is asleep.

CHAPTER 15

CHANCE 1997

18TH FEBRUARY

"Chance, Chance," I hear Lacey screaming for me, as soon as I enter the school gates. I push my hand through my hair, flicking it off my forehead as I walk towards her. She's jumping up and down looking like she's about to pee her pants. As I reach her, she grabs hold of my hand with both of hers while she continues her hysterical jumping. "Chance, have you heard of tamagotchi toys? Darren has one and they are so cute. I want one. It's a virtual pet and you can carry it in your pocket. You have to hatch the egg then feed it and look after it. It'll love you forever." She rushes through her explanation all in one breath before her big blue eyes stare into mine, expecting the same enthusiasm as she has. Last year being in different classrooms was horrible but this year they reunited us so I know it's going to be a great year.

"A tama what now?" I say, having no idea what she's talking about.

"Ugh. Come on, let's find Darren and he can show you," she rambles, and she yanks my hand, dragging me across the courtyard in search of Darren before the school bell rings. It's a minute before we find Darren and it's not hard as he is surrounded by a circle of our classmates, all wanting to see his new toy. Lacey pushes through the crowd, manoeuvring herself so she's right next to Darren and she leaves space so I can stand next to her and see what all the hype is about.

"Darren, show Chance your tamagotchi," she pleads, desperately wanting me to see this toy.

"Here, he's about to hatch," Darren says, holding it out so everyone can see. In his palm, he holds an egg shaped plastic device connected to a keychain. It has a tiny screen with an egg on it. Everyone's eyes are zeroed in on it. The bell rings but no one moves. Everyone is determined to see this creature hatch. When it does, the crowd erupts in cheers like it's the coolest thing to ever happen.

"Come on everyone. Get to class," Mr Lark yells, breaking the bubble we were all in. Everyone disperses heading to their classes and chatting about the coolest new toy out.

"I'm gonna ask my parents if I can get one when we get home," Lacey tells me, as she skips next to me.

"It is pretty cool," I admit. I wonder if I can convince Mum to buy me one.

"See, I told you so," she sings, sticking her tongue out at me which has me trying to pinch it with my fingers. Her giggles continue all the way to class and I laugh along as I chase her.

On our walk home together Lacey says, "I heard from Leo that Darren said his tamagotchi poops and he has to clean it up."

"What?" I reply, laughing, not quite believing her.

"Yeah. Apparently it looks like a chocolate hershey's kiss," she tells me, staring at me with a straight face. I can't help it and we both crack up laughing, picturing a hershey's kiss poop and Darren cleaning it up. As we get to our houses, we both vow to ask our parents straightaway if they can buy us one.

LACEY

18TH FEBRUARY
Dear Diary,

I really want a tamagotchi. I asked Mum and Dad and they said we'll see. I will keep bugging them until I get one as I can't live without one. They are the cutest thing ever. I'm not sure about cleaning up the poop side of things but at least it isn't real poop.

I think I'll name mine Linka after the character from Captain Planet. She's the planeteer who has the wind ring and she's my favourite. If my hair was a bit lighter, I reckon I'd look exactly like her.

I can't wait to get a tamagotchi. It will be like I'm finally getting the pet I always wanted. Linka will be all mine and sleep with me in my bed.

I have to cut this entry short as I need to write a list of chores I can do to help convince my parents to get me my tamagotchi because I need one like now.

Desperately in need of a tamagotchi,
Lacey

CHANCE

23RD FEBRUARY

I'm waiting at the weeping willow to meet Lacey so I can show her my brand new tamagotchi Mum gave me this morning. She took my pocket money this week and put it towards it. Holding the white small device in my hands I stare at the screen, the egg stares back at me. I'm anxiously waiting for it to hatch. I hear Lacey's soft footsteps crinkling the grass in her approach so I move my hands behind my back to hide my new toy.

"Chance, look what I got," Lacey announces, as her own tamagotchi dangles from her finger.

"I got one too," I exclaim, showing her my own.

"Has your egg hatched yet?" she asks.

"Not yet. What about yours?"

"Nah, I'm still waiting," she says, as she folds her legs under her and sits in her usual spot with her back against our tree trunk. Taking a seat beside her, we both get lost staring at our new devices and wondering when they will hatch. "I named mine Linka," she tells me.

"From Captain Planet?"

"Yeah. Have you thought of what you'll name yours?

"No, I hadn't thought of naming it," I tell her, honestly.

"You should name him Wheeler from Captain Planet," she suggests, and I nod, agreeing because Wheeler is cool. I pull out my walkman I carried with me and hold out an earphone for her to take. We silently listen to the music while waiting for something to happen. It isn't long before Lacey's finally hatches and mine follows soon after. We get distracted with cleaning up their poop, feeding them and putting them to sleep.

Before we realise, it's getting dark so we stumble back home slowly so we don't bump into anything as we aren't looking where we are going. We are too busy keeping an eye on our new virtual pets, not wanting to miss a single moment.

LACEY

23RD FEBRUARY
Dear Diary,

I can't tell you how excited I am. Mum finally got me a tamagotchi. My baby hatched today and her name is Linka. I love her so much and I can't get enough of her. I'm going to have to wake in the middle of the night to make sure she's alright, especially since it's her first night being more than an egg.

I told Chance to name his Wheeler because I'm sure Linka and Wheeler are destined to be together like Chance and I are destined to always be in each other's lives. I can't see us ever being apart. If it ever happened, I think the world would stop spinning.

Eww gross, I checked on Linka and she had pooped. It's cute because it looks like a chocolate hershey kiss but still poop is poop and poop is gross. I'm willing to sacrifice myself and deal with the poop because I love Linka so much. I'm glad it's virtual poop so I don't have to deal with the smell.

The fighting began earlier tonight. I should have known when I came home from hanging with Chance it wasn't going to be a peaceful night. Dad had his beer box with him in front of the TV and he wouldn't come and join us at the table for dinner.

Mum was yelling at him because he lost yet another job. She said if he gave up drinking then he could possibly keep one. I don't understand how drinking affects his work. I do know the beers have been making him more angry lately. I don't like Dad when he's angry. I want my Dad back like he used to be but I don't know how to fix him.

Dad's yelling is louder now. I'm not even sure if it's at Mum or the TV but I might try to sneak over to Chance's earlier tonight.
    Goodbye for now,
Lacey

CHANCE

28TH FEBRUARY

We got our tamagotchis on Sunday and it's now Friday and we are both exhausted. Lacey sneaks into my room most nights and then we take turns waking through the night to check on our virtual pets to make sure they are okay. I think this is more extreme than when Bronco was a puppy.

The bell rings for lunch which forces all the kids out of their desks and rushing out of the room to go eat. We are the last kids in the classroom so I patiently wait for Lacey as she puts her books away in her wooden desk and grabs her tamagotchi out. She steps out in front of me and out of the corner of my eye, I see something on her light blue dress, right where her butt is.

"Lacey!" I whisper yell at her, which has her lifting her eyes from her tamagotchi to my face.

Her brows pull together asking, "What?"

"Your dress has blood on it," I tell her, trying to force the worry away. We learnt about periods last year when our class had special lessons in the education van. They ushered us in and a yellow giraffe named Harold taught us all about puberty. The lesson couldn't have prepared me for seeing the real thing but then again I'm a guy not a girl.

"Whaaatt?" Lacey's own worry seeps into the air as she tries to turn to see the back of her dress, grabbing it to try and twist it into view. She places her forgotten virtual pet on her table trying to see behind her. I pull my school jumper over my head and put my arms around her waist. Her scared eyes linger on mine as I tie my jumper arms into a knot across her hips at the front to secure it and hide the back of her dress.

"Don't worry Lace. No one will see it now. Let's go to the nurses' station," I tell her, threading my fingers with hers and giving her a slight tug to shift her feet. I catch sight of her beloved Linka on the desk so I put it in my pocket where my own sits.

Together we walk, ignoring all the laughter and noise filling the air as everyone sits around on the concrete eating their lunches, unaware of the turmoil Lacey is going through. I can't help but worry for my best friend. One of the other girls, Fiona, got her period during school last year and everyone laughed and mocked her. I didn't want that for Lacey so I'm going to protect her as best as I can. As we silently walk to the nurses station, it makes me sad thinking of the way Fiona was treated over something she couldn't control. Knocking on the wooden door frame, we get the attention of Nurse Timmons. Her friendly smile glances between us as she places her salad on her desk.

"Is everything okay, you two?" she asks, unsure what we are here for.

"Aahh, it's Lacey," I stutter, unsure of what to say. I can feel Lacey's body tremble as she stands with her side pressed next to mine. Nurse Timmons eyes bounce to Lacey and then she steps forward and kneels in front of her, causing Lacey to follow her with her eyes.

"What's the matter Lacey?" she asks my best friend, and I squeeze her hand to encourage her to talk.

"I'm uh bleeding down there," Lacey whispers, as she points to her private parts. Nurse Timmons shows Lacey a warm, friendly smile as she takes her other hand, leading her into the room.

"Is this the first time?" she asks Lacey, and she nods. I try to release her hand so she can follow Nurse Timmons on her own but she holds on tighter so I follow her into the small room as she takes a seat on the vinyl bed. Nurse Timmons moves away from us and hunts through her many drawers until her search brings her across what she's after. She holds out her hand, giving Lacey a new pair of underwear and some white square thing. I don't want to see Lacey's underwear so I distract myself with the posters on the wall about the importance of cleaning your teeth twice a day while the nurse and Lacey talk. A minute later, Lacey releases my hand as she slides off the bed taking the things the nurse gave her and heading to the bathroom.

When she's gone, Nurse Timmons turns to me and says, "You're a good friend Chance. I'll be back in a minute. I'll give Lacey's mum a call." I pull out Wheeler, my virtual pet and check on him. I can't believe I let Lacey talk me into naming him. It made Lacey happy for us to have them both named Wheeler and Linka. I think if she had it her way, we would have a collection with Gi, Kwame, Ma-Ti, Linka and Wheeler. She'd probably want another collection of all the bad guys too. There's nothing stopping Lacey when her mind gets set on something. I'm about to pull out Linka and check on her when Lacey walks in. Pushing Wheeler back into my pocket, I stand as Lacey walks back to sit beside me.

"How did you go?" Nurse Timmons asks her.

"Good," Lacey replies, then she adds, "Did you ring my mum?"

"Yeah I did sweetie. She's on her way now to come and get you," she tells her, as I thread my fingers with Lacey's. I squeeze her hand again and she leans her head on my shoulder while we wait in silence, not knowing what to say in this situation. Her mum arrives and wraps her arms around Lacey as soon as she sees her. We walk hand in hand back to class to grab Lacey's bag for her to head home with her mum. Lacey's mum takes her bag from her hands and before she leaves, she turns to me and wraps her small hands around my waist, resting her head against my neck while I squeeze her back.

"Thanks Chancey," she whispers, before releasing me. A small sad smile tugging at her lips.

"Anytime," I tell her, as I let go and watch her leave. The bell for the end of lunch rings and I realise I haven't eaten. It doesn't worry me. I'm more worried about the fact we are growing up and I feel like things are going to change between us now.

LACEY

28TH FEBRUARY
Dear Diary,

I'm officially a woman and I want a refund. Some of the other girls in my class have already gotten their period and they act like it's not a big deal. Well I'm here to tell you it is in fact a big deal, especially when your first introduction to womanhood occurs and you have no idea what the hell is going on.

Poor Chance looked like he was going to faint when he saw the blood on my dress. I've never seen him so pale before. He reminded me of a ghost. He was so sweet, giving me his jumper and tying it around my waist before anyone else saw. He walked me to the nurse's station and held my hand while the nurse rang my mum.

The nurse gave me this bulky pad thing and a new pair of underwear to put on since mine were ruined. It was like a horror scene. Plus she told me to put it in my underwear but did the nurse think to tell me to have the sticky side against my underwear? No, she did not so I stuck the sucker to my vagina. Yes, you read that right. I stuck the sticky side to my skin and let me tell you it was worse than ripping a bandaid off. It hurt like a B word.

When I got home, Mum explained I need to place the sticky side against my underwear so it holds it in place. I think they need to better prepare girls because learning all this stuff in the heat of the moment was not a good experience. Plus I have a vague memory of the giraffe in the van mentioning this stuff but I was so horrified by them talking about penises, I zoned out and missed the period part.

So here I sit with a hot water bottle against my belly because Mum said it would help with the cramping. She's gone to the supermarket to get me some supplies. I can't wait for this to be over. Mum informed me this will happen every month like clockwork. What kind of joke is this?

I don't feel like I've turned into a woman. I feel like I've been given the short end of the stick. Why doesn't Chance have to worry about bleeding out of his penis for one week of every month for the rest of his life?

At least tomorrow is the weekend and Mum said I can stay in bed for the whole day if I want to. I might need to check in with Chance. I hope he doesn't think I'm bleeding to death.

Ugh, I hate the world today,
Lacey (officially a woman)

CHANCE

1ST MARCH

Linka is dead. I tried to keep her alive but I was out of my depth, trying to care for two virtual pets. I didn't even know they could die. I'm pretty sure Lacey doesn't know either. I was tired last night from worrying about Lacey and then trying to care for the two virtual pets. I slept through the night without waking and checking on them. Wheeler was still alive but poor Linka was gone when I woke up this morning. I hope Lacey isn't mad. I've quickly hatched another egg but it is still in the baby stage and won't grow much more before Lacey comes searching for Linka. It's Saturday and we always meet to walk to the dairy to spend my pocket money. I'm hoping we are still meeting today although I'm not sure what to do about this baby version of Linka.

Stressing about what to do, I almost miss the light tapping on my window. I know it's Lacey. I fling the curtains and her wide smile shines at me as she waves her hand back and forth. Sliding the window open, I tug her into my room.

"You could have used the door?" I tell her, when she's standing in front of me.

"Where's the fun in that? Anyway, I'm used to the window now," she says, in regards to her climbing into my room most nights. I decide to be brave, bite the bullet and spit out what happened to Linka.

"Lacey, can you sit on my bed please?" She jumps on the bed, looking innocently at me.

She must sense something about my expression because her own face drops and she asks, "What's wrong?"

"It's Linka."

Her eyes light up, "Oh did you find her? I thought I'd left her in my desk at school."

"She's dead," I spit out.

"Whaaattt? They can die?" she screams, jumping to her feet. I pull her device out of my pocket and drop it into her hand. She examines the screen, taking in the baby version of a new virtual pet. "I didn't even know they could die," she says softly, her butt falling back onto the bed as she tenderly holds her tamagotchi with both her hands.

Taking a seat right next to her I say, "I didn't know either. I thought they'd live forever."

"This blows," she says, staring at her new virtual pet.

"At least you can think of a new name for this one," I say, trying to find a way to look for the positive in the situation. Her face whips my way, eyes wide, slight smile across it.

"That is so true. If they keep dying and rehatching then we can get through all the planeteers in no time. I think I'll name this one Ma-Ti because I feel like I need his heart power to help me grieve Linka."

"Are you doing okay?" I ask, unsure if I should mention the fact she was bleeding or not. Her cheeks redden as she nods. "Does it feel weird?" I ask, curious.

"Yes. The pad things I gotta put in my underwear are weird. To be honest, it feels like I'm wearing a diaper," she says, which has us both laughing and lightening the mood.

"Let's go to the dairy and I'll buy you some ka blueys. They always cheer you up," I tell her, as I sling an arm around her, pulling her in for a side hug.

She wraps both her arms around my waist, turning her head into my chest mumbling, "Thanks Chancey." I raise my other hand and rest it against her head, holding her to my chest for a beat longer.

"Anytime," I tell her, before I release her and pull her to stand.

"You'll have to tell me about your first boner now," she blurts out and I'm sure my eyebrows hit the ceiling. She stares at my shocked face and adds, "Fair's fair," her cheeky grin growing when she places her hands on her hips, showing she means business.

"Fine," I sulk.

"Pinky promise," she demands, holding out her tiny hand, her teeny pinky pointing at me. I roll my eyes but give her what she wants, stretching my own pinky to wrap around hers. She lifts her thumb and then says, "And lock it." I let out a huff pushing the pad of my thumb to hers and locking our pinky promise. With a smug smile across her face, she skips out of the room laughing, "Come on Chance, Ka blueys await us." I join in her laughter because she's right, fair's fair I guess.

LACEY

1ST MARCH

Dear Diary,

I have so much to tell you. Where do I begin? Firstly, Linka died. I know, right? Why didn't anyone tell me our virtual pets could die? I know we didn't read the instructions but I'm sure someone would have filled us in by now. It's okay because now I have Ma-Ti and with his heart power I feel braver, like I can take on the world.

Chance and I got some ka blueys today. I don't think I'll ever tire of these lollies. Chance gave me an extra one too and I'm going to eat it before bed. I don't think Mum will be happy if I go to bed with a blue mouth but I'm living recklessly today.

I think Chance felt bad about Linka dying and the period drama. He did save me the embarrassment of everyone seeing my stained dress so I'm thankful. I didn't think he'd ever agree to telling me about his first boner. I was half joking when I suggested it. I guess it's what best friends do, tell each other everything. Plus I think it will be good information to have. There's only so much a girl can learn from the sealed sections of the Girlfriend magazines I buy with my pocket money. I need to tell Chance to come with me to Whitcoulls sometime to get some new magazines. I need to update the posters on my wall. There should be a new Backstreet Boys one out this week and I can never have too many of Howie D.

Howie D has all I have to give,

SARAH DELANY

Lacey

CHAPTER 16

CHANCE

19TH APRIL

It's autumn now. Tilting my head I see some of the leaves of the weeping willow are turning yellow. It won't be long before the tree sheds its leaves for winter like it does every year. By then it will be too cold to sit out here under the tree but for the time being, it's fine to sit out here in my jeans and t-shirt. Earlier in the day Lacey and I went to ECM in town where we bought a CD single each. Mum got me a discman as a treat last month so now we can buy CD's instead of cassettes. I'm thinking of giving my walkman to Lacey so then we both have something to listen to music on. I need to buy more CDs for my collection so I have more music to listen to. We can't burn CD's on the radio either so I will have to save some of my pocket money.

Thoughts of Lacey magically make her appear. I'm distracted by the music and thoughts swirling in my head so she manages to surprise me. She offers me a genuine smile before folding her legs and sitting next to me, her back against our tree. She tugs the headphone out of my far ear and lifts it to her ear so she can listen along. Her light laughter drifts into my ear as she hears Mariah Carey's 'Butterfly' play. She always makes fun of my love for Mariah but lately she hasn't said anything. Her simple laugh says everything without saying a word. We sit without talking, with the song on repeat until she's tired of the song and holds the CD case she bought today. I sigh, pressing the open button on my discman and retrieving my CD and place it carefully back into its case so it doesn't scratch. Taking her CD from her fingers I push it into the slot, closing the lid and pressing play.

Handing the case back to her, she flicks it open, pulling out the cover insert so she can see the song lyrics and I know I'm in for a long afternoon. The thing about Lacey and new songs is, she'll make sure the cassettes or CD's she buys have the lyrics on the insert. She'll spend the rest of the day listening to the song over and over until she has every word memorised. She flicks out the folded leaflet and holds it between us so I can see the words too. She's obsessed with the Backstreet Boys and for some strange reason she always makes me sing Nick's part. She could sing every word herself if she wanted to as she knows all of their songs word for word but I think it's her way of including me. I wish she wouldn't give me Nick's parts as he is one of the main singers so I end up having to sing a lot.

'All I Have to Give' is their newest hit and she was extremely excited about it because they each sing a clear part of their own. When it gets to her one true love's part, (her words, not mine) I hear her sigh Howie's name before she sings along with his voice, reading the lyrics from the sheet.

Lacey and I often have days like this lately. We don't talk much, content to sit in silence with each other. I think knowing I'm there beside her helps, even though I know she doesn't want to talk about anything. The fighting between her parents has gotten worse so nearly every night she creeps across her lawn and climbs into my window. For a while she stopped but I could tell she wasn't sleeping as she had dark circles under her eyes and she'd fall asleep at lunch time.

I didn't want to draw attention to it so all I said to her was, "I'll keep my window unlocked for you every night if you need it," then I squeezed her hand and walked the rest of the way to my house, leaving her at her front door. Nearly every night since she's taken me up on the offer.

I feel Lacey shiver beside me, her lyric sheet lying across her lap now, not needed anymore. It's no wonder she's got the lyrics down pat, I think she forced me to listen to it over a hundred times.

"Let's head home," I say, tugging the headphones from each of our ears and she nods, standing as she brushes the dirt off the back of her shorts. She bends down, grabbing the cover insert, refolding it and sliding it back into the case. There's a sadness lingering around Lacey and sometimes it seeps into me because I don't know what to do about it. I want to see her smile so I say, "You want to take my discman for the night?" holding it out for her to take. Her eyes light up and it makes me realise I've missed that about her.

"Really?" she squeals, and the shrill sound makes my heart smile so I can't help but nod, knowing I've done something simple to make her smile. "Oh Chancey, you're the bestest," she tells me, as she pulls me into a hug, clinging to me for a second as I squeeze her tightly.

Releasing each other, she steps back, grabs the discman like her life depends on it and pushes both headphones into her ears before pushing play. We walk back to our houses with the sound of Lacey belting out the song filling the air. We high five each other as we near the spot where we split off into different directions. Once I get to my back door, I continue to watch my best friend. Keeping an eye on her until her voice fades with the closing of her own back door, knowing I made her happy.

Stepping through the front door, Mum lets me know dinner will be ready in a minute and sends me to go wash my hands. I walk into my room and set my Mariah Carey CD on my desk and then move to the window, unlocking it like I usually do. I don't think I'll need it unlocked tonight because I'm pretty sure Lacey will fall asleep with her beloved Backstreet Boys serenading her.

LACEY

19TH APRIL
Dear Diary,

Today was a great day. Chance and I went and picked out CD's for us to play in his discman and I finally got 'All I Have To Give' by the Backstreet Boys. I've wanted it for soooo long.

Chance let me borrow his discman so I could listen to it all night. I'm so excited. I'm quickly writing to you and then I'm jumping in bed to listen to my one true love's voice. Howie is so cute. I love his hair. I hope he never cuts it. I wonder if I'll grow up to marry someone who looks like Howie D? I hope so.

Okay, it's short and sweet tonight as I want to get back to Howie's voice but I'll write more later. Let's hope his voice drowns out the fighting tonight.

Howie's future wife,
Lacey

CHAPTER 17

LACEY

24TH SEPTEMBER

Dear Diary,

Dad lost yet another job. The fighting is constant now and I climb into Chance's window every night because it's so bad. Chance keeps my mind off it but as soon as I walk into my house, I feel a sense of dread wash over me.

I wish Dad could keep a job. Mum yells about his drinking so much I think alcohol is the problem. I can't remember the last time I saw him without a drink in his hand. He usually comes home at night carrying a box and sits himself in front of the television with them.

I spend as long as I can out of the house now, wanting to spend as much time as I can with Chance laughing and feeling like myself. Like a kid. I've thought about running away but then I'd have to beg Chance to come with me because I can't leave him. He wouldn't dare leave his mum and she doesn't deserve to be abandoned so it stops me from asking him. The idea pops into my head daily, at least it's nice to daydream about. I wish I could run away to the beach and not have a care in the world. Sometimes it feels like it's too much for a kid my age to deal with.

The fighting has stopped for the night so I might try to fall asleep before they fight again otherwise I'll need to climb in Chance's

window. I hate bothering him every night and interrupting his sleep. I wish my life was different. I miss how my dad used to be.
  Goodnight,
  Lacey

CHAPTER 18

CHANCE 1998

26TH JULY

The phone rings from the kitchen so I race to answer it.

"Hello?"

"Chance, wanna meet me outside?"

"Sure Lace. I'll see you in a minute," I say, before hanging up the phone.

"Mum, I'm heading out to meet Lacey," I yell, as I pass her in the lounge on my way to the front door. I drop to the floor and pull my sneakers on.

"Okay honey," she calls back, as I'm closing the door behind me.

I walk along the footpath and sit on the grass between our houses waiting for Lacey to appear. I hear her door open a minute later and she comes hopping along. She's got her new favourite toy with her. Her skip-it. It's pink of course. Lately every time I meet up with her she has it hooked around her ankle. She wasn't good at first, she doesn't have much coordination. You have to swing it with one leg and jump over it with the other. I helped her figure it out but while I played with it, I got hooked and Lacey didn't like the fact it came naturally to me. Now she's spent the last two weeks practising in all her spare time so she can be better than me. Everytime we play together, she brings it along to see who can get the highest score as it records your skip count on it. I try to let her win but most of the time the competitiveness in me takes over and I forget I was going easy for her sake. Hopping over to me now, I can tell she's concentrating hard as her eyes stay focused on her feet, her tongue peeking out the side of her lips.

"Watch out Lace," I yell, before it throws her sync off and the hard ball whacks her in the shin. I can't help laughing as she leans down to rub her leg.

"Chance, I was on a roll," she whines, making me laugh harder at her.

"Give me a turn. I'll beat you easily," I taunt, as I try to grab it off her ankle. She shuffles out of my reach then tries to run with it still around her leg. She swings it around again but it slows her down and it's easy to catch her. I grab her around the waist, lifting her in the air as I twirl her and the pink device flies around with her. Her laughter hits my ears, making my smile grow.

The hum of her dad's car halts her laughter so I slow my swings, placing her back on her feet. I slide my arm over her shoulders, holding her close. Her dad slams his door as we watch him make the trek to the front door of the house with his usual pack of beer in his hand. My hand tightens around Lacey's shoulder. We stand there holding our breath while he enters the house. Releasing our breath, the tension disappears from our bodies as he disappears from view. Lacey's dad was always this man we looked up to but now he's someone I feel I need to keep Lacey safe from. I often hear yelling from their house in the evening, they don't try to hide it anymore.

It's made Lacey more withdrawn. I try my best to keep a smile on her face but sometimes I watch her retreat into her head and it's a place where I can't follow her so I have to wait. We sit in silence while she comes out of it or else I'll try my best to distract her so she doesn't feel the need to retreat in the first place. On the bad days, I offer to play elastics with her. We usually drag two of my kitchen chairs outside as Mum is worried we might break something with all the jumping inside. Lacey is better at it than me so she has to show me all the moves and explain what to do. She plays a lot of elastics at school with the other girls so she gets a lot of practice. No boys at our school would be caught dead playing it. At school the girls take turns holding each end with their legs but because it's just me and her, we need the chairs. I'm about to ask her to hand over her skip-it so I can have a turn when we hear her mum and dad yelling at each other. Her mum must have seen the beer.

"Want to go climb our tree?" I ask, trying to get her away from the house so she won't hear them as much. Her face drops and it's the expression I like least on her.

"Nah I want to beat you on this today," she says, lifting her gaze to meet mine. Her head held high. I nod, holding out my hands for her to give me the device. She unhooks it from her ankle before we hear the front door of the house slamming, causing us both to jump. Stunned, we watch her dad storm out to his car, jump in and peel out of the driveway. Once he's gone, Lacey doesn't move, she stands frozen in the same spot gazing at the driveway where his car was.

"You want to play elastics instead?" I offer. Her eyes travel to the sky, inspecting the weather but it's blue skies above for as far as the eye can see.

"Okay," she replies, her sad eyes turning my way.

"You grab the elastics. I'll grab the chairs," I tell her, as it's what we usually do. She nods and we rush off to our houses. Meeting back minutes later, we hook her pink elastics around the wooden chairs. We continue playing until the sun sets, as it's one game Lacey never tires of.

"Bye Lace," I say, before we part ways.

"Thanks Chance," she says, knowing I was distracting her with the elastics. I think she caught on to what I was doing a while ago because on the days we play elastics, she doesn't say bye. She always says thank you. I nod in reply, carrying the chairs back into the house. I have dinner and get ready for bed. I read my book until Lacey climbs through my window. On the elastics days, it's always a given she'll be climbing through my window. It doesn't bother me. I like having her close and knowing she's safe. When she climbs into my window, she hops in my bed, turns out my lamp and we silently fall asleep. No words needed, being together is enough.

LACEY

26TH JULY
Dear Diary,

Dad left today after a fight with Mum and he hasn't returned. He doesn't usually leave and not return so it's making me worried. Mum didn't mention him leaving over dinner. I'm not sure if she knows I saw him leave or not.

Chance was so sweet today. He always knows when I'm feeling the worst as he pulls out the elastics card, knowing I can't resist them. They are my favourite game to play. I wish he would play at school with me but he won't. He said it's not cool for the boys to be seen playing elastics so I have to split my time. Some days I'll play with him at lunch and then other days, I'll play elastics with the girls. Some days I'll even quickly play elastics at first break to get a hit of it to last me until my next fix. It's so addictive.

I would write more but I'm nearly out of pages in this book. I'll have to ask Mum in the morning to buy me a new one. I will write again when I get my new diary. I'm going to Chance's now to get some sleep.

Night,
Lacey

CHAPTER 19

LACEY

27TH DECEMBER

Dear Diary,

We're having a change of scenery today. Instead of writing to you in my room, I'm writing to you from outside. I am currently seated with my back against our trusty old weeping willow tree. I think the name for the tree is fitting as weeping is what I am doing right now.

My parents, seconds ago, informed me they are getting the dreaded D word. Yep. Divorced. I don't know many kids with divorced parents but Josh from school told me once his parents are and he hates it. He currently lives with his dad because his mum moved away and he misses her like crazy.

That will be me soon but I'll be the one moving away. They told me Mum and I are going to live with Nana. I don't want to move again and I don't want to move away from Chance.

Chance. How am I supposed to tell my best friend I'm leaving him and I don't know when I'll see him again. Who's going to protect him while I'm gone? I know we made up with Theodore and are technically friends with him now but I still worry in the back of my mind he will hurt Chance if I'm not around to keep him in line. Who else is going to threaten the kid's goolies? It's for his own good as well as Chance's.

Sorry the pages I'm writing on are getting wet but I can't stop the tears. It feels like my heart has cracked in half.

I wonder if Chance's mum would adopt me. She's always mentioning I'm the daughter she never had so I'm sure she'd be more than happy to. The downfall is I'd miss my mum terribly if she left without me.

I don't want to tell him but I heard his back door slam shut so I know he's probably seen me run here and is following me. I'll have to tell him now when he sees the state of me. Wish me luck.

Heartbroken,
Lacey

CHANCE

27TH DECEMBER

"Lacey, come back here," I heard the faint yelling of Lacey's mum calling out to her, so I peek out my open window to see what's going on. Lacey's wild hair thrashes behind her as she runs along her fence line. Whenever she runs in that direction, she is always headed to the same place. Our weeping willow tree.

"Mum, I'm going out to the tree," I call, hoping Mum will hear me from wherever she is in the house. I heard a faint reply so I know she did hear me. I open the back door and the wind catches hold of it when I let go, slamming it shut behind me. I glance at the clear blue sky, not a cloud above me. It looks like we are in for an awesome summer. I always love summer with the hot weather. Lacey and I usually go to the river where we are allowed to swim with all the other kids from the neighbourhood. Walking to Lacey and my favourite spot, I catch sight of her sitting against the old tree with her diary leaning against her knees while she furiously writes. She wipes her face with the back of her hand which has my heart rate picking up. I can tell she's crying from here and seeing Lacey cry isn't a new thing. For some reason I have a bad feeling in my gut I'm not going to be able to fix whatever it is that is causing her tears today.

Her bloodshot eyes stare at me when I reach her and I raise my brows in a silent question, making fresh tears stream down her face. I sit next to her and pull her head against my chest, wrapping my arms tightly around her. She squeezes me back so tightly, it makes my heart ache knowing whatever she tells me is not going to be good. We sit for a long time, her head buried against my chest with both of our arms embracing each other. Her soft sniffling fills the silence around us. I'm scared to ask but I rip off the band aid anyway.

"What's wrong Lace?" I whisper, which makes her shake her head against me, signalling she's unwilling to tell me yet. "Okay, we can stay like this for now," I tell her, squeezing her even tighter. The shade from the weeping willow protects us from the sweltering summer sun and as we sit there, the shadow moves along the grass. Time passes as I continue to hold her while she's unwilling to voice what's wrong. A light breeze swirls around us, giving me a nudge to ask her again.

"You ready to talk yet, Lace?" Her hands gently release my waist so I untangle my own hands, dropping them to my lap as I watch her scrub her hands down the tear soaked skin of her face. She gazes at the sky for a minute before closing her eyes and taking a deep breath.

"My parents are getting a divorce," she whispers into the breeze, hoping it will take the truth away with it. My heart sinks at her words but I try to put a positive spin on it.

"It's for the best then they won't be fighting all the time," I try to reason with her.

Her head drops to her knees and I hear her breathing loudly before she grunts, "You don't get it. They are getting divorced which means separate homes, Chance." She lifts her head, staring into my eyes as if she's trying to get me to read her mind so she doesn't have to say it out loud.

"So is your dad moving out?" I ask, coming to the logical solution Lacey and her mum would stay here next door to me. She sadly looks at me as a tear drips on her cheek, shaking her head no.

My heart rate picks up speed as I ask, "Your mum is moving out?" The tears flood down her face as she nods and my gut twists. My eyes burn, already thinking I know the answer to the next question but needing to ask it.

"Are you going to live with your mum?" I whisper, as a tear of my own betrays me and slides down my cheek. She sadly nods while she wipes my lone tear away with the pad of her thumb.

Her soft skin slides against mine wiping the moisture away as she says, "We're moving to my nana's house near Dunedin. It's in the South Island." The burning in my eyes intensifies as we stare at each other. Both of us let the realisation of the situation sink in. We are getting pulled apart. Neither of us expecting it and neither of us ready for it. As fresh tears stream down both our faces, I pull her onto my lap. She wraps her whole body around mine as she shakes with emotion. I lean back against the cold bark, letting my own emotions slide down my face, unashamed of the falling tears.

"I don't want you to go," I admit, which brings a new wave of tears.

"Me either," I hear her muffled reply, as her face is squished against my chest. We cling to each other, our tears and sniffles surrounding us as the sun sets in the sky. We don't dare move and it is how our mums find us when it's dark out, still wrapped in each other's arms.

"Aww kids," I hear Lacey's mum stutter, as their soft steps through the grass get closer. We both look up and I take note of the tears on both their faces. "It'll be okay," she tries to say.

Lacey cuts her off, screaming, "NO IT WON'T," and a new round of tears race down her face. Her mum takes a step back like Lacey's words have wounded her.

"Come on Lacey, I'll walk you home," I tell her, helping her off my lap. She lowers a hand to help me stand, then she picks up her forgotten diary and pen. Hand in hand, we walk back towards her house and when we get to her back door, I give her another hug. "Goodnight Lace. I'll see you in the morning." She nods, then watches me as I walk to my own house. Our mothers talk between themselves near Lacey's fence before my mum comes home. As she enters, she wraps me in her arms and I let out even more tears. After I've exhausted all my tears, I go have a shower and wash the remaining tears away under the hot stream. Once I'm changed, I leave my window unlocked as it's part of my normal routine but I don't know if I'll need to do it anymore as the reason for it has been resolved.

I hop into bed and flick my lamp off, not in the mood to read tonight. I lie there staring at the glow in the dark stars on my ceiling Lacey gave me for Christmas. How could it have been a few days ago? Christmas was such a magical and happy day and is so far away from how I feel now. After she gave them to me, we raced to my room with the step ladder and she handed each star to me, directing me on where to place it. How fast things can change.

It feels like forever before I drift off but then the rustling of my curtains draws my attention to my window where I see a familiar figure climbing through. Her soft thud hits the carpet, before she lightly steps beside my bed, flinging the duvet off and climbing in. She lays her head on my chest, wrapping her arm around my waist and covers us again without saying a word. I wrap my own arm around her. Lacey and I don't usually sleep wrapped around each other but I think we're both scared the other will disappear if we don't have contact. I need to hug my best friend right now. It's how we fall asleep. Holding on tightly to each other, hoping with all our might, our friendship will last the distance.

CHAPTER 20

CHANCE 1999

2ND FEBRUARY

Today's the first day at my new school. Dressed in my new uniform Mum ironed specially for today, I walk into the hallway where Mum waits with her camera to take some pictures of me. She said she has a couple more slots on her film so I have to give my best smile so we can get a good photo. Knowing her, she will take it to the photo lab to get developed today so they are ready by tomorrow. I stand up tall, a large smile spread across my face with teeth showing. After a couple snaps, she declares she's out of film. Thank god, I hate having to force a smile for photos. I grab my backpack from the floor and sling it over my shoulder.

Nervous, I follow the footpath, the sound of my clunky footsteps filling my thoughts. I wish Lacey was here. It hasn't felt the same without her. Mum said I have to get used to her not being around and I should embrace it as it will give me the opportunity to make new friends. I don't want to make new friends, I was fine with the best friend I had.

"Chance," someone calling my name has me whipping my head behind me. Theodore comes running up to me. "Hey bud," he says, slapping my shoulder, his laboured puffs filling the air.

"Hey."

"Are you excited for high school?" he asks.

"Not really. You?" I ask him, not able to muster the same excitement he has.

"I can't wait. Do you think there will be heaps of pretty girls there?"

"Who knows," I laugh, but it's Lacey's face filling my head when he mentions girls. We fall into an easy conversation as we walk the rest of the way to school. If you didn't already know our history, you wouldn't think Theodore used to bully me.

"Could you call me Theo now? I think Theo sounds a lot cooler and older, don't you?" he asks.

"Sure Theo," I say, testing out his new nickname which has him smiling and slapping my shoulder again. Walking through the gate together, I realise how much bigger this school is than my primary school. We arrive earlier than we needed to so we wander around the school, looking at all the buildings not knowing what any of them are used for. The bell ringing signifies it's time for us third formers to congregate in the hall. Pushing shoulder to shoulder through the double doors, we all rush in and Theo and I catch sight of Darren and Miles from our old school. Greeting them, we all take seats on the cold wooden floor, following the lead of others doing the same. Everyone chats amongst their little groups and an excited buzz fills the air as we nervously wait to find out what happens next. Darren and Miles fill Theo and I in on what they did over the summer holidays. They both ask where Lacey is and a pain fills me at the sound of her name.

"Her parents got divorced so she and her mum moved back to the South Island where her nana lives," I tell them. It was right after Christmas last year she told me they were leaving. I keep my eyes on my lap while they talk between them but I can feel their sad eyes on me. Everyone who knows me and Lacey, knows we were inseparable from the first day she moved in next door to me.

A booming voice over a microphone silences the room, "Good morning students. I'm Mr Abbott, your third form deputy. Today we are going to run through what will happen this year. It will be a lot different from primary school. You'll be assigned a tutor group. These are formed from the four houses we have here at school. This is filled with students from all different year levels and it's where you go for roll call when the first bell rings. Fifteen minutes later, a second bell will ring and you will head to your first period lesson," he says, glancing around at all the students. "You'll also be assigned a core class who you will go to your everyday classes with. There will be a different set of taster classes each term. These classes are for you to try out and see what you enjoy and then next year you will pick two of these to focus on for the whole year. Make the most of your taster classes this year as it will help you decide what you want to study in the future." Mr Abbott keeps talking for about ten minutes, telling us about the school values and what is expected of us. I zone out and think about what Lacey is doing and if she has started her new school yet. Before I know it, he's calling out names of students to stand and assigning them to their class groups. Luckily Theo and I end up in the same group which puts the first genuine smile on my face today. At least I won't have to tread this scary new chapter of my life alone after all.

Sorting out our classes takes forever so by the time we are splitting apart from the rest of the students, it's already the second period. The day goes surprisingly fast. I guess the learning of new faces and names plus trying to remember where classes are and what we need to bring for each class is a lot. It leaves little time, if any, for Lacey to invade my thoughts again. There's a time here and there when I think Lacey would have said something funny. I think I'm coming to terms with the fact she won't be around any more and I am going to have to accept it whether I like it or not.

Lunch time arrives and I spend it playing handball with Theo, Darren, Miles and a few of the new guys they have become friends with today.

On the walk home, Darren and Miles join Theo and I and we all agree to meet in the morning at the local dairy as it's a central location between all our houses so we can walk to school together every day. We split up once we arrive at the dairy, all of us going off in different directions. As I get to my house, my eyes glance at Lacey's house. Memories surface and I let them flood my mind. Remembering how her boofy head would run along the fence line, showing me she was on her way to our tree. My feet of their own accord lead me to the weeping willow now. The thick green foliage hangs low, creating a shelter of sorts from the outside world. I drop my backpack on the grass below and climb through the branches like Lacey and I would do most afternoons. A few branches up, hidden from the view below, I find what I'm looking for. I run my fingers over the uneven bark. The L + C we engraved in our tree so many years ago. We did it to show the tree belongs to both of us, not realising there wouldn't always be an us here to enjoy it.

I get lost in the moment, staring at the disfigured bark, missing my best friend. It isn't until I feel the first drops of the changing weather I know it's time to head inside. Mum will be mad if I come home soaked in my new uniform on my first day. Jumping down, the soft grass breaking my fall, I grab my bag and sling it over my shoulder. Walking faster towards my back door, I glance once again at Lacey's old bedroom window before sighing and disappearing into my house.

LACEY

2ND FEBRUARY
Dear Diary,
I hate it here. I want to go back to Chance. Back to my old room. Back to my tree. Our tree. Will I ever see Chance again? I tried

ringing Chance a few times, remembering his phone number off by heart but Mum said I couldn't ring him all the time because of the phone bill. The times I did ring no one answered so he wouldn't even know I had rung.

I've thought about writing letters to him but I can't think of anything exciting to write. Nothing is going on here worth telling him about. I hope the kids are still being nice to him. We were about to go to high school together and with my leaving he was on his own. Well he has Theodore but the kid is a major pain in the butt and I can't trust him to have Chance's back. Not like I could and always would.

I hope his first day at his new school went alright. It should've been us walking into those new school gates together. I hate the new school I'm at. The uniform sucks. It's a bright red jumper and I swear the skirt looks like a blimmin Scottish kilt. Like who in their right mind thinks this is a good uniform for kids to wear? I don't know what the skirt is made out of but it itches like crazy.

I didn't make any friends today because everyone already knows everyone else. They all came together from the one primary school in this freakishly small town. Now I'm the outsider again. Although I never felt like an outsider when I had Chance by my side. I was always worrying about how to protect Chance and without me realising, he was protecting me in a way as well.

I miss my best friend. I don't think any of these new people will do.

Hating this new life already,
Lacey

CHAPTER 21

CHANCE

3RD APRIL

Saturday was always the day Lacey and I would walk to the dairy to spend my pocket money. Thinking about it now, I never realised we always spent mine on lollies to share and hers was reserved for her *Girlfriend* and *Teen Beat* magazines. At least she shared her posters with me I guess, but it was always after she'd taken the ones she wanted so I got her reject pile.

Lying on the grass in my yard, I stare at the clouds, trying to see what images I can decipher from the white fluffiness above. Tilting my head to the left I think I can make out a rabbit riding a dragon but then it also could be a camel with an Arabian rider.

"Chance?" I hear someone call from close by, so I push myself to sit until my eyes land on Mr Connelly.

"Hey, Mr Connelly," I say, as I push to stand while he walks over to me. I take in his haggard appearance. His now greying hair which was once a dark brown and the scruff on his face tells me he hasn't shaved lately. His clothes hang looser on his frame than usual so I suspect he's lost weight. His blue eyes are a painful reminder of my best friend I desperately miss. Although his eyes now hold a sadness I've never seen on him before. Mr Connelly was always a giant force and the way Lacey would look at him was like nothing else I'd ever seen. It was pure happiness in a glance.

Now he is a shell of the man he once was. The permeating smell of lingering liquor surrounds us the closer he gets.

"You good Chance?" he asks, and I nod, not knowing what to say to this man who has changed so drastically over the years.

"I saw you out here and I thought you might like this," he says, as he hands me something I didn't see him holding before. I take it from his fingers and one glance at the photo has me throwing my head back in laughter. I realise it feels good to laugh because I haven't laughed like this since Lacey left.

"It's very Lacey, isn't it," Mr Connelly says, his own smile upon his face. I stare at the photo of Lacey with her face screwed up in clear disgust. I'd take a guess it's because of the ugly uniform. I can tell her hair is still not brushed and it brings an ache to my chest, not realising I would miss her bird's nest of hair if it ever left.

"It sure is," I reply, holding out the photo for him to take back.

"No, no, you can keep it. Her mother sent me a few and I thought you might appreciate this one the most when I saw you lying out here from the window." I feel the burn in my eyes, with unshed tears as I will my body not to let them fall. I don't want Mr Connelly to see me cry, especially if it's going to be reported back to Lacey. I'm not lucky because his next words tell me he saw the emotion I tried to hide.

"It's okay to miss her Chance. I miss her too," he tells me, raising his hand to my shoulder and giving it a squeeze.

"Thanks Mr Connelly."

"You're a good kid, Chance. You were always a good friend to Lacey which I'm grateful for," he says, squeezing my shoulder again before walking back the way he came to his house. Holding the photo, staring at it, it makes me smile again and I hold it carefully as I race inside calling for Mum. She's in the lounge reading a book when I find her and show her the picture.

"Aww she looks like she's grown a bit," Mum says, and I notice her own tears arrive on her lash line. She always did think of Lacey as a daughter and often told her so.

"Mr Connelly said I could keep it," I tell her, as she looks at me.

"I think I might have a frame for it. Let me have a look," she says, handing the photo back to me as she stands to go in search of a photo frame. She returns a minute later, silently taking the photo from my hands and placing it in the white frame. She squeezes the back in then presses the little black sharp metal bits into place.

Handing it back to me, I thank her as I take the wooden frame back to my room and place it on my bedside table next to my library book *The Subtle Knife* by Philip Pullman. Admiring the new addition to my room, I can't help but laugh and this time it's followed by a sigh because I could have all the photos in the world of her but I'd still miss my best friend. Nothing beats the real thing.

CHAPTER 22

CHANCE

15TH APRIL

Dear Lacey,

I'm writing you this letter because a pinky promise is a pinky promise. Plus you made me lock it too and I'm not one to break promises, especially to my best friend. Here it goes. I got my first boner. I woke up this morning and it was there. There I said it. I have fulfilled the pinky promise law. We didn't promise I had to go into detail so the pinky promise is complete. Possibly burn this letter after you read it so there isn't any evidence of this conversation ever happening.

If nothing else I hope this puts a smile on your beautiful face. I miss your face and all your different smiles. I miss the dark freckle above your right eyebrow. I miss the chicken pox scar between your eyes (my mum was right about it scarring if you scratched it.) I miss your shaggy hair. Is it wrong for me to hope you still don't brush it? Is that weird? Are you still wearing pink wherever you go?

Is it wrong for me to hope you haven't changed much? I'm being selfish, I know but I don't care. I don't want to miss any part of my best friend's life. If you've changed then I've missed something and thinking I've missed something important makes me upset because I don't want to miss anything.

I'm rambling and if you were here, you'd call me out on it but the gist of it is, I really miss my best friend. I've missed you since the minute you drove away and every minute thereafter.

Your dad saw me being a loner by myself out in the yard one day and came out and gave me a picture of you in your school uniform. The uniform is horrendous. I feel sorry for you having to wear it every day. Question: Does it itch? It looks like it does.

Theo, yes Theodore, goes by Theo now. Apparently Theodore wasn't cool enough for high school so he is now Theo formally known as Theodore. Well he's gone girl crazy. You should see him flirting with all the girls. I don't think he's any good at it because most of them get the same look on their faces you used to have when you'd look at him. You know the look I'm talking about, where you scrunch your nose like something stinks? Yes! That look.

And no, for your information, I don't flirt with any girls. I'm scared they might give me the same look if I even tried.

High school is a lot different to primary school, isn't it? What's your school like? Have you made some new friends? I hope you're okay, Lace. I miss you terribly. I know I already said it but I wanted to drive the point home about how much I miss you.

Well you know where I live so I'm hoping you'll write me back. I walked over and got your address from your dad so I could send you this letter. Since I have a photo of you in your uniform, I asked Mum for one of me to send to you. Hope you like it. I framed the one of you your dad gave me. It sits on my bedside table so I get to see you every morning and night. I'll admit sometimes I even talk to your photo like you're sitting in my room with me. Hope that's not weird.

Well I better go.
Your best friend,
Chance.

LACEY

12TH MAY

Dear Chancey,

I can't believe you wrote it in a letter and sent it. You know how they check letters before they let prisoners read them and send them? What if someone read your letter? Someone could have intercepted your letter at the post office and read what you wrote before sending it to me? Now there's a random person in the world who knows you got your first boner.

Thank you for taking the risk in sending me the tidbit of information. It is much appreciated and yes, the pinky promise is complete.

I miss you too, like you wouldn't believe. It's been hard to make friends because the town we are in is small and everyone knows everyone else. I have become close with a girl named Calliope, although she's no Chance.

Yes I still love pink. I think something pretty drastic would have to happen for me to not love pink anymore. I haven't changed at all so you don't need to worry. Mum does make me brush my hair a bit more as a few of the girls at school mocked my hair when I started and I didn't want to keep getting mocked so it forced me to brush it more although I hate doing it.

Thanks for the photo. You look like you've grown. Are you taller? And since you framed my photo, I asked Mum to get me a frame the next time she is at the mall and she said she would.

On Saturdays I walk to my local dairy to buy my ka blueys so our tradition is still alive and well. I hope you are okay and I hope Theodore (I refuse to call him Theo) is treating you well and not ditching you for any shiny new people. If he does I may have to hitchhike there and kick his butt.

I miss you Chancey. Keep writing please and I'm sorry, I can't burn your letter. I need it as evidence in case you ever try to deny it.

Write back.
Your best friend forever,
Lacey

CHANCE

7TH JUNE

Dear Lace,

I hope you were joking when you said you weren't going to burn my letter. BURN IT NOW!! And if a random person is reading our mail, I'll have to make it extra boring so they don't get any joy out of it.

Have you heard the Backstreet Boys' new song 'I Want it That Way?' I'm sure you have. Are you still obsessed with Howie? Still hoping to marry him one day? I bought the cassingle and listened to it over and over under our weeping willow tree. Now I know all the words but it's a secret I will take to the grave.

Theo and I went to the movies last Saturday and saw Never Been Kissed. Have you seen it? You will love it so you should watch it if you haven't already. Theo groaned about going to watch it but I dragged him to see it as you would have dragged me to go see it. He didn't mind once he saw all the girls lining up and buying tickets for it. I swear his hormones have exploded this year.

He's growing a moustache. Can you believe it? He's going to be shaving soon, the way it's growing. I think it means he will have a hairy back when he's an adult if his moustache is anything to go by. Don't worry, my face is still baby butt smooth so you aren't missing out on much.

Theo and a few of the other guys I hang out with want me to try out for the school soccer team next week. I guess it could be fun if all my friends are playing. Are you going to join any sports teams?

How are things at school? Are you still friends with Calliope? I saw your dad again the other day. He looked better, he had shaved his face and gotten a haircut. His clothes looked half decent this time so he must be recovering.

Anyway I better run. Theo is coming around so we can shoot some hoops.

Hope to hear from you soon,
Chance x

LACEY

28TH JUNE
Dear Chance,

Yes! Of course I've heard 'I Want it That Way'. I begged Mum to take me into town as soon as it got released so I could buy a copy as I had to have it. I learnt all the words too.

It sounds like you and Theodore are becoming good friends. I must say I did suspect he would be a hairy adult like his namesake Theodore the chipmunk. Has he managed to sweet talk any girls into going out on a date with him yet? Are there any girls you like?

No sports for me. Nana has been quite sick lately and isn't improving. Mum is worried even though she tries to hide it from me. I love listening to Nana talk about back in the day. The stories are so funny. Growing up she didn't have a car so she and her two brothers had to walk five miles to school and five miles home every day. I'm not sure how far five miles is but it sounds pretty far. I hope when I'm her age I can tell my grandkids about all the things we did when we were young.

Yes I'm still friends with Calliope. She is pretty cool. We went and got a second piercing in our ears. Mum wasn't too impressed. She said I'll be full of holes soon but I like them. I think I'll pierce my ears more as I get older.

I've never had a girl as a friend before so it is nice. I can talk to her about stuff you would cringe at so at least she listens with a straight face. I'll have to get her to watch Never Been Kissed with me as I haven't seen it yet.

Dad rings me every week to see how I'm doing. He mentioned he got a new job and he reckons he is going to stick with it this time. Time will tell I guess. He might come visit me sometime if he can manage it too. Would be good to see him. Wish I could see you too.

Mum finally got me a frame for your photo you sent. I've got it on my bookshelf in my room. I feel like your eyes laugh at me every time I put my school uniform on now. You guessed it, the skirt itches like crazy.

Good luck with soccer. I know you'll be amazing,
Lacey

CHANCE

13TH JULY
Happy Birthday Lace,
I hope this arrives in time as I didn't want to miss your birthday on the twenty-second. I can't believe you're fourteen. I've added

five dollars in the envelope for you to buy yourself some ka blueys or put it towards one of those Girlfriend magazines you love so much. Do you still read those? Did you get any cool presents this year? Are you doing anything special for your birthday? I wish they hadn't closed Georgie Pie then you could have gone there. I sure do miss their pies.

I made the soccer team. I play centre midfield so I need to be fit so Theo and I go for a run a few times a week after school to increase our fitness. Theo plays goalie. He may look like he'd have butterfingers but he is surprisingly good. I think it's the ticket he needed to get the girls to notice him. Now they are, he's getting a big head about it. I wish you were here so you could pop his big head. I don't think he would have such a huge ego if you were around. You always could keep him in line.

You asked if I like any girls and the answer is yes. There's a girl called Hannah who I think is pretty. I'm too chicken to ask her out. She asked me about my scar the other day and I told her I got mauled by a wild boar when I was younger. Her eyes got so big, I thought they might pop. I ended up laughing and telling her the truth but you would have thought it was funny. Unfortunately she hasn't talked to me since.

Don't poke too many holes in your ears okay, I don't know if you would suit the punk rocker image popping into my head. Are you brushing your hair?

I hope your nana feels better soon.

Miss you tons,

Chance x

CHANCE

12TH SEPTEMBER

Dear Lacey,

Are you okay? I never heard back from you. I hope my last letter arrived in time for your birthday. Sorry I didn't write sooner to check on you, I got busy with soccer and homework. I can't believe how much homework they give us at high school. I thought primary was bad but this is crazy.

Please let me know you received my letter. I hope they didn't steal it at the post office because I included $5 for you. They have x-ray machines to check every envelope and I'm guessing they saw the money and took it for themselves. If that's the case, I hope you enjoyed your birthday. I better not send any more money in case it goes missing again.

You haven't put any more holes in your body, have you? I hope you aren't turning into a pin cushion. The soccer season is nearly finished. We possibly have two games left. We won our division and made it into the semis so we have to play this week and if we win, we get to play in the finals. Wish us luck. Hope to hear from you soon.

I miss you,
Chance

CHANCE

17TH OCTOBER

Dear Lacey,

Are you avoiding me? I've tried ringing your house but no one answered. Mum doesn't like me ringing too much because of the phone bill. I'll use my pocket money and buy a phone card so Mum doesn't have to worry about the cost.

I still haven't received a letter from you so I'm not sure if you are receiving mine or if your replies are getting lost in the mail. I hope no one is reading our letters. They aren't like a daytime TV soap opera my mum watches or anything.

The leaves on our weeping willow are growing back now. It'll be back to being fully covered with leaves in no time. I climb it most days but it isn't as fun without you. I mainly sit out there with my discman and listen to music while thinking about you.

We didn't make the final for soccer this year. The guys on the team reckon we will come back bigger and stronger next year and take out the championship. Our coach said we did amazing for our first year playing together.

I got the trophy for MVP for the year. Can you believe it? I was their most valuable player. I scored a lot of goals which was a big factor in my getting the award. Funny to think I joined because the guys pressured me. I thought it would be a good way to pass the time as I have a lot of free time now you are gone.

Darren said he's changing schools next year. He is heading to Saint Stephens which is an all boy school in the city so we won't see him at school and unless we happen to see him around the neighbourhood, we probably won't be able to spend much time with him anymore. I hate when things have to change.

I hope you write back because I really miss my best friend.
Love,
Chance

CHANCE

21ST NOVEMBER
Dear Lacey,

What's going on? I think this is the third or fourth letter now gone unanswered. I haven't heard back from you since before your birthday.

I even went and knocked on your dad's door and asked if you were still alive. He said you were probably busy helping your mum as your nana is still sick. I hope she's okay. Is she the reason you aren't writing? You still want to be my friend right?

We had a Halloween disco at school the other week. It was quite fun. I dressed as a werewolf while others went as ghosts, witches and vampires. Most of the guys were too scared to ask the girls to dance so the girls danced with the girls and the boys danced with the boys. You would have loved it if you were here. You could have gone dressed as a pink fluff ball. Do you still wear pink? I hope so.

Theo and I are still going for our runs. It's to keep our fitness levels up but we've cut it down since we don't have soccer at the moment. We are making sure we don't get too unfit and will be ready for next year. We want to win the championships and get some trophies.

I hope you still want to be my friend Lacey because I miss you terribly. It's not the same without you and I find myself thinking about you constantly. I hope you are okay.

I don't know how long I can keep writing these unanswered letters. I'm running out of things to say.

Love,

Chance

P.S. Please write back to me.

CHAPTER 23

CHANCE

23RD DECEMBER

I bounce my basketball in the gravel driveway as I pass the time. School's out for the year and I survived my first year of high school mostly unscathed. Without Lacey it was hard but I got into a routine without her. Theo and I have gotten closer. I have yet to call him my best friend because it would mean I was replacing Lacey. No one could replace her or even come close to her. It's overcast today, grey clouds are scattered across the sky. With the gloominess in the air it doesn't even feel like Christmas is in a few days. Christmas isn't a happy occasion for me this year. Whenever I think of Christmas all I can think of is Lacey getting ripped away from me. I can't believe a whole year has passed already.

I get lost in the mesmerising rhythmic beat of the ball bouncing against my driveway. I hear an engine in the distance but my back is to the road and my eyes are focused on the ball. As the familiar hum gets closer, I realise it's Lacey's dad's car. I turn my head as he pulls into their driveway. He parks and turns the engine off, but remains in the car. I can't see him behind the window tint, but I wait for him to exit. I usually wave hello when I see him. I hold the ball at my hip, waiting. He takes longer to emerge from the vehicle than usual. He slams the door closed and turns my way.

The biggest smile spreads across his face as he looks at me. It's been a long time since I've seen him smile like that.

The sound of a second car door slamming has my brows pulling in. Confusion sets in. They must have gotten out on the opposite side of the car because I can't see them. I lift my hand in my usual hello gesture to Lacey's dad which he returns, his smile still plastered on his face. My body leaves my hand hanging in the air as I'm drawn to the small body that makes an appearance around the back of the jeep. Sucking the air from my lungs at the sight. Her small hands wrap around her waist, her head tilted downwards like she doesn't want to look up. Her blonde hair is a lot smoother than when I last saw her and it covers her face from view. Was she always this small? The bouncing of the basketball breaks through my trance as I absently let it drop.

"Lacey?" I whisper. My brain is not functioning properly. She's here. Her eyes finally lift up. Even from this distance I can see a brokenness in her I've never seen before. "Lacey!" I scream, my feet taking off on their own to get to her. It takes her a second but she releases her waist, pushes off with her feet and is running towards me. Within seconds I'm by her side and she leaps into my open arms. Her body simultaneously wraps around me as I press her head against my neck with one hand, my other wrapping around her waist. I spin us around and around with the momentum until we slow.

I can feel the fast beating of our hearts against my chest. A sigh leaves my body as my soul relaxes. It's as if it realised a piece was missing and it's been reunited with it, making me whole again. We stand in silence for a few minutes, neither of us talking. It isn't until I hear the soft sniffing I realise Lacey is crying. She's clinging to me so tightly I can release both my hands without dropping her. I pry her head off my neck so I can stare at her face. Tears stream down. There's the freckle I missed and the chicken pox scar I remember. Her wet lashes shimmer at me.

"Lace?" I ask, because her tears are not happy ones. She shakes her head, her sign it's too painful to talk about yet.

"Her nana passed away," her dad's voice interrupts our reunion, which sends streams racing down her face. I wipe the warm moisture away with the pads of my thumbs before bringing her head back to the crook of my neck, holding her there. "I'll let you two catch up," her dad sadly says, as he rubs her back then leaves, heading to his house.

"Our tree has missed you," I softly say, wrapping my arms back around her and carrying her towards the back of our yards. When I get to our favourite place, I lean against it with my back while holding Lacey. Her cries surround us and I continue to hold her, letting her release it all. She finally turns her head out from my neck, looking out into the yard.

"Nana had cancer and they didn't tell me. She kept getting worse and they still didn't tell me. They told me near the end when they knew she didn't have long left. They said they didn't want me to worry," she tells me. I squeeze her tighter in my arms. Her tears have all dried for now.

"Dad suggested to Mum I come stay here for the summer so here I am," she says, leaning back on my lap to look into my eyes.

"I'm happy you're here but I'm so sorry it's under these circumstances," I tell her. I'm not sorry she's here after being missing from my life for the past year.

"I've missed you Chancey," she tells me. One side of her lips pulls up in a sad smile.

"I've missed you too," I say, pulling her back into my arms and kissing the top of her head. We sit in silence for a while longer before Lacey talks again.

"The funeral was last week. I'm sorry I haven't written you back lately. I got busy helping Mum with Nana after school and on the weekends."

"Don't worry about that. I'm here for whatever you need," I tell her, giving her a squeeze.

"Thanks, Chance. I felt bad about leaving Mum but she said she would be okay and wanted to go through Nana's house by herself and get it sorted. Plus I couldn't give up the chance to come see you and Dad."

"I'm glad you're here. I think I've already said that but I mean it," I chuckle.

"Well you've got me for the whole summer."

"You wanna see my mum now? She's been missing you as much as I have."

"Yeah, let's go. I've missed her too." She stands and hops off my lap, holding her hand out to pull me up. I grasp her hand, stand up and we walk hand in hand back towards my house.

Turning the handle of the back door I call out to Mum, "Mum where are you?"

"I'm in the living room," she replies. I pull Lacey behind me until Mum comes into view. She's sitting in her rocking chair reading. She looks up when she feels me enter the room and her eyes move to the figure behind me.

"Oh Lacey, sweetie," she gasps, dropping her book and rushes to Lacey, encasing her in her arms. I catch sight of Lacey's smile before Mum squeezes her face to her chest. "Let me look at you," she tells Lacey, as she holds her out at arm's length looking her over before saying, "You look more beautiful than ever."

A blush creeps across Lacey's cheeks before she says, "Thanks. It's good to see you again."

"Are you and your dad doing anything for dinner? Why don't you come over here tonight for dinner? The both of you," Mum asks.

"I'm not sure if he had plans. I can go ask him now if you like?"

"Sounds great," Mum says.

"I'll be back in a minute," Lacey tells us, giving me a small smile before walking to the front door and walking out.

"Oh Chance you must be so happy to see her," Mum gushes, as she claps her hands together.

"Yeah I am Mum," my smile beams at her.

"How long is she back for?"

"For the summer. Her nana died so her mum thought it might be good for her to come spend time with her dad for a bit," I tell Mum, watching as her face drops.

"Aww that's sad to hear. Hopefully they can come for dinner and I can make my spaghetti bolognese she loves."

"That would be nice Mum."

"I'll go see if I have the ingredients while we wait for her to come back," she tells me, as she walks to the kitchen in hunt of what she needs. I follow her down the hall so I can look out the window to see Lacey when she returns. I sit at the kitchen table where I have a view out the window. My leg bounces in anticipation of her return. It's about fifteen minutes later when she comes running out of her house towards mine. I go to meet her at the front door but she's already closing it behind her when I get there.

"Dad said dinner sounds good," she huffs out, between breaths.

"Awesome. Let's tell Mum because she's hunting for ingredients to make spaghetti bolognese."

"Aww yum, my favourite," she squeals. I smile because my best friend is back, she's happy and we are the reason for her happiness.

Lacey and her dad left a few hours ago to head home. We are going to hang out tomorrow and catch up properly. I'm lying in bed, trying to calm myself down from the adrenaline running through me from her being back. I heard Mum head to her room over an hour ago so she's probably fast asleep by now. I'm lying in the dark hoping I drift off to sleep soon.

Tap, tap, tap. The familiar knocking on glass has me lifting my head in the direction of my window. Throwing the duvet back, I spread the curtains open. I'm greeted by the biggest smile on Lacey's face. I push the window open and move back for her to climb in.

"I didn't know if you'd still be awake," she whispers, after she's climbed in. I decide to leave the window open as there's a cool breeze swirling through, cooling against my clammy skin.

"Couldn't sleep," I tell her, hopping back into bed and she follows like old times. We've both grown so don't have as much free space in the bed as we used to. Lying face to face, our hands under our heads, we stare at each other.

"I've missed this," she whispers.

"Me too," I whisper back. We continue to stare at each other, smiling. My heart beats fast in my chest. I want to pull her close since I haven't had her near me in so long. I stretch out my arm in her direction and whisper, "Come here." Her smile widens as she wriggles over into my open arms. I wrap my arms around her while she rests her head on my chest and squeezes my waist.

"I hope the summer goes slow," I barely hear her mutter.

"Me too," I reply, with a satisfied smile on my face. We hold onto each other tightly until our breathing evens out and we fall asleep.

CHAPTER 24

CHANCE 2003

7TH JANUARY

"Yo Theo, pass another beer," I yell over the music to my friend, as he's sitting by the chilly bin. A bunch of our classmates made their way to the riverside where we all hang out these days. It's not much to look at. A river runs through the town and this section happens to be where the teenagers congregate to get away from prying adult eyes. I think it's one of those unspoken rules teenagers can come out here to party and drink and the adults turn a blind eye to it as long as no one causes any trouble. It's where I spent many summers with Lacey during my younger years.

The strip of water runs along the green grassy bank. There's a big tree hanging over the edge of the water where a big tire swing hangs. It's always been there and through the years others have replaced the rope as it's frayed. People use it to swing out over the water then jump in. With it being the last days of summer before school, some of the tipsy teenagers are making use of it and enjoying the heat of the stream before the chill of winter makes it too cold to swim in.

Laughter draws my attention back to Theo who has Missy sitting on his lap. Those two have gotten close over the summer break. I wonder if it's a summer fling or if it'll carry on when school begins. Theo isn't the type to have a girlfriend so I'm surprised Missy has lasted this long. While I'm distracted looking at Theo, I tilt the dripping wet can to my lips letting the foamy beer slide down my throat with a big gulp. Long tan legs with teeny jean shorts step into my view. My eyes roam upwards, taking note of the hands on her hips which tell me she's already in a mood.

"Chance, can I talk to you?" her whiny voice rings in my ears. I see Theo pop his head to the side so I can see him making stupid faces at me, behind her back, trying to make me laugh.

"I got nothing to say to you Emma," I keep my face neutral, trying my best not to laugh at Theo behind her.

"Please. It won't take long I promise," she pleads with me. Looking into her eyes, I let out a sigh. Pushing myself to stand I catch the small smile on her lips as she leads the way, with me following behind. I quickly tip my head back, finishing the cool drink and then squashing the can and throwing it to Theo. Emma walks close to the river, passing the teens on the swing until no one is around to overhear us. She plops herself on the grass so I follow suit and do the same. I rest my chin on my denim covered knees.

"What do you want, Emma?" I ask, with an uninterested tone, hoping she gets the hint.

Twisting her fingers together, her head bowed, I hear her whisper, "I'm sorry, Chance." Letting out another sigh, I let my eyes close. I'm tired. Tired of having the same conversation we've been having since Christmas Eve when I found out she'd been cheating on me.

"I know you keep saying it Emma and I keep telling you, it's okay. We are over so there's no need to keep apologising."

"I made a mistake. Can't we give us another shot?" she asks, with hope in her voice. I turn and look at the girl who I had been going out with since last summer. I had feelings for her once upon a time but now all I feel is betrayal.

"What's my nickname?" I ask her, staring into her sad eyes as I see the emotion surface when she realises what I'm alluding to.

"No second chances," she whispers, followed by a sniffle. My friends nicknamed me when we were younger when they realised I could hold a grudge like no other. Once you cross me, I have no sympathy for you and you won't get a second chance. I'm not sure if it was a coping mechanism I created to protect myself. Before Lacey left me, I would have given her a million chances to make things right. Now I have a cold exterior others find hard to crack at times.

"That's right Emma. No second chances. I don't want to get back with you. Please stop. I will be cordial when I see you in the school halls but I don't want anything to do with you and that's on you." I stare back out at the river while I listen to her soft whimpers beside me. It isn't long before she realises I'm done with the conversation and she stands and runs away. I let my forehead drop to my knees, breathing deeply.

"I thought you could use this," Theo's voice sounds from over my shoulder. I lift my head as he sits beside me, handing me another beer. I snap the pin back and gulp a huge mouthful, swallowing before I nod at him in thanks. We sit in silence for a minute before he asks, "She still hounding you to get back together?"

"Yeah. You know me."

"No second chances," we say in unison, before we crack up laughing. He wraps his arm around my shoulder while we laugh, giving me a sideways hug.

"In all seriousness, you deserve better than her and there are plenty of fish in the sea. You with your love of sea creatures should know this," he laughs at the end to lighten the mood. Theo always knows the right thing to say to keep me from falling too far into a downward spiral. He's had first hand experience, helping me out of one a few years ago. I quickly jump up, dust off my jeans and lean down to offer him a hand.

"You're right. There are plenty of fish in the sea when I'm ready. Right now, I'm in the mood to forget all about girls so let's go get shitfaced."

"That's the way," he says, wrapping his arm back over my shoulder and leading the way towards our group of friends, where our alcohol awaits.

As we stumble up my gravel driveway, I slip on the tiny dark stones. I try to catch myself with my hands before I fall but Theo's arms are there, pulling me upright.

"Chance, you're tripping over your own feet. You sure you don't want to crash at mine?" Theo asks, as he helps me right myself.

"Nah I'm fine," I say, as I stand there swaying.

"Come on, I'll give you a boost," he tells me, as he moves to stand right under my window. When I'm sober, I can get into my window no problem, but after the amount of alcohol I had, I'm in no shape to attempt climbing in by myself. I shimmy the window I left unlatched so I could climb back in undetected by my mum. The wood grates along the edges like it usually does but in the dead of night, it sounds louder. I'm hopeful Mum will be fast asleep. I often wonder if she knows how much I've snuck out this summer.

"One, two, three," Theo loudly whispers beside me, before he's squatting with his joined hands waiting for me. I grab hold of the window frame and step into Theo's hands for the extra push I need. Awkwardly, Theo pushes me through the window where I slither to my carpeted floor and lie on my back, staring at the glow from the dark stars on my ceiling. I swing my head to the side as Theo's blurry face comes into view, hanging onto the window frame.

"You good? Do you need help getting to bed?"

"Nah, I'm gonna lie here for a minute then I'll be good," I tell him, as my bout of energy slips out of me fast. Too tired to move, even with help.

"Okay, message me tomorrow," he says, before I hear the thud of his feet hitting the grass under my window and then the tinkering of his steps on the gravel driveway. Gazing at the bright glowing stars above me, my eyes close but I shake my head from side to side, trying to keep them open. I haven't purposefully looked at these stars for a long time. They were always too hard to look at after Lacey left. I didn't have it in me to remove them, needing to keep a part of her with me. Blowing out a breath, I let my eyes close to thoughts of Lacey which I always try to push aside.

"You drink now? How times have changed. Damn, you are way heavier than I remember," I hear someone say in gibberish whispers, but my heavy eyes won't open so I ignore the somewhat familiar voice speaking to me. Rolling over on my side, I feel pulling on my arms but I'm too tired to move.

"So tired," I murmur, to whoever is trying to move me, wriggling to try and get comfortable in my spot.

"Ups a daisy, Chancey," my foggy brain hears, but the alcohol makes it hard to make the connection. Something niggles in my mind but I can't figure out what it is. I give in to the pulling of my hands, helping them but shifting my weight to stand. Swaying on my feet, I drop my hands and they land on something soft in front of me. Automatically I grab hold of the small body in front of me pulling it in close, hugging it to my body. Breathing in, I take a deep breath.

"You smell nice," I say out loud, but the alcohol has numbed my senses more since I climbed through my window.

"Not what you used to say," the voice says back, before I'm falling backwards, taking the smaller body with me. Luckily my bed breaks my fall and I instantly relax, wrapping my arms around the body entwined with mine. My brain foggily thinks this isn't such a good idea, but at this moment, my liquored up veins don't care. While cuddling the comfortable teddy bear to me, my thoughts wander back to Lacey and I drift off, whispering her name.

Pounding behind my eyes wakes me before I even open them. Peeling them open, I look at my window as a warm breeze blows in. My fuzzy head has snippets of Theo pushing me through it last night and I'm guessing I forgot to close it before I fell asleep.

Squeezing the pillow in my arms, I vaguely remember something warm being wrapped around me but it was my pillow. Funny how things are different with alcohol in your system. Banging on my bedroom door has me wincing as it makes my head pound louder.

"Chance, you awake in there? It's nearly lunchtime," Mum yells through the closed door. No wonder the air blowing through the window is so hot, if half the day has already gone.

"Yeah, I'm up," I yell back, hoping my mum doesn't open the door. I don't think my headache could take my mum's twenty questions right now about why I'm sleeping the weekend away. Listening, I hear her footsteps retreat from my door. I roll to my back and stare at my white ceiling with the old glow in the dark stars. I should take those down. I'm getting too old for glow in the dark stars. Puffing out a breath I think about how my life has changed this past year. I never used to drink but this summer I'm drunk nearly every weekend. I use it as a release to forget for a minute. To forget my ex girlfriend who cheated on me and to forget my best friend who left me. It's been four years now since her and her mum moved away when her parents split. One day we were together and happy and then the next we weren't.

Shaking my head I rid my thoughts of Lacey. I've learnt over the years it's a lot easier if I don't think of her. Thinking about her brings nothing but sadness and at the moment, I'm already feeling sorry for myself. The alcohol I consumed has done a great job of making me feel crap anyway. Sliding my feet onto the floor I push myself to stand and stretch my arms over my head. Holding it until I feel satisfaction flow through me. I don't know what it is about a good stretch when you wake after a long sleep but it sure does feel amazing. After grabbing something to eat and a shower, I feel more awake. I ring Theo from my landline and ask him to come over so we can shoot some hoops. Tying my sneakers, I grab the old brown ball from my cupboard and make my way outside bouncing it while I take shots at goal as I wait for Theo to arrive.

Theo and I are still on the school soccer team and we have been since our first year at high school but we enjoy playing basketball from time to time. Theo joined the school team but I prefer to play for fun. I don't have it in me to play competitive basketball. It's not to say I don't give him a run for his money when we play donkey because I'm pretty good, if I do say so myself.

"Chance," I hear Theo's voice call to me, as he walks up the driveway. I pass him the ball and he jogs while pretending to fend someone off before shooting and missing. I chuckle before gathering the ball and we fall effortlessly into a game like we usually do.

"How'd you pull up this morning?"

"Didn't get up until lunch but not too bad," I tell him.

"You were pretty wasted."

"Think Emma wanting to talk made me want to drink more," I confide in him. Every time I think about her cheating on me, it makes me so mad. I wish she had told me before she hooked up with someone else. I would've preferred to get broken up before she cheated on me. I'm dreading going back to school because everyone knows we've broken up too. I'm not sure if they know all the details yet but it won't be long before it's spread around. High school is gossip central.

"You wanna go to a party tonight?" he asks.

"Down at the bank again?"

"Nah, I heard Kyle's having a party tonight so everyone is heading there instead. He moved into the big red house on Sommersby Road last week so wants to break it in, his words not mine." Kyle is one of the guys in our year at school.

"Sure. Let's go then," I tell him, before taking a shot at the hoop. We continue playing well into the late afternoon when the heat from the sun lessens.

"I'm gonna head home and get ready. I'll come back for you later," Theo tells me, before we slap our hands with our handshake moves. He walks off in the direction of his house while I take a few more shots. On the last one I miss it and the ball bounces off the metal hoop and falls close to Lacey's wooden fence. I make my way to retrieve it, my eyes lingering on her window. I feel the same anger simmering I usually feel when I think of Lacey. I can't get over how she threw our friendship away. It was a few days after she left when Theo came around to see me. He dragged me from my wallowing and nicknamed me no second chances.

It was a way for him to try and perk me up but over time it's made the anger and resentment I feel for her fester. No matter what I do, every time I look at her house I feel the anger burning inside me again. Letting out a sigh, I turn my back on the familiar house and walk to my own.

"Mum, is it cool if I go to a party with Theo tonight?" I ask, as she stands at the stove, stirring something in a pot for dinner.

"What time are you thinking of being home?" she asks, turning to look at me.

"Twelve?" I ask, closing an eye and showing her all my teeth.

"Fine. No later than twelve," she says, shaking her head as she turns back to the pot. I walk away when I hear her say, "And thanks for asking this time instead of sneaking out like you have been." I roll my eyes as I bang my fist against my forehead in embarrassment. Of course she knows I've been sneaking out. It's hard to get anything past my mother these days.

Theo rings a few hours later saying he's on his way. I tell Mum goodbye before leaving and she reminds me to be home by twelve. Closing the door behind me, I jog to meet Theo who smiles when he sees me approach. He hands me a big full coke bottle while he holds another.

"Knicked some Black Jacks from Dad's cupboard and made us a mix," he tells me, as he unscrews his lid and takes a skull. I follow his lead with my own bottle and nearly gag on the liquid as it burns my throat.

"This crap is foul," I tell him, holding the bottle away from me like it offends me.

"That's all I have. You could try scabbing off someone at the party but you know everyone is usually stingy with their drinks," he reminds me. "Plus after a few skulls, you probably won't taste it anymore."

It isn't long before we arrive at Kyle's house. Everyone at school lives pretty close to each other so most people are within walking distance. We see a few people from school as they stagger their way towards the house. It's only 8 p.m. so I'm surprised they are already drunk. I tell Theo about my curfew and he's happy for us to be home by twelve as he's still recovering from last night. People greet us as we walk around the back of the house to where everyone is already drinking. A few people are inside but it looks like the majority of the party is outside. Kyle's house is surrounded by bushes so the neighbours can't see the underage drinking taking place. Music can be heard softly coming from the closed glass doors leading indoors.

"Hey Theo," Missy says, as she comes up behind him, wrapping her arms around his neck and kissing him on the cheek. A smile lights his face as he turns to give her a hug and it makes me wonder if he has feelings for her. Seeing them happy together makes an ache form in my chest as I miss the feelings I used to feel when I was with Emma. Now all I have in me is anger and disappointment and I don't know how to get rid of either feeling. I thought I was happy with Emma but the more I look back at our relationship, the more I think I used her as a distraction. Looking at it from a distance, I wonder if what I felt for her was even real to begin with. In all honesty I haven't felt like myself since Lacey left. What I thought I felt for Emma pales in comparison to how I feel about Lacey. She left a void inside me and she is the only person who can fill it.

Taking a skull from my bottle, I let thoughts of Lacey sour my mood. Unable to shake off the sad thoughts, I let them invade my head. I leave Theo and Missy when they make out and grope each other. I don't want to be surrounded by that right now, not in my current state. I find a spot under a lemon tree in the corner of the yard, away from everyone so I lean my back against it and take another skull of the foul liquid, letting the burn creep down my throat. I don't know how long I sit there wallowing. Theo finds me later on and I'm half way through my bottle.

"You okay man?" Theo asks, as he takes a seat next to me.

"Yeah, thinking about Lacey. You know how it goes," I say to Theo. He knows I get in these moods from time to time since she left. It has happened several times over the years. Theo is the person I confide in about missing Lacey and he has become a great friend in her absence. Far from the bully he once was.

"Come on. How about we find you a pretty girl to talk to and take your mind off things?" Theo suggests. Shaking my head, it feels heavier than usual.

"I wanna be alone," I moan, taking another skull. The burning feeling is absent this time.

"Well I can't leave you alone in this state so up you get," Theo mumbles, as he hoists me up with his hands under my armpits. I stumble forward before he steadies me by grabbing my forearm. "You good bro?" he asks, and I lazily nod. "How about I hold it for you?" he says, grabbing the half empty bottle from my grip. Scanning the crowd I see it's grown a bit since I last was paying attention to it. It's darker now too and a breeze floats by, cooling my clammy skin.

"What time is it now?" I ask him, which has him glancing at his watch.

"Before ten. You been sitting here the whole time?" he asks, and I nod in reply. "Well come on, I heard Luke say they saw some girls here from St Bernadette's. Someone new could lift your spirits."

"Lead the way," I tell him, which has him smacking me on the back, smiling. I follow him through the groups of people as we make our way around the yard. He meets up with Missy again but whispers something in her ear before leaving her behind as well.

"I can't see any new girls out here. Let's check inside," he says, which has me shrugging my shoulders because at this point I don't care. My bed feels like a nice place to be right now. I hope I can find a comfy spot inside and rest until Theo is ready to bounce. He slides the glass door open and the noise hits us as we enter. It's extremely muted outside when the door is closed. The music is much louder now we are inside. Shutting the door behind us, we look around at the squished crowd in here. The heat in here makes the room feel stuffy. The trickle of sweat on the back of my neck makes my t-shirt cling to my torso. I lift the hem of my shirt to wipe the sweat off my brow before it drips into my eyes.

"There they are," Theo whispers near me, which has me glancing around before looking in the same direction. My hand slowly lowers, dropping my shirt as I catch sight of a black haired girl checking out my stomach. I watch mesmerised as she bites her lower lip before her eyes raise to mine. Her eyes are so deep and blue they have me catching my breath for a minute before she turns, disappearing into the crowd. Shaking my head for a bit, I try to rid myself of the familiar feeling.

"You okay Chance? You look like you've seen a ghost," Theo says, squeezing my arm to get my attention.

"Yeah I'm good. The girl looked familiar, didn't she?"

"Which one?" he asks, looking back to the crowd where the girls are talking and laughing.

"The one with the black hair," I say, as my eyes search, trying to locate her.

"I don't see a girl with black hair."

"I swear she was right there. She must have run off," I tell him, but his brows pull together.

"You sure you aren't seeing things because you're drunk?" he asks, and I shake my head.

"No, I swear there was another girl there," I argue.

"Oh well, there are plenty of girls there to talk to. Come on," he says, as he pulls on my arm, leading me to them as the song changes. The girls scream and sing along so instead of talking, Theo dances along with them and pulls me into their inner circle.

He hands me back my bottle, smiling while we dance with the girls for a few songs. One girl with brown hair keeps looking over her shoulder at me and smiling while Theo holds the hand of another girl as she dances along to the beat with him. The heat of the room mixed with the amount of alcohol I've had makes the buzz I was feeling more pronounced. Closing my eyes, I sway as I feel hands run up my torso. At the feel of the touch, I open my eyes and see the brown haired girl looking at me. My brain, too heavy to think, grabs the girl by the hand, pulling her close to me as we dance. I don't know how long we dance as one song flows into the next. My bottle is nearly empty so I chug the remainder, dropping the plastic bottle onto the carpet.

"Theo?" I hear the high pitched squeal over the music, which draws my hazy vision upwards. Missy stands there with glistening eyes staring at Theo who is dancing with another girl. His face drops as he sees Missy and he lets go of his dance partner. Missy stumbles away and Theo follows her, calling her name in pursuit. Losing Theo clears my head and I excuse myself from the girl with brown hair, telling her I need to go to the bathroom. She turns back to her group of friends while I stumble away, down the hallway in search of a toilet. Opening a few doors I find a closet and then an empty bedroom. The third door I open has me stopping in my tracks when I hear the tiny voice.

"No, don't." I step closer into the darkened room and feel my hand around the wall for the light switch. Finding it I flick it on, closing my eyes to the blinding light. As they adjust to the brightness, I take in the scene before me. A guy I don't know has a girl pinned to the bed. "Help," I hear her plead and the one word sobers me up. I rush to the bed and pull the guy off her.

"What the fuck man?" I ask him, as he staggers back off the bed.

Snarling at me he says, "She's asking for it man. You can go after me if you like." His words make me see red. I quickly glance to the small figure on the bed, hugging her knees to her chest, her black hair hiding her face from view. She's visibly shaking and it makes my head pound in my ears. Without thinking, I punch the guy in the face. He fights back, hitting me in the cheek. Blood pours from his nose when I hear a crack after I get a clean shot on him. Tackling me to the ground, we wrestle, pounding on each other, trying to get the upper hand.

In the background, I hear someone yell, "Theodore," but it doesn't properly register as I'm too busy trying to beat this guy.

"What the," I hear Theo's booming voice, right before his hands wrap around me, pulling me off the guy. Theo's tight grip on me stops me from grabbing the guy again as he runs out the door. "Calm down," Theo says in my ear, as he faces me towards a wall, holding me tightly. My loud breaths can be heard in the room as I close my eyes and focus on bringing my breathing under control.

"Clear out everyone. Fight is over," I hear Kyle say, ushering what I'm guessing is a crowd out of the room. "You okay?" I hear him ask, and before I can respond, thinking he's talking to me, I hear the small voice from before.

"Yeah I'm okay now," the voice says. Theo tightens his grip on me at the same time my brain registers what he already knows. My breathing speeds up and his grip tightens further.

"I know. You need to calm down before I let you go. She's shaking as it is and I don't want you scaring her even more," he whispers softly so no one else can hear. I scrunch my eyes tight as I feel my body burn but I push it all away. She's here. She's scared. She's shaking. She's here. She was nearly.... I can't finish the thought without the anger returning, so I push it to the side. She's here. She's really here. In and out. In and out.

"I'm good," I tell Theo.

"You sure?"

"Yeah," I tell him, which has him loosening his grip on me. I take a deep breath in before turning around and facing the girl of my past, who I thought would always be in my future. The girl who I've longed for but at the same time hated for leaving me. We stare at each other now. Her blue eyes are so distinctive and recognisable to me, I don't know how I didn't realise it was her earlier. Minutes pass as we stand staring at each other but neither of us wanting to be the first to speak. I see Theo and Kyle exchanging looks out of the corner of my eye but neither says a word out loud. Kyle leaves the room as the sound of glass breaking draws his attention down the hall.

Blinking, I break the silence, "Are you sure you're okay?" My voice comes out quieter than I wanted, but I'm unsure how to approach the girl who was once my best friend.

"Yes. Thanks for helping me," she says, holding eye contact. I nod in reply, not knowing what to say.

Her eyes flit to Theo next to me, "Thanks for your help too Theodore," and I hear his huff.

"Umm I go by Theo now and you're welcome," he tells her.

"Whatever you say, Theodore," she replies, rolling her eyes which has my lip twitching because it's something the old Lacey would have said. My hazy brain can't join the two. There's my best friend from the past and then this new black haired girl I don't know at all. Before Theo can say anything, which I know he will, because it's what these two do, bicker and fight like an old married couple, I interject.

"Come on, I'll walk you home."

Her eyes widen before she stutters out, "Oh ah no, that's okay. You stay. I'll be fine."

"It wasn't a request, Lacey. Let's go," I demand, my voice getting firmer with her. Theo grabs my forearm, which makes me turn to him, where he shakes his head in warning. I turn back to Lacey and try to get my drunk brain to take in details of her. She's still shaking so even though she may put on a confident front, she hasn't recovered from what happened. "It's fine Lacey. Let me walk you home," I say, lowering my voice, trying for a gentler approach.

She raises her eyes to mine, searching them for a minute before nodding.

"You coming or staying?" I ask Theo, before taking a step towards Lacey.

"I'm gonna stay. I need to find Missy," he says, and I nod, acknowledging he has his own mess to sort out. I hold out my hand for our custom handshake before leading the way with Lacey following behind me.

Walking out the front door, the cool air hits me and is such a contrast to the heat in the house. I push my hands in my pockets as we slowly stumble along. I'm not sure how much or if Lacey has had anything to drink but the alcohol is still swirling in me, making my steps slower than usual. I notice Lacey hugs her arms around her waist. I'm not sure if it's to fend off the cold air or if it's to do with what happened tonight. Lost in our thoughts we don't say much to each other and it isn't long before we are standing in front of her house. I have so many questions I want answers to but one question beats the others.

"How long are you back for this time?" I ask, as I keep my eyes pinned on her house, not wanting to look into her eyes right now, before all my questions spill out of my mouth.

"I'm back for good," she says, the wind carrying her voice away with it. She's back for good. I keep my breathing even, not wanting to show any emotion.

"Okay," I reply, not knowing how I'm supposed to respond to the information she gave me. Especially while drunk. Part of me wants to demand how she could walk away and leave me so easily while the other part of me wants to take her in my arms and tell her how much I missed her and to make sure she's okay. Neither part wins. I stand there numb, not saying or doing anything.

"Okay, umm, thanks again I guess," she stutters, as she walks quickly to her front door like she's trying to escape the awkwardness that is us. I stay rooted to the spot while she opens her unlocked door and disappears behind it. It's several minutes later before I force my feet to move and walk to my house. I catch sight of the light in Lacey's old room but don't linger. Opening my own front door, I close it behind me and check on Mum.

"I'm home Mum," I whisper into her darkened room.

"Thanks honey. Did you have a good night?" her sleepy voice asks.

"Yeah, it was good," I lie.

"Get some sleep," she tells me.

"Goodnight."

"Night honey." I close her door before heading to my own room. I don't turn on my light instead I traipse to the window and peek through the curtains at Lacey's window where the light is still shining. I can't see her but I stand there, hidden in the shadows hoping to catch one more glimpse of her. Time ticks by as I wait and my eyes droop so I give up. I kick my shoes off and throw myself onto my bed on top of the covers. It isn't long before the remaining alcohol in my system pulls me into slumber.

LACEY

7TH JANUARY
Dear Diary,

Well surprise, I'm back Chance. It's not the way I wanted him to find out I had returned. I couldn't think of a worse possible way. He looked so angry and I don't blame him. How am I supposed to explain to him I was young and dumb and plain embarrassed from our last interaction. I should have talked to my best friend instead of running away from him.

Now I'm running away from my mum. Her new boyfriend and her new baby on the way was too much to handle. I had to get away from them. I couldn't handle them being all lovey dovey all the time, while inside I wanted to scream.

I missed my dad so thought the change would do me some good. He's doing a lot better now. He said he attends AA meetings regularly and hasn't had a drop of alcohol in years. I've been standoffish with him since I came back a few days ago. It's not his fault, I think I'm standoffish with everyone now.

I snuck out to go to this stupid party because I overheard Theo and Chance talking about it when they were outside playing basketball earlier. It was an added bonus Theo mentioned Kyle's address otherwise I would have gotten lost trying to find it. It was easy enough to blend in with the crowd as there were girls from another school there.

The stupid guy dragged me into the room when I'd run away from perving at Chance. Damn, he grew up and got muscles and abs. I don't remember ever feeling like my best friend was hot. He was always Chance to me and I loved him. Now, damn, the boy is the definition of hot.

I'm extremely lucky he walked into the room when he did because I was struggling to fight the asshole off. I should take some self defence lessons or something, they could come in handy.

Sorry if the writing is wobbly, my hands haven't stopped shaking. I don't want to be alone right now but I doubt Chance would appreciate me climbing through his window like old times.

I peeked out my window and the lights are off in his room so he's probably already asleep. I don't want to tell my dad as he'll wrap me in cotton wool and won't let me leave the house until I'm thirty.

The shaking is still not stopping. Be brave Lacey. Okay, I'm going to do it. The worst he can do is turn me away but at least I would have tried, right. Here goes nothing. I'm going to change into my pyjamas then run to Chance.

Wish me luck,
Lacey

CHANCE

Tap, tap, tap. The faint noise pulls at my brain, drawing me from sleep. Tap, tap, tap. Is that the window? I lazily stumble to the window. Throwing the curtains open, I let my eyes adjust to the dark and then I see her. Letting out a sigh, I push the window open, letting the cool night air flow into my room.

"What do you want, Lacey?" I ask, not in the mood for this after the night we've had. The shock of her being back is too much to take. She wrings her hands and I notice the slight shake as she wraps them around herself before speaking.

"Umm I know I don't have a right to ask but could I stay with you, please? I don't want to be alone after everything that happened tonight," her shaky voice says, and I let out a sigh again. I could never deny Lacey, no matter how mad I was at her. I grab her hand and then pull her through the window.

"This doesn't change anything," I tell her, and she nods, before following me to the bed. A year ago Mum got me a double bed as my legs hung over the side of the single and she was worried I would fall out every night. Climbing into the bed, she follows and I turn to face the wall, giving her my back. I don't have it in me to look at her right now, knowing I'll demand answers from her. I don't think she's in any state to give them to me.

I stay as still as I can, trying to feign sleep. I control my breathing, hoping she will think I've fallen asleep. She keeps wriggling, I'm guessing to get comfortable. Having her so close after all this time has sobered me up as I listen to any sign she's still awake. It feels like I lie there forever, waiting to hear the signs of her sleeping soundly but it's not what catches my attention. Her soft sniffles have my ears perking up and I close my eyes, letting out a deep breath. Turning around, I see her back is facing me so I slide my hand under her neck and drag her small body towards me. Wrapping my arms around her tightly, I hold her back to my front.

"You're safe now, Lacey. Let it out if you need to," I whisper into her hair. Her hands cling to my arms as her body is taken over by shudders, and her gentle cries fill the night. I squeeze her tighter into my body as she draws her knees up so she's curled into a ball while I hold her from behind. I don't know how long she cries but I don't say another word, letting her get all her emotions out in silence. Her body finally relaxes as her cries turn into sniffles and then into soft breaths. Closing my eyes, I breathe in her strawberry scented hair, so foreign to me yet so familiar. Pulling her closer into me, I let myself relax and for a moment, I relish having my best friend back even though I know in the light of the morning, this moment will dissolve.

Stretching my limbs out, I feel instantly good and my muscles relax. Sleepily I roll on to my back as thoughts of the night before come flooding into my mind. Lacey. My eyes pop open as I sit, looking at the side of the bed where she is. Well was. She isn't there any longer. The fluttering curtain draws my eye to the open window. She snuck out while I was sleeping. She was here, wasn't she? I wasn't so drunk my mind was playing tricks on me, was I?

No. She was definitely back. Different but back. I still don't have the answers to all the questions swirling in my head. Most important of all is how she could leave me without saying a word. Letting out a sigh I rub my forehead, a headache thrumming behind my eyes. I obviously wasn't as important to her as she was to me. I stand and walk to my window, letting my eyes gaze at the house next door for a minute. Many memories are wrapped up in her house. With her. Huffing, I force the window closed before turning back to my bed. I toss and turn for a bit before I fall asleep again.

CHAPTER 25

CHANCE

29TH JANUARY

Today's the first day of my last year of high school. I'm finishing school this year and I'm not sure how I feel about it. I'm excited but also hoping the year goes slow so it doesn't have to end. I have no idea what I want to do with my life when high school finishes. I haven't seen Lacey for the remainder of the holidays. I thought I caught glimpses of her but then when I looked again, she wasn't there. She hasn't sought me out and I haven't gone looking for her. I have hung out at our tree a lot more than I usually do in the hopes she may come to our spot but she never did. I'm not sure if she is going to be attending the same high school as me. It was the plan when we were little but times have changed. I told my mum Lacey was back and she said she hoped we could rekindle the friendship we once had. I never told her what happened between us, I said we had a fight and left it at that.

Looking in the mirror, I straighten my navy tie. Yes, being my final year they make us wear ties with our uniform. Thankfully Mum took time over this summer to show me how to tie it. I examine my crisp white shirt and navy slacks. Releasing a breath, I smile at myself before heading to the bathroom to put gel in my hair. Mum always asks why I bother with the gel because my hair apparently looks like I have bed hair even when I spend an obscene amount of time on it. Her words, not mine. Fixing my hair into its messy state, I meet Mum in the kitchen for my required first day of school photo.

"Aww Chance. You look so handsome," she gushes, as she looks me over. My face heats at the compliment.

"Thanks Mum."

"Say cheese," she says, holding her camera while I put the biggest smile on my face.

"Cheeessseee," I say, hearing a few clicks of the button. Hopefully one of the photos is good.

"Are you and Theo walking to school together?" she asks, as she places her camera back in its case.

"Yeah, he shouldn't be too far away," I tell her, as the phone rings, right on cue. I walk over and lift the landline phone off its cradle.
"Hello."

"Chance, leaving now. See you in five," Theo quickly says into the receiver, before hanging up. He rings every morning before school, letting me know he's on the way so I've got time to gather my things and wait outside for him. I hang up the receiver and Mum turns to me, holding out an old ice cream container which serves as my lunch box.

"Thanks Mum," I tell her, leaning down and giving her a kiss on the cheek as I take the ice cream container from her. I walk back to my room, place the container inside and then fling my school bag over my shoulder.

"I'll see you later," I yell to Mum, as I head to the front door, waiting outside a minute before Theo joins me.

"Hey," I say, as he walks to me.

"I hate the first day of school," he groans, and I chuckle as he says this every year. He gets the end of summer blues every year. It's like clockwork, he will walk into school, see a pretty girl and it'll be the end of his blues. This year he has something going with Missy so I'm guessing things will change. Although I don't think she has fully forgiven him for dancing with another girl at Kyle's party the other weekend.

"You and Missy good yet?" I ask, as we fall into step next to each other.

"I don't know. On one hand, I like her but then on the other, I don't want to have to answer to anyone, you know?" he says, holding his hands and moving them up and down like he's weighing up his options.

"Guess it depends how much you care about Missy. I reckon if you want to be single, it's better to tell her now than to string her along and hurt her later," I reply honestly, my experience with Emma creeping into my mind. Theo must catch a look across my face as he pats me on the back.

"Sorry bud."

"I'm over it. I don't think you should hurt Missy if she's not what you want," I tell him, and it makes me realise I haven't thought of Emma since Lacey returned. How easily I forgot about Emma when Lacey came back into my orbit. Will she always have this effect over me, I wonder. We fall into an easy conversation the rest of the way to school and I push thoughts of Lacey to the side. Theo knows she's a sore spot so doesn't mention her which I'm thankful for.

Walking through the school gates, we make it with time to spare. The bell ringing is our signal to head to our tutor group where we will get assigned our new timetables. I hold out my hand to Theo for our handshake then I'm off to the art room where my tutor group has been since I started here. Tutor groups consist of students from all different year levels. I think it's a way for the older students to part some of their wisdom onto the younger kids.

Stepping into the art room, the familiar scent of paint and turpentine hits me. Students file in, one after another, taking seats where they can. I take a seat next to Kyle, giving him a head nod as I pull my stool out. While Ms Ferguson takes roll call, I pull out my sketch pad and draw. I don't think I'm any good but it gives me something to do and helps calm my nerves a bit when I'm stressed.

"Cool octopus," Kyle says next to me, which makes my lip lift into a small smile. I have an obsession with sea creatures, even after all these years.

"Thanks," I reply, admiring my work before continuing to sketch the tentacle I was working on. Taking a break from my drawing, I glance around and check out the new kids in my tutor group. Fresh faced and getting their first taste of high school. They are always nervous but excited, like they have all the time in the world. It's a different feeling now as it's my last year. I'm already getting sentimental, knowing in the not too distant future my life will change. I'll be out in the big bad world and I'll be like these newbies. Nervous but excited about beginning a new stage of my life.

The first day of school is always the same. Meet your teachers and classmates for each subject. The teacher usually goes over the curriculum as well but there's never much learning happening on these days. It's still hot out even though the end of summer isn't too far away, and by morning break I'm already feeling the heat. Theo catches up with me as I'm chatting to Kyle while he kicks his hacky sack. We usually spend our break times out on the school field and the first break today is no different.

"Have you seen her yet?" Theo asks, before taking a bite of his apple.

"Who?" I ask, as my eyes follow the small ball as Kyle keeps it from dropping.

"Lacey," he whispers, so Kyle can't hear. My head whips his way as I suck in a breath like he sucker punched me.

"She's here?"

"Yeah, she was in my chemistry class. Called me Theodore again. Wish she'd cut it out," he moans. My lip twitches at his annoyance. They always butted heads. Even after all the bullying stuff was behind us, I don't think Lacey fully trusted Theo. One thing about Lacey I could always count on, she had my back even when I didn't have my own. Until the day I couldn't anymore.

"Have you talked to her?" he asks.

"Nah, I haven't seen her since the party," I tell him, which is exactly what I've been telling him every day he's asked me. I don't mention the part where she climbed in my window the night of the party. I don't know why I kept it a secret as Theo and I usually don't keep secrets from each other.

"Well you may want to talk to her bud. Sooner rather than later," he says, biting his apple again.

"Why?"

"Emma sat next to her in chemistry and they looked pretty chummy by the end of class. Wouldn't be surprised if Emma laid out all your history before Lacey even mentioned her name. You know the girl has got her claws in you," he tells me, smiling at his joke. I don't want to think about Lacey or Emma or the two of them together so I steer the conversation away from me.

"You seen Missy yet?"

"Ugh. Yes and I swear the girl looked straight through me like I was invisible. I don't think I've seen such a cold look before," he says, as he pretends to shiver for emphasis. I crack up laughing.

"I'm telling you. You gotta choose. Are you in or are you out? It's the first day of school and you don't wanna be like this the whole year," I tell him, leaning back on my hands as I stretch my legs out in front of me on the green grass.

"You're one to talk. Think we both need to sort out our girl problems," he says, raising a brow at me and I roll my eyes in return. I know he's right. I need to talk to Lacey but I don't want to be the one to make the first move, especially after she hurt me by leaving. I think I'll leave it for another day or possibly two and hope she will make the first move instead. After all, she broke us so she should be the one to fix us.

I've gone most of the day not crossing paths with Lacey. She's the only new girl in our year which means her name is on everyone's lips making it hard not to think about her. I heard her name whispered behind me in class and it floated my way numerous times through the hallways. Everyone is wanting to know about the mysterious new girl. They don't know she's my best friend. Or was my best friend. Ugh I don't even know what she is to me anymore. I heard a couple of guys talking about how pretty the new girl is and Theo gave me this look. The look that says you need to sort your stuff with her before someone else comes along and steals her.

I voiced my feelings about Lacey once and I don't mean my best friend feelings, I mean the feelings where I can't stop thinking about her and want her as more of a friend feelings. It was Theo I voiced them to. It was right after she left me. I had a moment of weakness and let out my secret. I have never let myself be weak again. Theo has kept my secret, it's how I know I can trust him. He never mentions it out loud but he does in the way he looks at me or the way he's talked about Lacey in the past. Today he doesn't come outright and tell me to go get the girl, but he implies it. It's exactly what he's implying with the look on his face. He's not blind, he knows Lacey is pretty and she'll be catching the eye of the other guys at this school. Some of these guys can't control their hormones and have to go after every girl they see. Like I said, I don't have it in me to fix what is broken with Lacey, not today. I want to focus on getting through my first day of school. I'll tackle it tomorrow.

Finding myself on the school field at lunch time playing soccer with my mates, I forget about all my worries over Lacey until the guys randomly gather in a circle.

"There's the new girl," Luke points out.

"Where?" Dominic asks.

"Over with Emma and Billie. Guess you haven't got a shot Chance, if Emma is in her ear," Luke says.

"We should call you no chance instead of no second chances," Kyle pipes in, which has the guys laughing.

"Ha ha very funny," I say, not finding it funny at all. "Can we get back to soccer now?"

"Yeah come on guys, you can ogle the new girl later," Theo says, trying to get their attention off Lacey for me.

"I'm planning to do a lot more than ogle her later," Luke says, and I roll my eyes because he thinks he's got all the game in the world. It hardly ever works but a tiny part niggles at me because this time it could be Lacey who falls for his weird charm.

Instead of strangling Luke I dribble the ball away which has the others breaking the circle and chasing after me. I score in the unattended goal which I know is a cheap shot but I don't care. I succeeded in getting their attention away from Lacey. We play for the rest of lunch, running back and forth around the field, not keeping score but enjoying the fun of playing and mucking around with our friends again. I've been able to watch Lacey out of the corner of my eye. She sits cross legged, pulling at the grass while listening to Emma talk. They watch us play and after I score another goal, I run around with my hands in the air, celebrating.

The guys on my team high five me and as I'm lost in the moment, smiling wide, my gaze flickers to Lacey. Her head is down so she doesn't see me looking but Emma does. Her own gaze turns harsh as she realises it was Lacey I was looking at and not her. I quickly avert my eyes but I see the movement of Emma's head as she turns to look at Lacey. She looks at Lacey like she's appraising her, trying to see what I see. It makes the hairs on the back of my neck stick up but I ignore it for now and continue with my game.

As the bell signals the end of lunch I pull my singlet out from under my shirt, using it to wipe the sweat from my face. My eyes find their way to where Lacey was sitting, to check if she's still there and my eyes lock on hers. I watch as her cheeks redden from being caught. It brings a sense of deja vu and I remember how before the fight began at the party, I caught her checking me out before she ran away like a chicken. At the time, I didn't realise it was Lacey but now with her looking at me, it has made the memory resurface. My best friend was checking me out. I want to focus on the fact for a minute but I can't because our stare off is broken by a pissed off Emma tugging on Lacey's arm, dragging her away.

"You need to fix it and soon before Emma does something," Theo whispers to me, so the other guys can't hear. I let out a sigh knowing he's right. I still can't help but feel it should be Lacey fixing things and not me.

The last class of the day rolls around and I'm disappointed I haven't shared a class with Lacey. I walk along the ramp to where my English class is. Mr Rodgers stops me and a few other students at the door before letting us enter.

"Grab a number from the hat and find the desk with the matching number," he instructs, shaking his baseball cap at us. Dipping my hand in, I pull out the first scrunched up paper I come to. Opening it I find a black nine scribbled with a line underneath it. Glancing around the room my heartbeat increases as I see her. Lacey. She's already seated at a desk with Luke next to her. He has his arm stretched out across the back of her chair, with a huge smile spreading across his face as he talks to her. Something I know he's been wanting to do all day.

Her eyes begin moving away from him and before she can catch my eye, I stare at my paper like it has something interesting on it. I refuse to be the one to make the first move. Peeking out of the corner of my eye I scan the numbers on desks as I move around the room, trying to locate number nine but I'm finding it hard to concentrate with her so near. Instead of continuing my search, I decide to stand at the back of the room and wait until all the desks are filled. It doesn't take long for the room to fill and one seat is left.

"Chance, what number have you got?" Mr Rodgers asks, looking at the clipboard he has on his desk.

"Ah number nine sir," I say, walking down the aisle of desks towards him.

"No, I've got nine," I hear Luke say, which has me turning my head his way. He still has his arm across the back of Lacey's chair which makes my nostrils flare.

"Both of you bring your numbers here," Mr Rodgers tells us. I hike my bag higher on my shoulder before handing over my number to him. He looks at it and hands it back. Luke makes it to us and hands him his paper.

"Luke, yours is a six. The line goes at the bottom of the number. Chance here has a nine, see?" he explains, grabbing my wrist so I can hold my paper for Luke to see.

"Damn it," Luke mutters, before he adds, "Want to swap?"

"There will be no swapping. Now go to your seats. You're over here Luke," Mr Rodgers directs Luke to the desk near the door and it's then I realise I chose the seat directly next to Lacey. Releasing a breath, I take my time walking towards her before slumping into my seat. I don't look at her or say a word. I don't even know what to say so instead I choose to do nothing. I don't know if she's chosen to tell people we know each other or not. I haven't heard any whispers of my name joining the rounds with hers so I think it's safe to say she hasn't. The only person who knows I was best friends with Lacey is Theo and I can't see him telling anyone.

Mr Rodgers is talking but I find myself too distracted to listen. I noticed earlier Lacey has tried to get the black dye out of her hair. It's more orange than her usual blonde but I prefer it over the black. It makes me want to ask why she made such a drastic change with her hair but I bite my tongue. Her pen taps her desk absentmindedly as her focus is on the front of the class where Mr Rodgers stands, talking.

"I'm sorry to say but there are no free passes in this class this year. We have a lot to get through and what better time to start than the present. Here's your first assignment," Mr Rodgers informs us.

"Ughhhh," a unison drone fills the room, as everyone realises we are going to have to do work today instead of having a cruisey last period on the first day.

"This assignment will count for five percent of your total mark. It may not sound like much but it does add up so I expect you to take this seriously. If you can get off to a good start with this assignment then it gives you a good foundation for the year," he tells us, as everyone pulls out pads or pieces of paper to write notes on. I notice Lacey is one of those prepared students who already has her stationery as she pulls out a bright red book with a hard cover, opening it to the first page. "Take a sheet and hand it on," Mr Rodgers tells the people in front, as he hands them each a stack of papers. The sound of shuffling papers fills the room as people pass them down the lines then read what the assignment is about. Lacey receives the stack from Grace in front of her and slides one off the pile onto her desk before handing them to me. As I grab the papers from her, my hand gently touches hers and I feel a shock run up my arm. We both still, laser focused on our hands and where they touched. I can feel my own chest rising and falling as I try to keep my composure. From the corner of my eye, I can see her chest doing the same. When she lets go of the papers, our weird moment is broken and I turn, passing them behind me as I take my own copy. Reading through the bold wording on the sheet, I try to focus on the assignment brief and not on the fact a slight touch from Lacey set my skin on fire.

"Now most of you have probably read through the assignment already but I'll quickly go over it. You are to write a letter to your younger self. You can frame it anyway you wish but the gist is to give yourself some advice. Something you know now you wouldn't have known back then or you wish you had known. You can choose whatever age your former self is you are writing to. Please do not write to your former self of last week telling them not to eat the two day old leftover chicken as I don't want to spend my time reading about how you spent a couple days camped out on the toilet," Mr Rodgers says, making us all laugh. It's so specific, I assume someone wrote that as their assignment in a previous year.

"You have the next few weeks to get it done. There will be no extensions as it's the beginning of the year and I expect you all to get stuck in right away. This is not the time to slack off. It's your last year of high school before you are sent off into the real world so how about we make it a good one," he tells us. Mr Rodgers continues talking and informs us of the expected assignments we will have to complete for the rest of year and how much each assignment will be worth toward our final grades. The scribbling of pens fills the room as everyone rushes to write all the information. When he's finished, he lets us brainstorm ideas for our first assignment for the remainder of class.

The bell signals the end of the day and Luke lets out a big, "Yes," as it does and I can't help but feel the same happy energy as him at having this day be finally over. The weird tension swimming around Lacey and I is making my brain hurt. I don't say a word to her as I push my papers into my backpack and rush to leave the room. I notice she takes her time, not in a hurry like I am. Exiting the room, I breathe a sigh of relief before Luke flings his arm across my shoulders as we walk.

"So did you talk to her?" he asks.

"Talk to who?"

"Man, the new girl of course," he says, as he shakes his head at me in disbelief.

"Nope, didn't talk to her at all."

"You've got no game. I don't know how you scored Emma," he says, laughing. When he notices I'm not laughing with him he adds, "And we will not mention her. Got it." It's my turn to shake my head at him. We join Theo out the front of the gymnasium. It's our usual meeting spot after school before we walk home together.

"Rough first day?" Theo asks.

"Why do you say that?"

"Your face is all scrunched up like something stinks," he replies.

"Yeah it's Luke," I joke.

"Ha ha. Nah he knows he's got no shot with the new girl, if he can't even talk to her. My chances are looking better already," Luke says, before slapping me gently on the head, making me duck before he runs off to catch his bus home.

"What happened?" Theo asks, as we fall into step, making our way out of the school gates and onto the main road.

"I got seated next to her in English and I'm stuck there for the whole year. We didn't talk at all," I tell him.

"You can work up to talking to her. Find out why she cut you off in the first place," he reasons.

"I don't know man."

"You know the Chance I knew back in the day was joined at the hip with Lacey and I didn't think I'd ever see the two of you apart. Now I've lived with you separated and you're a good friend, don't get me wrong but I always get the feeling like you're not completely happy and we both know it's because Lacey has been missing from your life. She's back now, so why not take a chance and talk to her at least," he says, softly.

"We'll see man," I tell him, but I don't add the fact I'm scared. I'm scared because what if I lay my heart on the line for her and she doesn't feel the same or she doesn't want to be my friend anymore. What am I supposed to do then? I don't think I could take it if she rejected me again. One rejection is all I can take from her.

"You know you could talk to her now. Look," Theo says, pointing ahead of us. I follow his finger and see her walking about fifty metres in front of us, all by herself. She has her hands tucked into the straps of her bag, holding them as she walks. Her sleek shiny hair so different to the bushy mess she had years ago and it makes me realise so much has changed.

"Another day," I tell him softly, as I watch her walk the rest of the way home. She doesn't notice us walking behind her and doesn't turn our way when she enters her house.

"See you tomorrow bro," Theo says, patting me on the back as I walk up my driveway and he carries on to his house.

"Laters," I yell, opening my own door and heading to my room before flopping on my bed, thinking about how so many things have changed and wishing I could go back in time to when it was all simpler.

CHAPTER 26

CHANCE

3RD FEBRUARY

"Chance, don't forget to take your jacket to school. It's supposed to rain today," Mum calls from the kitchen, as I'm about to leave. I traipse back to my room and grab my puffy black and white sports jacket from my closet. The bulkiness of it will make it impossible to fit in my backpack so I fling it over my shoulder.

"Got it. Bye Mum," I yell back, heading to the door again. Walking outside I see nothing but blue skies stretching in front of me so I think about dumping the jacket inside but then change my mind. The weather can change drastically within minutes here so it's best I take it just in case, especially if Mum says there's supposed to be rain.

Walking alone today since Theo has a dentist appointment, I make it to school earlier than usual. When Theo and I walk together, we tend to walk at a slower pace, laughing and joking. Since I'm early I head straight to the art room. The door is always open as the teacher lets kids come in to finish art projects before school if they need to. I sit in my usual seat and pull out my notepad where I keep my random drawings. I finished the octopus last night so now I'm working on a turtle. I'm so focused on drawing I don't realise the bell has rung until Kyle is tapping my shoulder to get my attention.

"You're in the zone today," he chuckles. Dropping my pencil and glancing around the room, I notice everyone chatting and laughing.

"Guess I was zoned out," I tell him, laughing to myself.

"Did you hear Luke asked Lacey out yesterday?"

"What?" My heart rate increases and I contain myself before I freak Kyle out by turning into the Hulk. "Ah, what did she say?" I ask, keeping my voice calm. I focus on my breathing, keeping it even while I wait for his reply.

His eyes dance with laughter before he says, "She told him she didn't think there was room for her in the relationship as his ego takes up a lot of space." It has a smile stretching on my face as it's a classic old Lacey remark.

"She sounds funny," I say, chuckling.

"Yeah she sounds like she'd be a blast to date," Kyle adds, which has me raising an eyebrow at him. "What? If Luke is out of the equation, I might have a shot."

"Sounds like you might luck out too," I taunt, hoping it will change his mind about her.

"Maybe. Maybe not. I might wait, I don't wanna get shot down like Luke," he chuckles. "Oh, did you see Miles? They went to the Philippines for the Christmas holidays and they got back last Friday so he missed the first week of school."

I gulp before saying, "Awesome. I'll try to catch up with him before first period."

I put away my drawing supplies as I need to rush out of the room as soon as the bell goes. I'd completely forgotten about Miles. When we started high school, it was me, Theo, Miles and Darren who all came from the same primary. The same primary Lacey attended. Darren went to an all boys school at the end of our first year so it wasn't a factor but with Lacey back, it slipped my mind Miles would know her.

The bell rings out so I quickly say bye to Kyle as I embark on my task to find Miles before first period. Searching through the groups of students, I finally spot Luke with a circle of guys from our year. I jog over to them, letting out a breath when I see Miles at the centre.

"Miles," I call out, a genuine smile on my face.

"Chance. How's it going man," he says, stepping towards me, slapping my hand before giving me a quick hug hello. The second bell rings, sending everyone scattering to their classes, not wanting to be late but I'm willing to risk getting detention to keep my secret.

"Good man. Where's your first class? I'll walk you," I tell him, slinging an arm around his shoulder, dragging him away from our friends.

"I have chemistry first," he says, making me wince. I wonder if it's the same chemistry class Theo and Lacey have together.

Walking together, I check to make sure no one is within hearing distance before saying, "I wanna catch up man but I need you to do me a favour," I blurt out, feeling like a crap friend for putting my drama on him.

"Yeah man, anything, you know that?" he says, a worried look on his face.

"Have you heard about the new girl yet?" I ask, and he laughs.

"Man, are you here to call dibs? I didn't think my gorgeous face would have a chance. Everyone is talking about her," he jokes.

"It's Lacey," I say, quietly.

"What?" he yells, stopping in his tracks.

"Yeah I know," I say, dragging him along.

"When? How? What?" he stutters.

"I don't know. All I know is she's back but I haven't talked to her and no one knows our history or that we know each other," I tell him, biting my lip. He stops again, turning to me.

"So if you don't know her then I don't know her?" he asks, tilting his head to the side and catching on to what I'm trying to say.

"Yeah. You know, I wouldn't stop you from talking to anyone but could you not mention you went to the same primary as her and tell her to not mention it either, if you do talk to her," I blurt out. He stares at me for a few seconds before letting out a sigh.

"What happened with you two? Back in the day, you couldn't say one of your names without the other as you two were a package deal." I let out a sigh of my own as we keep walking, slowing our pace as his class comes into view.

"We grew apart," I lie, but he sees right through it.

"This is fate's way of giving you another chance," He says, before adding, "You know you turned into no second chances when she left but the people who know you two know you looked at her like she hung the sun in the sky. You would have given her a million chances if she messed up. It's not too late to find the boy who looked at her like that," he says, before patting me on the back and walking away, not waiting for my reply.

The second bell rings, "Shoot," I mumble to myself, before turning on my heels and racing to my own class.

At lunchtime we play our usual game of soccer as the sun is still shining although there are a few clouds in the sky.

"Did you hear?" Kyle asks me, as I dribble the ball past him.

"What?" I call, letting my voice trail behind me while he tries to catch me.

"Miles knows Lacey." This stops me in my tracks and gives him time to steal the ball. His laughter flits behind me as he races the other way and I have to chase after him.

"How does he know her?"

"Their mums know each other or something he said," he responds, before I manage to steal the ball back, letting out the breath I was holding. I dribble the ball back, shooting and scoring a goal before he catches me this time. As my team cheers, I turn and catch sight of Emma sitting in the same spot she sits in every lunch time. Next to her sits Lacey and on the other side of her is Miles. He says something to her, making her laugh loudly.

"How about we play a game of girls against boys?" Kyle suggests, loud enough for Miles, Emma and Lacey to hear.

"How is that fair?" Luke asks.

"We could always mix up the teams?" Kyle says, looking at me for confirmation.

"I guess so," I reply.

"I'm in. I'm on Chance's team," Emma says, as she bounces over to me. A few more girls sitting with them come and join in too.

"Lacey and I are on Kyle's team," Miles says, as he narrows his eyes at me. It might have something to do with the fact Emma has hooked her arm with mine.

"Cut it out Emma," I say quietly to her, unhooking her arm as gently as I can while trying not to draw attention to us. Rolling her eyes at me, she crosses her arms as she stands her ground next to me.

"Teams are pretty even. Let's play," Kyle calls out, and his team kicks off.

I can't find my usual enthusiasm, not with Lacey and Miles laughing and joking at the back of the field. The distraction gives Kyle's team the ability to get past me and score, sending his team into hoots and hollers. We reset and our team kicks off this time. Kyle tells Lacey to change positions and move to a forward position. Miles encourages her so she nervously steps forward. Luke kicks the ball and passes to Emma who toe hacks the ball which smacks Lacey right in the face, causing her to fall backwards. Before I realise it, I'm standing over her, having raced right to her when she fell. Everyone else follows suit and soon she's surrounded by a crowd. Bending down, I help sit her up as bright red blood drips from her nose.

"Shit Lace you okay? Your nose," I say.

"What do you mean Lace?" I hear snapped behind me from Emma, and I wince realising the old nickname slipped out. Lacey holds her fingers to her nose and then inspects them, seeing the blood. Someone thrusts some tissues into her hand and she holds them to her nose.

"I'll help you," I offer. Effortlessly I pull her to stand as my gaze falls to her neck. Without thinking, I grab the black cord so I can inspect it. It's what dangles from the end of it that catches my attention. The rough pink stone from so long ago is now polished and smoother in some areas. A hole has been drilled into it so the black cord could be threaded through to make the necklace. She kept it. All this time, she kept it. I hold the stone gently in my fingers, forcing myself to keep my breaths even. My gaze slowly rises to Lacey's deep blue eyes and I catch the shimmer of sadness she's containing.

"I'll take you to the sick bay," Miles cuts in, which makes Lacey wrap her soft fingers around mine, prying them off the stone. I didn't realise I was still holding it until I felt her touch. A shock hits my fingertips but it doesn't last as she releases my fingers as soon as I've let go of the stone. Miles narrows his eyes at me for the second time today as he wraps an arm around Lacey, dragging her away from the field and away from me. My feet are rooted to the spot, watching them leave. The crowd around us talking amongst themselves.

"Come on, let's get back to the game," Kyle suggests, nudging my shoulder with his, breaking me out of my trance.

"Lace huh? When did you two become so friendly?" Emma snaps.

"Drop it," I tell her, before turning my back on her.

"I have a right to know if my friend is going behind my back," she demands, and it has me stopping in my tracks and turning to her.

"You don't have a right to anything when it comes to me and leave Lacey out of this. Stop trying Emma because you and I are through. You made it pretty clear you were done with me when you went behind my back and cheated on me," I shout, hearing a few gasps. I lift my head and see the crowd I thought had dissipated, listening closely to Emma and I argue. Huffing, I shake my head as Emma's face turns a bright red. I'm over this day and want to be alone so I walk off the field and don't stop walking even when I hear Luke and Kyle calling after me. Grabbing my bag and jacket, I head to the art room because at least I know I'll get some peace in there.

Sliding onto a stool, I pull out my notebook and let my mind wander as my hand automatically makes the movements it needs to without much thought. She kept the random stone I happened to trip on one day. All these years and she still has it. She even made a necklace out of it so it was always close to her. Pulling myself out of my thoughts, I can hear my rough breathing as I fight to keep myself calm. My body is on fire from holding in the emotions I don't want to feel. I can't even pinpoint which emotions I'm feeling at this point as they are all tangled together. I sit stewing until the bell goes and then slowly gather my things before heading to my PE class.

Miles catches me in the locker room as I'm taking my time getting changed and he's rushing in late, puffed from running here. He looks at me, waiting for me to ask about her but I bite my tongue. We get changed silently until his anger unleashes.

"Lacey's fine by the way," he tosses out.

"Hmm," I grunt.

"Seriously dude. Get over yourself. What is wrong with you?" he bites at me.

"Stay out of it Miles. It doesn't concern you."

"No, it doesn't. When I've got an old friend crying on my shoulder about my other old friend who is completely stupid by the way, it drags me into it," he argues. My laboured breathing returns as my eyes whip to his.

"There he is," he says, his tone softer than it was.

"Huh? Who are you talking about?" I ask, my brows furrowing.

"The Chance who loves that girl more than anything and can't bear to see her hurt. The Chance who hated when someone hurt her. The Chance whose world revolved around her. He's in there but I don't know why you won't let him out," he huffs, shaking his head.

"You wouldn't understand," I reply, pulling my sports shirt over my head.

"Understand what? That you're being a stubborn ass," he taunts.

"She left me," I roar, surprising myself with the volume. We stare at each other, Miles eyebrows raised at me.

Closing my eyes, I take a deep breath to calm myself before repeating, "She left me. She left me without a second thought."

"Why don't you talk to her? Ask her why she left?" he suggests.

My skin heats again, "Why is it up to me to talk to her? I'm not the one who broke us."

I turn to leave before I hear Miles reply, "You could be the bigger person and try to fix it." I rub my forehead as I leave the locker room, closing my eyes for a second. I walk right into someone which has my eyes flashing open and my hands grabbing them to stop them from falling.

"Sorry I...," my words die on my lips, as I realise it's Lacey standing in front of me. How long was she standing there and how much did she hear? I peel my fingers off her forearms, scanning her face. Her nose and cheek are bright red and one eye has a slight purple tinge under it, suggesting it will bruise.

"Chance," her small voice says, and I hold in the sigh my heart wants to make at the sound. I'm not ready for this conversation.

"Is your nose okay?" I ask instead, seeing the tears she's holding in on her lash line.

"Yeah. It still hurts but the bleeding stopped," she says.

"Good. I gotta go," I say, before rushing away, not stopping even when I hear her call my name.

I can't shake the funk I'm in for the rest of the afternoon and it doesn't help my mood when I step out of my last class and the heavens open and rain pours down. I guess Mum was right, I think to myself as I chuck my jacket on. I'm glad I haven't been lugging it around all day for nothing.

I walk home in the rain by myself. It makes me miss Theo as he always makes the walks home more enjoyable. As I avoid a newly formed puddle, I catch sight of a girl walking ahead of me. She's soaked as she walks with her arms wrapped around her waist, trying to keep warm. I know it's Lacey without seeing her face. Letting out a sigh, my feet pick up pace until I'm jogging to catch her. I stretch out and tap her on the forearm so she stops.

"Hey," I say, her eyes widening at my touch.

"Oh hey," she says, her teeth chattering from the cold, as the wind whips against her wet face. Without thinking, I unzip my jacket and drop my hood. Shaking my arms out of it, I step closer to her. Wrapping it around her, she slips her arms in. Her hands are lost in the sleeves as the jacket is giant on her. Staring into her eyes, I move closer, causing her breath to hitch as I grab the bottom ends of the jacket. I hook the zip in and slowly slide the zipper all the way to the top. Maintaining eye contact, I pull the wet hood over her drenched hair. Without a word I tuck her hair in, my fingers grazing her neck. It's as if the world has stopped moving. My index finger hooks into the collar of her white shirt, fingering the black cord. Lifting it I raise the stone from where it lays hidden under her shirt. I grasp the pink stone like I did at lunch time. My eyes break contact with hers to inspect it. It's definitely the same stone. We don't say a word as the rain pelts us. My white shirt is now soaked through but all I feel is warmth. My skin is burning from being so close to her. She feels so close but yet it's like a million miles are between us, keeping us apart.

Crackling of thunder breaks my trance as she jumps and I bring my gaze back to hers. I tuck the glass rock back under her shirt, letting my finger run along her wet skin as I trace a raindrop along her collarbone. I blink a couple times, stopping myself from doing anything crazy like pulling her into my arms. I grab the jacket strings and tighten them, making the hood close in around her face so nothing but her eyes, nose and mouth are visible. I don't know whether to laugh because she looks ridiculous or to sigh because even looking like this, she's gorgeous. Lightning shimmering across the sky has us both gazing upwards.

"Let's get home," I say, turning to walk in the direction of our homes.

"Chance?" she stammers, but I don't have it in me mentally to have this conversation right now. I'm already drained from the day.

"Another time okay? Let's get out of the rain," I softly tell her, seeing her head droop forward in acceptance. We carry on walking the rest of the way in silence. The splattering rain fills the air with the occasional thunderous outburst. I slow my steps to keep in time with her. We arrive at my house and both stop. Turning to me, she pushes her hands through the sleeves so she can unzip it.

"Keep it on. You can borrow it if it rains tomorrow," I offer. Her eyes drop to my soaked white shirt, clinging to my skin. Her eyes trail over my torso while I watch her cheeks redden.

"Thanks," she says, as her eyes lift back to mine. I nod my head, taking a step towards my house which makes her feet move towards her own house. I don't dare look back, opening my door and leaning my back against the closed door, feeling as if I ran a marathon.

"Chance. Didn't I tell you to take a jacket?" Mum's voice breaks me out of my thoughts, as she stands staring at me with her hands on her hips.

"Yeah. I lent it to Lacey," I stammer, pushing away from the door and heading to the bathroom.

I avoid Mum's gaze as I see her eyes soften, "Oh honey, did you two make up?"

"Not yet," I tell her.

"I wish you two would hurry up before I have to beat your heads together," she threatens. I roll my eyes at her before shutting the door and shutting her out. Peeling my wet uniform off, I step under the hot stream and let it wash away the emotions boiling inside me.

LACEY

3RD FEBRUARY
Dear Diary,

I have so much to tell you. Miles was at school today. I didn't know he went to the same high school as no one mentioned him last week. He told me he was in the Philippines for the Christmas holidays and got back last Friday.

You should have seen his face when he entered chemistry this morning and saw me sitting there. He raced over and gave me the biggest hug. Emma was looking at us funny and when Miles let me go, she asked if he was my boyfriend. We both laughed and before I could tell her we went to primary school together, he cut in and told her our mums knew each other so we had grown up together. Well we did grow up together I guess but I don't think our mums have met before.

Emma kept looking between us so I didn't say anything to Miles. I know he said it for a reason and I don't trust Emma after what happened today. On the way to second period Miles said Chance didn't want people to know Miles and I went to primary school together and it dawned on me. Chance doesn't want anyone to know he knows me. I waited for someone to say something about Chance knowing me but no one said anything. I know I messed up and I think a part of me thought if I came back, I could fix things easily but every time he looks at me, I see the anger lurking in his eyes. The look he gives me makes me too nervous to even broach the subject with him. One day I'll grow some balls and do it.

I hung out a lot with Miles today but I never should have let him talk me into playing soccer with them. I joined in thinking it would give me a reason to be closer to Chance and help break the ice. Well I nearly broke something. My nose. Stupid Emma. I'm sure she kicked the ball at me on purpose.

It was so embarrassing. It felt like my whole head got whacked behind me and then to fall as well. Ugh. I wanted to cry so bad from the pain but I held it in until Miles got me to the sick bay. Chance was running hot and cold today. He initially was worried about me and then he saw my damn necklace. I've worn the stupid thing for years since I left so I forget I have it on most of the time. It happened to be showing when he was near. I couldn't tell what he was thinking when he saw it but he froze like he didn't know whether to stay or to run. Luckily Miles dragged me away. Chance called me Lace. I don't think he realised he did it. Emma looked pissed when she heard so I'm sure others did too.

The way she was hanging all over him proves she's not over him. I'm not sure how he feels about her. I wish I could ask him. I bawled my eyes out to Miles about how much I miss Chance and how I messed up big time. I never told him what happened and he never asked. He's been such a good friend to me today. I went to return his jumper to him he'd left with me in the sick bay and I overheard him and Chance arguing in the locker room about me.

My heart sank when I heard Chance scream about me leaving him. He sounded so hurt and I don't blame him. I don't know how to fix us. I miss my best friend.

When he caught up to me in the rain, I didn't know what to expect. I didn't expect his jacket, that's for sure. I was already soaked through so more rain wouldn't have made a difference. I didn't voice my opinion because as soon as he put his jacket on me, it was like being wrapped in his arms. His jacket was so warm and it smelled like him. A reminder from a time long ago.

I'm not sure he was aware of what his touch did to my skin. His fingertip tracing my skin lit my whole body on fire. I've never felt anything like it before. When I saw his white shirt clinging to his skin and I could see his muscled torso, my fingers itched to touch him but I restrained myself at the last second.

It's as if my heart wants my best friend back but my body wants him as more than my friend. It's a cruel twist of fate. I now have him as nothing but want him as everything.

I dont have anyone to talk to about these feelings either. I would have talked to my best friend about it back when we were friends but now I can't even do that. I don't think I would have talked to him about feeling this way. It would have made things majorly awkward. I probably would have done what I'm doing now and written in here. Like a coward.

Why can't things be simple again? Everything was so simple when we were younger. We would play and laugh. We'd hold hands and hug without second guessing everything. Now I can't even look at him without worrying he may see me. Or if I catch his eye, I wonder what he's thinking. In the past he'd give me a look and I would know his thoughts instantly, without any words spoken at all.

I messed up and broke us like I heard him say. I want him to forgive me. Why is I'm sorry such a hard thing to say? Would he even forgive me? What if he says no? I think him rejecting me would be even worse than not knowing. I'd rather live without knowing his answer because it's easier to live with hope. If he rejected me, I would be crushed. I don't think I'm prepared to deal with a rejection from him. Not from Chance.

Enough rambling from me. I need to ice my face again before bed. Dad said he thinks I'll have at least one black eye by morning if not two. At least the redness has faded. He thought I'd gotten into a fight but when I said it was a fight with a soccer ball, he laughed because he knows I have no coordination when it comes to sports. It was nice to laugh with him too. We haven't interacted much with each other since I've been back so it was a pleasant reminder that the dad I love is still there.

He said he'd take me shopping over the weekend to get some paint for my room as the bright pink walls I've had since we moved here are giving me a headache. Don't get me wrong, I still like pink but I'm not as obsessed with it as I once was. There's only so much pink you can look at before you feel a bit nauseous.

Okie dokie, I'm off to grab ice. Pray my face isn't too bruised tomorrow.

Sweet dreams,

Lacey

CHAPTER 27

CHANCE

8TH FEBRUARY

Bouncing the ball on my driveway, I see Mr Connelly's jeep pull into their driveway. I glance over quickly before carrying on with my one man game. I hear more than one car door open and close so I know Lacey is with him. It's been a weird week with us and we still haven't talked about what happened, neither of us wanting to make the first move to change our situation.

"Hey Chance," I turn at the welcome I receive from Mr Connelly.

"Hey Mr Connelly," I return, waving. Lacey looks at her feet while she waits for her dad at the back of the jeep. He opens the back door and I watch as they gather some paint tins in their hands.

"What are you doing?" I ask, my curiosity getting the better of me.

"Lacey here was over the pink in her room so wanted a change," he tells me. My eyes flick to Lacey watching the pink on her cheeks grow.

"Hmmm," I murmur mainly to myself, as I'm lost in thought.

"We could use another pair of hands if you've got nothing better to do for a few hours," Mr Connelly asks.

"Dad, I'm sure Chance has better things to do," Lacey says, but I cut her off.

"Sure. I'm not doing anything. I can help," I tell him, which has Lacey's face flashing my way but I don't look at her.

"Great. We'll be done in no time with an extra set of hands," he says, placing a can on the ground, slamming the car door shut then picking the can up again. I fling my basketball towards my house, watching it bounce until it stops in the flowerbed without moving. Walking towards Lacey, I stop in front of her.

"Here, I'll grab those," I softly tell her, as I replace my fingers with hers around the handles so I can carry the cans.

"Ah thanks."

"No problem," I reply, following her dad into their home. I haven't stepped foot in their house for years and a sense of deja vu washes over me. It's exactly as I remember it. Not much has changed over the years, it's probably because Mr Connelly was living here alone. He's an if it ain't broke why fix it type of guy so I can't see him worrying about the interior decorating.

I walk the familiar steps to Lacey's room. It's a shorter distance now with my longer strides. When we were little it always felt like I couldn't get to her room fast enough. Opening her door, she leads us in and I can understand why she wants the walls painted. The bright pink was too much when I was little but I accepted it because it was Lacey's favourite colour. Now it looks quite sickly.

"Let's get to it," Mr Connelly says, placing the paint tins on the covered carpet where they've thrown old sheets to protect it from any paint splatters. They've removed her bed and dresser so it's easy to cover every inch of the walls. Mr Connelly lays out paint brushes, rollers and trays. He cracks the lid open and stirs the paint with a long block of wood before pouring some into the trays. The colour is a bright yellow and I feel my lip tug up as I'm not sure it's much better than the pink in the brightness department.

"So are we covering all the walls?" Mr Connelly asks Lacey.

She gazes around at the walls before saying, "Yeah I think so," which tugs at my heart a bit. It shows we've grown and changed from the people we were when we were younger. It hurts because there's a chunk of her life I missed out on. I never thought I'd see the day she gave up pink on purpose. I used to beg her sometimes to pick something other than pink. Now she has, I don't think I'm entirely happy about it. We get to work, dipping our rollers in the paint and rolling them up and down, watching as the pink disappears, replaced by yellow. We work quietly with Mr Connelly occasionally asking us questions about school when the silence is a bit much for him. With the three of us working, it doesn't take us long to get all four walls covered with two coats of yellow paint.

"Thanks for your help Chance," he says, patting me on the back as he exits the room, taking some of the rollers and trays out back to wash them with the hose.

"Yeah thanks for helping," Lacey says, when the two of us are alone in the room.

"You're welcome," I reply. "What made you decide to get rid of the pink?"

"Things change I guess," she says, her eyes dropping to the carpet and I can't help but feel she's not talking about the colour of her room when she says it.

"I guess they do," I reply. "I better go."

"Bye," she says.

"Bye." I hurry from the room and find Mr Connelly walking through the front door.

"Are you off home already, Chance?"

"Yeah, unless you needed something else?"

"Nah, we're good. Thanks for your help," he says, patting me on the shoulder.

A thought comes to my mind and before I can stop myself, I ask, "You couldn't get Lacey out of the house tomorrow, could you? I want to make a surprise in her room for her."

His smile grows before he says, "Yeah, I'm sure I can get her out of here for a few hours in the morning if it suits you?

"Perfect. Thanks Mr Connelly. See ya later."

"Bye Chance." I head back to my house and ask Mum if she's got any large cardboard. She points to the box from our new vacuum and luckily it's big enough for what I have planned. I take it with me to the kitchen table and using a craft knife, I slice the cardboard and manage to cut myself four decent sized sheets to work with. I spend the rest of the day entranced in my project. Mum drops off food to the table intermittently, not wanting to disturb me too much as I'm in a zone. It takes me the rest of the day to get it done and by 10 p.m. I'm done and have it all sorted for tomorrow.

My alarm wakes me early Sunday morning so I won't miss when they leave the house. I play basketball outside as an excuse to keep tabs on them and will be able to see them leave. I bounce the ball up and down my driveway for about ten minutes before Lacey walks out, followed by Mr Connelly. He gives me a wink and a head nod as he walks to the driver's side. I take it as my cue the coast will be clear in a minute.

They drive off and I race back to my room, grabbing my supplies before carrying it all over to their house. I turn the knob on the door, thankful Mr Connelly left it unlocked for me. I turn the handle on her door and walk in. Setting my things out, I crack the lid off the paint tin I brought with me. I forgot I needed something to stir it with so use the knife I bought with me instead. I'm sure Mum won't notice one is missing. The rich blue colour mixes together as I stir it. Grabbing one of the cardboard stencils I made, I use tape to hold it against the wall while I paint over it. The royal blue makes a nice contrast against the yellow. I complete one then move on, taping the next one and so forth until I've finished all four.

I sit on the floor and wait a while to ensure they've dried before I remove the tape carefully from the stencils so as not to peel the new paint off. Slowly removing them from the wall, I take in my art work and I'm amazed at how great it worked out. There staring back at me are my drawings of an octopus, a turtle, a jellyfish and the seahorse I drew last night. I hope she likes them. I've placed two on either side of her window. I hope when she looks at them, she looks out across the yard and sees my own window and thinks of me. I pack my things and leave everything as it was and make my way back home. I busy myself with homework while silently hoping she likes her surprise when she sees it.

I'm woken by the familiar tap, tap, tap against my window. Rubbing my eyes, I flick the blankets off and trudge to the window. Opening the curtains, I don't even look to see who it is before unlocking it and lifting it. I already know it's her. Greeting me is Lacey in a pink silk pyjama set of shorts and button up shirt. I guess we can paint over the pink in her room but she still loves it enough to wear pink. It has me hoping that part of her will always remain.

"Can you talk for a minute?" she asks.

"Yeah sure. U wanna come in?" I gesture to my room.

"Ummm, can we go out to the tree instead?"

"Okay," I say. I step back from the window, wriggle my feet into my sneakers and pull on a jumper. Jumping out the window, I land beside her. We walk quietly to our tree, the still of night surrounding us and a light breeze in the air. Once we get to the tree, we both climb onto the lowest hanging branch, straddling it and facing each other.

"Sooo," I say, breaking the awkward silence.

"I wanted to say thank you for the paintings on my wall. It was a surprise when I got home. A good surprise," she says, smiling at me.

"You're welcome."

"So you still like sea creatures huh?"

"Yeah, always."

"Guess some things never change."

"I guess so," I reply, watching her as she wrings her hands. Closing her eyes, she inhales deeply before letting it out slowly.

Opening her eyes she says, "I never thought there would be a day where it would be hard to talk to you." My own breath puffs out, knowing exactly how she feels.

"I know what you mean."

"I'm sorry you know, for leaving like I did," she softly says, as moisture rushes to her eyes.

"You leaving me hurt a lot. You didn't give me a chance to talk to you and fix things before you ran away," I tell her, being honest.

"I know. If I could go back in time and change things, I would."

"Was it as easy as it looked?" I ask, dropping my gaze to the tree branch we are seated on.

"Did what look easy?"

"Leaving me and not looking back," I raise my eyes to hers, watching as a tear runs down her cheek.

"Leaving you broke me," she stutters out, before giant sobs take over. Wrapping her arms around her waist, my fingers itch to pull her into my arms but I force them to remain still.

"Then why did you do it to me? To us? You didn't break yourself, you broke me too," my voice rises, as the anger bubbles under the surface.

"I'm sorry, Chance. I wasn't thinking straight after my nana died and I know it's not an excuse but you saw what I was like that summer. I felt like I was on this horrible grieving rollercoaster ride and I couldn't get off," she blurts, wiping the tears now streaming down her cheeks. She takes a breath before continuing, "All I felt was numb and sad unless I was with you. You made me feel happy and all I wanted was to feel something other than the sadness I was drowning in. I wanted to cling to the happiness I felt when I was with you."

"You didn't cling to me. You wrecked me," I confess, as my own eyes water.

"I'm sorry, Chance. I'd give anything to change it. Please forgive me," she pleads.

"Did it mean anything to you? Did I mean anything to you?" I ask, as my tears fall.

"You mean everything to me. You're my best friend."

"Was your best friend," I reply, causing her to lean back as if I physically hit her.

"You'll always be my best friend," she says softly.

"I gotta go," I say, feeling overwhelmed by this conversation. Flinging my legs over the side, I jump down, hit the grass and walk away.

"You promised me," she yells, stopping me in my tracks. With my back to her, she continues talking as I hear her jump from the tree to follow me. "You promised me if I messed up, I'd get unlimited chances because we both knew I would mess up." I close my eyes, breathing in and out. Remembering a time long ago when I said the exact thing to her. "You aren't this no second chances person you pretend to be. Where's the boy I know? The boy I love?" she stutters. The anger bubbling inside, rises up and I can't contain it as I lash out at her.

"You destroyed him," I yell, before turning as the tears fall along her skin.

"I'm sorry Chancey," I hear carried on the wind, not sure if she said it or my mind is playing tricks on me. I race to my window, hoisting myself inside and shutting the window. Throwing the curtains closed, I rip my jumper off and kick my shoes off before falling onto the edge of my bed and tucking my head in my hands as my emotions take over. I haven't cried since she left me years ago. Ever since her betrayal I always hold my emotions in. It began as sadness but slowly turned to anger swirling around inside me. Her leaving changed me and even though I want to forgive her and take her in my arms, it's the small part deep inside of me holding me back. That part is scared. Scared to risk getting hurt again, especially by the girl I love.

LACEY

8TH FEBRUARY

Dear Diary,

What have I done? I tried to fix things and talk to him but he's so angry. I've never seen Chance lash out with anger before. It surprised me. I know he has every right to be angry at me. It's all my fault. I wish I could take it back.

He did this amazing mural for me so I thought now would be the time to fix things between us and have this conversation. It's been a long time coming. I think I read the situation wrong and it wasn't the right time at all.

I wish I had someone to talk to about things. Mum is too busy with her new family to be worried about me. I need some advice on how to fix things and make everything better again. I want to go back to how we used to be.

I know the old Chance is still in there but he's also changed. I've changed too and I often wonder how I can go about getting the old me back. I don't know if she exists anymore. When I'm close to Chance, I feel more alive than I have in years. He brings the girl from the past out of me, without even trying.

I wish he could be the boy I love and know is still inside of him. I need to work on my assignment and write about what advice I'd give my younger self. Well for starters, I'd tell her what a complete idiot she is. I don't know what advice I'd offer because I don't know what to do now.

I'm sorry, my tears have wet your pages and blurred the ink tonight so these pages will never be reread. It could be a good thing as the heartache I feel is too much to bear a second time around.

I'll be crying myself to sleep tonight.
Heartbroken,
Lacey

CHAPTER 28

CHANCE 2000

10TH JANUARY

It's been amazing having Lacey back for the summer. We've had a lot of fun, spending every waking moment at the riverbank, swinging in the old tyre while chatting and laughing about everything. It's been like old times. Lacey has had moments of deep sadness consume her which is understandable. I wish I could help her, I don't know how to take away her pain or make things better so I sit and hold her until the sadness passes. I feel like we've changed since we've been apart. We've both grown. I had a major growth spurt this year because I'm a lot taller than Lacey now. When we were younger, we used to be closer in height. When I'm with her, my heart picks up pace and I don't think I'll ever love another girl as much as I love her. I'd do anything for her.

She climbs in my window every night since she's been back. Most nights we sleep soundly side by side but then some nights, I hear her trying to hide her sniffles, so I'll pull her close and hold her the best I can until she falls asleep. I told her to talk to her mum and dad about how she's feeling but she keeps reassuring me she's fine. I'm not too sure, I know the loss of her nana has hit her hard and she's still struggling with her parents' divorce.

It's been a few weeks since Lacey has been back now and I can hear the familiar shuffling of her pulling herself in through my window. I leave it open for her so she can come and go as she pleases. It's so hot these days Mum doesn't question if she sees it open constantly. My lamp is on as I've been reading so without looking, I lower the covers so she can climb in and pull them back to cover herself. I hook my arm underneath her, pulling her close while I continue to read.

"Read to me like you used to when we were little," Lacey whispers, which has a smile spreading across my face at the memory.

"Okay," I reply, finding the right spot and reading out loud to her. "Turn the page," I tell her, when we finish reading each page. She turns the page quickly then burrows her hand back under the blanket. I begin reading again but stutter when I feel Lacey's fingertips slip under my shirt. The heat from her skin sets mine on fire, causing my brain to stop thinking.

"Lacey?" I ask, as her palm moves against my torso.

"Hmm," she softly replies.

"What are you doing?" I ask, rolling on my side to face her, the book now forgotten. I scan her face as she looks at me, the deep blues of her eyes shining under the light of my lamp.

"I love you Chance," she whispers, causing my breath to catch.

"I love you too, Lace," I tell her.

She shakes her head before raising her palm to my cheek, "No, I love you like I have feelings for you. I think I always have," she confesses.

My throat dries before I croak out, "I feel the same way." Staring into each other's eyes, we both lean forward, pressing our lips together. It starts out slow then turns into a frenzy with each of us trying to get as close to the other as we can. Lacey pulls off her t-shirt and reaches for my boxers which has me halting.

"What are you doing? We don't need to do that," I tell her.

"Please Chance. I want my first time to be with you," she pleads, and in her eyes I see the Lacey I've always loved. The one who I would give anything to and the one I could never deny.

"I don't want it to change things between us," I tell her.

"It won't," she begs, leaning down and kissing me again. I get lost in the current. I have the girl of my dreams in my arms and I don't stop to question if this is the best idea.

"You okay?" I ask Lacey, as we both put our clothes back on. I can feel she's pulling away from me but I don't question it.

"I'm fine Chancey. I'm sore but I've heard it's normal. We should get some sleep," she softly says, curling into my arms.

"You sure? Do you want me to get you anything?

"No I'm okay," she tells me.

"I love you Lace."

"I love you too Chance."

I fall asleep easily, thinking I finally have the girl I've always wanted and I don't need to hide my feelings anymore. She loves me back. Everything has fallen into place. It's like one of those fairytales Lacey always made me watch when we were younger.

The next morning the sun hits my face, waking me up. My arms are empty and the bed is cold. I sit and look around but there's no sign of Lacey. She's gone. She left after what happened last night without talking to me. There have been other mornings when I have woken up alone so I don't question it too much.

"Chance, I need you to come with me to the mall today to try on new shoes for school," Mum yells from the other side of my door, as she bangs on it.

"Okay Mum. I'll get ready," I tell her, changing my clothes then brushing my teeth. I slept in so it's after ten in the morning. As we head to the car, I glance over at Lacey's house and see her dad's car in the driveway. I'll go see her when I get back, I tell myself.

Mum takes longer in the mall than I hoped. She buys me school shoes and then decides to buy me some new clothes as I've grown a bit more than she expected me to. After clothes shopping, she drags me to the supermarket so I can help carry all the heavy groceries. It is late in the afternoon when we get back. I help her lug in the groceries and unpack them.

"I'm heading to Lacey's," I tell Mum, as soon as the final item is put away in the cupboard. Jogging over to her front door, I knock because her dad's jeep is gone from the driveway. There's no answer so I guess they have gone out and I decide to hang out at our tree for a bit so I can see as soon as they return. It's over an hour before I hear Mr Connelly's car door slamming shut. I race to catch them before they get inside but when I see Mr Connelly alone, my stomach drops. My sixth sense kicks in, telling me something isn't right.

"Mr Connelly, is Lacey home?" I ask.

"Chance, did you and Lacey have a fight?" My brows pull together as I shake my head.

"No. Why?" I ask, as my heart picks up pace.

"She was crying this morning, begging me to take her to the airport so she could go back home to her mum. She didn't want to spend her last two weeks here. I thought something happened between you two to upset her," he states, but I shake my head again as I feel the blood drain from my face.

"She left me? I mean she left already?" I stutter.

"Yeah, I dropped her to the airport. She wanted to go straight away and she managed to get a flight for this afternoon," he casually says, not realising his words are cracking me open.

"Chance? You okay son?" he asks, concerned. I realise why when I taste the salty tear on my lips. I turn and race away as I hear him call after me. I run back to our tree, hiding at the base so no one can see me. No one witnesses me break down over the girl who I love most in the world. Who I thought loved me too but now I know she doesn't. If she loved me, she wouldn't have broken me.

CHAPTER 29

LACEY 2003

9TH FEBRUARY

Dear Diary,

I can't get the image of Chance from last night out of my head. He hates me. He hates me. I knew I'd hurt him in the worst possible way but I didn't realise the extent of it until I witnessed his anger last night.

Him crying in front of me broke my heart. Seeing him vulnerable took me back in time to when he used to get bullied as a kid. This time, it was me who caused him all this hurt and pain, not a bully. I don't blame him for hating me. What I did was unforgivable. I didn't mean to hurt him. I was selfish and couldn't care less what any of the repercussions would be.

I woke up the morning after 'the event' and I felt more broken inside. I remember glancing at Chance looking so peaceful and for the first time in my life the cold, hard truth slapped me in the face. I didn't deserve him, not after I'd taken from him and used him to make myself feel better. All I'd wanted was to feel something instead of the numbness I felt since Nana died.

I was embarrassed of what I'd done and how I had acted, ashamed I treated my best friend so badly. I did the only thing I could. I ran. I ran as far away as I could, all the way back to my mum.

I spent the next few months crying myself to sleep every night because I knew I'd wrecked it all. He hadn't tried to call and no letters arrived so I knew deep in my bones he'd let me go. It's not what I wanted. I wanted to stop hurting and feel something other than the pain. It didn't help Mum checked out as well, she was physically there but not mentally or emotionally. She didn't notice I wasn't coping.

It wasn't until the principal rang her about all the school I was missing, she realised something wasn't right. She made me see a therapist and she helped me to come to terms with losing my nana. I still had the hole in my chest from losing Chance and I didn't think anything could ever fix that.

Once Mum came out of her fog, she realised she didn't have Nana to worry about or a husband, so she decided to give dating a go which leads us to more pain. She has a new boyfriend Doug and she's currently pregnant with their first child. They would gush over everything pregnancy related and I felt left out. It's why I asked Dad if I could move back in with him. I feel like she is starting a new family and there's no room for me in it.

I guess I have a habit of running when things aren't going my way. I should work on it, my old therapist would highly recommend it. I feel like Chance will never forgive me but I can't give up hope. We were best friends. I need to remind him that an epic friendship like ours can't be torn apart.

I'll make it right. I have to.

Hopeful,

Lacey

CHAPTER 30

CHANCE

14TH FEBRUARY

"What's been with you all week?" Theo asks, as we walk towards school.

"Nothing."

"Don't give me that crap. I know when you're in a sour mood. Who is it this time? Emma or Lacey?" he asks.

"I honestly don't think about Emma anymore," I tell him, kicking a rock sitting in my path.

"So it's Lacey then."

"Maybe," I reply.

"What's happened now?"

"We had a fight over the weekend," I confess.

"Over the weekend? And you're telling me now? What happened?"

"I'm not sure if we can ever be friends again," I tell him.

"You're an idiot."

"What? Why am I an idiot?" I demand, turning to face him.

"The girl is crazy about you, I can tell. Do you know how many times I catch her looking at you with those sad eyes of hers when you aren't looking? Let me tell you, it's a lot."

"Why are you always looking at her?" I ask. He stops in his tracks, turning his whole body my way.

"Do you not know how scared I am of the girl? Man, she gives me a look and I worry she might cut my balls off. I know you've forgiven me for the past but she knows how to hold a grudge. I gotta keep one eye on her at all times so I know if she's coming for me. Or my balls. If I catch her looking at me, I usually make a dash for it before she can call my name out. She refuses to call me anything but Theodore," he blurts out, and I can't contain the smile pulling across my face.

"Remember when she threatened your goolies?" I say, laughing.

"Don't remind me man. The memory is etched into my brain. Why do you think I'm worried about them now?" he confesses, and I laugh loudly. The first real laugh I've had all week. We continue walking to school, both reliving memories in our heads before he speaks again. "You know it's not too late to fix things. I know you don't want to tell me what happened between the two of you which is fine. I have watched you two for years and a friendship like yours isn't something you should throw away if you have a chance to save it," he tells me.

"Thanks man. I'll think about it," I tell him, which has him patting me on the back.

"And if you want, we can drown your sorrows tonight at Kyle's?" he offers.

"That sounds pretty good but I'll let you know for sure later on," I tell him, as we walk in the school gates, doing our handshake before parting ways.

Walking into English class, the period before lunch break, I catch sight of Lacey already seated at her desk. I let out a breath. I've ignored her all week, trying to avoid eye contact. The fight we had the other night opened all my old wounds and now the betrayal feels fresh again. It's hard to let it go, even though part of me wants to. The other part is scared I'll get hurt again. I've lived through it once and barely survived, I don't think I could live through it again.

Shuffling through the maze of desks, she looks at me when I pull out my seat. I unzip my bag, pull out my book and stare at it on the desk, hoping the teacher arrives soon. My skin prickles as I feel Lacey's eyes on me. My heart hammers in my chest like it does every time I'm this close to her. I force my breaths in and out, not wanting to show any weakness or let her know being near her still affects me. Tension swirls around us, as her eyes stay focused on me. I can't take it any longer and raise my eyes to hers. I watch the slight widening of her eyes before the smallest of smiles tips her lips up. I can't help but think she's gotten more beautiful..

"Hello class," our teacher greets, breaking the trance we were locked in. I shake my head to clear it and turn back towards the front of the room. I force myself to focus on the lesson but it's hard with Lacey right next to me. A few minutes into the lesson, she slides a piece of paper across the desk to me. I glance at the paper and read what it says. 'Do you think you can ever forgive me? Tick yes or no' with two boxes underneath for me to pick one.

The conversation from this morning with Theo floats in my head and I take a deep breath, trying to let some of the hurt I feel go with my exhale. I grab my pen and make a new box on her note, writing maybe above it. I tick the box before sliding it back her way. Her greedy hands grab at it, wanting to see my answer. She writes something else quickly before waiting until the teacher's back is turned before she slides it my way. Glancing at it, I read, 'Do you think we will ever be best friends again? Yes or no.' Again I create my own box, ticking it as I write I don't know above it. Checking the coast is clear, I slide it back to her.

She scribbles quickly again before pushing the paper back towards me, eager as she has my attention for the first time this week. I wait until the teacher isn't looking before glancing down. 'Do you miss me? Yes or No.' Letting out a sigh, I decide to be honest, ticking yes before pushing it back to her. I hear her release a sigh of her own. Writing again, she pushes it my way and I read the words 'I miss you too' before she takes the paper back and places it inside her exercise book. The teacher gives us notes to write from the board for the rest of the lesson so everyone quietly gets to work copying the notes. Lacey pushes her book on an angle to be able to write better. I do the same and we fall into a rhythm of glancing at the board and writing our notes. Lacey is left handed and I'm right handed and it was something she always loved because when we'd sit together in class, it meant she could hold my hand whenever she wanted and we didn't have to stop working, that way we wouldn't get in trouble.

Back then if the other kids caught sight of us holding hands, they would tease us but it never bothered us. Together we were unstoppable and we had a bond that felt like it was unbreakable until it wasn't. Missing the connection I used to have with her, I don't let my brain stop me as I use my pinky finger to graze the side of her hand. I hear the hitch in her breath as she feels it, so I do it again. She stills beside me, her writing forgotten as her gaze lifts to me. I lift my eyes to her, keeping a straight face as I wiggle my pinky under hers and link them. Her finger squeezes mine as a smile lights up her face. I turn back to my work and finish writing the notes with our pinkies joined and both of us holding on tightly. We remain in the same position until the bell rings and breaks our small connection. I untangle my finger and pack my stuff as she does the same. No words are spoken as we go our separate ways but a spark of hope has been ignited, lighting a way for us to find our way back to each other again.

LACEY

14TH FEBRUARY

Dear Diary,

I think I'm making progress. He held my finger today. I know it's the smallest thing in the world but it is a big step for us and it meant the world to me. It means he doesn't hate me. I know I said he did earlier in the week but I think there's still hope for us to find our way back to what we had before I ruined it.

He even answered the questions I wrote for him in English. I was expecting him to screw my note into a ball and throw it in the rubbish bin. I think even if he had answered the question without the finger holding, I would have called today a win. He said he misses me. Gosh, how I miss him.

I'll try to take it slow and remind him how strong our friendship used to be. We can't throw away years of friendship. We have to at least try. I need to prove to him I'm worth another shot. I won't let him down this time.

I don't know what my next step is and I wish I had someone to bounce ideas off about Chance. The only person I can think to ask is, dare I say it, Theodore. I wonder if he will help me?

I'm thankful in a way he had Theodore as a friend all these years. I think he's more than proved himself he's changed and he isn't the bully he once was. It's time I give him the benefit of the doubt and let our past go. If Chance can forgive Theodore for bullying him then I'm positive he can forgive me too with time. Next step is to talk to Theodore and see if he's got any perspective on the situation.

The landline is ringing so I better answer it before it wakes dad. I guess that's my cue to end this entry for the night.

Until next time,

Lacey

CHANCE

"Come on man, we need to get you home," Theo begs, but in my drunken state I'm adamant.

"No. I wanna see my best friend," I mutter.

"You know when I suggested drink

ing your sorrows away, I didn't think you were gonna skull half a bottle of vodka," I hear Theo say, as my vision gets hazy.

"Hey," Theo says.

"Hey back," I say, laughing.

"I'm not talking to you. I'm on the phone," he tells me. I squint my eyes to try and to focus on one Theo instead of the three of them.

"Yeah he won't budge. Wants to see his best friend apparently," he says, sounding annoyed. "I am annoyed because I wanna go home now," he says.

"Whoops, did I say that out loud?" I ask.

"Yes," he huffs at me, before turning back to his phone conversation. "So could you please help us out? I know it's a lot to ask but I need your help," he says, before the conversation becomes muffled and I can't hear any more.

"Are you not his best friend?" I hear someone say, but it's dark. I'll rest for a bit.

"Do you think it's a good idea?" Miles says.

"Well it's his own fault. If he didn't want anyone to know, he shouldn't have gotten wasted like this," Theo says.

"Who the hell are you talking about?" I hear Emma shriek. Her voice is like fingernails on a chalkboard.

"You'll all see soon enough," Theo yells, quietening all the voices around me.

"I hope you aren't mad at me in the morning for blowing the lid on your dumb secret but you left me no choice," Theo says closer to me.

"I miss my best friend," I confess, feeling him pat me on the back.

"I know bud. I know." Feels like a minute later before I hear voices again.

"Thanks for coming. I owe you one," Theo's voice says.

"What are you doing here? I thought you couldn't make it?" Emma says. I feel a soft hand slide across my forehead, combing my hair back with their fingers causing me to sigh.

"That feels nice," I say. A hand links their fingers with mine and even in my drunken state, I know who it is. "Okay, we can go home now," I say.

"I thought you were waiting for your so-called best friend?" Emma asks.

"I was. They're here now so I can go," I say, squeezing my best friend's hand.

"How drunk is he? Has he got imaginary friends now?" Emma asks, causing Theo and Miles to laugh. Well I think it's them laughing.

"What's going on?" Luke's voice cuts in.

"We're trying to get Chance home," Theo tells him.

"Are you two a thing now? Why are you holding hands?" I hear Luke ask.

"Duh. She's my best friend," I laugh, which causes the room to fill with laughter.

"Chance, you haven't opened your eyes for like the last hour. You don't even know who's sitting next to you," Emma says, laughing to herself.

"I don't need to see my best friend to know it's them. It's what makes us best friends," I state, causing more laughter.

"Okay, tell us who your best friend is then," Luke says.

"Shh it's a secret," I whisper, which causes more laughter.

"Don't worry, we won't tell anyone," Luke says.

"Tell them so we can go home, please Chance," Theo tells me.

The hand holding mine squeezes it before I say, "Fine. It's Lace." My confession causes gasps to echo around me. I try to peel my eyes open but they're so heavy. "Did I say something wrong?" I mumble.

"No Chancey, you didn't," Lacey softly says. "Let's get you home now."

"Okay Lace," I reply, finally able to open my eyes and see my best friend smiling at me.

"She's your best friend? You two don't even talk to each other," Emma wails, causing a drumming to sound through my head.

"They've been best friends since they were little," Miles says.

"Theo, can you help him? Hopefully we can get him to walk," Lacey says.

"I don't believe you're best friends. Stop lying," Emma's voice rings out.

"Yeah I don't believe it either. I think you're dating," Luke says. The room quietens at his accusation. I force my eyes to open more, vaguely seeing the people in the room surrounding us. All wanting answers. I didn't think my friends would be so invested in my life.

"Well we are invested," Luke calls, making everyone laugh.

"Stop thinking out loud," Theo tells me.

Squinting at the crowd I say, "Fine. Lacey has a scar on her right forearm from where she broke her arm, falling out of our tree on the day we met when we were six years old. She has another scar between her eyes from when I gave her chicken pox," I tell them.

"Aha, so you admit it was you who gave me chicken pox. I knew it," Lacey accuses, but I hear laughter in her voice.

"Rewind, the scar is from when she gave me chicken pox," I correct, laughing to myself.

"No, you can't take it back, you already admitted it," she says.

"Come on Chance. Let's get you up," Theo says. I wobble but Lacey comes underneath one arm, so I wrap my arm around her for balance, while Theo comes to my other side.

"Everyone make some room so we can get this life of the party home. You can ask him your twenty questions on Monday but I'd be surprised if he remembers," Theo says, walking and helping me move with him.

"Here Lacey, let me take his other side," Miles offers, as he and Lacey switch out from under my arm.

"It's cold," I mumble.

"Well it'll be worse when the wind hits you outside," Theo's voice says.

"No. I mean Lacey took the warmth away again. I'm always cold when she leaves me," I mumble some more.

"It's okay, Chance I'm right here," I hear Lacey say, quietly behind me.

"Don't leave me again. I don't like the cold," I tell her.

"I won't," she says.

Someone leans me against a wall which I sag against. It's nice here.

"I don't think he's gonna be able to climb in the window," Miles says.

"My house is too far, I don't think he will make it there," Theo says.

"Guys, I'll go home. Mum will probably ground me but it's okay," I mumble.

"He can come to my house," Lacey's voice says.

"You sure? Will you get in trouble for sneaking out?" Theo asks.

"It'll be fine. Better than his mum seeing him like this," Lacey says.

"Come on bud. We gotta do a bit more walking," Miles says, pulling my arm around him. We stagger towards Lacey's house and I feel less drunk but not enough to walk on my own. Theo and Miles help me while Lacey opens her front door.

"Try to be quiet," Lacey whispers, as they shuffle me down the hallway.

"In here," Lacey directs them, before a bright light shines in my eyes, blinding me.

"Lacey, sweetie, what's going on?" Lacey's dad's voice asks.

"Hey Dad, long story," Lacey says.

"Well we've got time."

"Chance here, as you can see, got drunk and the guys couldn't get him to go home so I had to sneak out to help," she explains.

"I thought I heard the phone ring earlier. Why didn't you walk him through his own door?"

"We didn't want him getting into trouble. Can you give us the third degree tomorrow please?" Lacey asks.

"Fine, get him to bed. Boys, it's late so why don't you crash here tonight. You can deal with your parents tomorrow."

"Sure thing Mr Connelly," Theo says.

"Lacey, show them to the spare room then go to your bedroom."

"No worries Dad. Thanks."

"Night kids."

"Night," we all say. Theo and Miles help me stumble down the hallway to the spare room and let me flop on the soft mattress.

"Here you go guys." I peel my eyes open to see Lacey handing them pillows and blankets. Their muffled replies drift away as my eyes close again and I fall asleep.

Peeling my heavy eyes open, the dark room spins around me as my head throbs in pain. Sitting makes the room spin more. Steadying myself for a minute I take in my surroundings. Seeing blankets and outlines of figures on the floor, I'm guessing I fell asleep at the party. I need to piss so I push myself to stand and stumble my way in the dark to the door. Opening it I step into the hallway in search of a bathroom. As I stagger down the hall, keeping my hands outstretched for balance, I feel a sense of familiarity. A light on shows me the bathroom so I relieve myself with my eyes half closed. I wash my hands when I'm finished and look around the room.

"Lacey's house?" I question quietly, wondering how I got here. I leave the room and venture back into the dark hallway. Not thinking clearly, I shuffle to Lacey's door trying to be as quiet as possible. Turning the handle I push the door open then close it behind me gently. Glancing to the bed I see her curled on her side, facing the wall. I still have my shoes on so I kick them off, before lifting her blanket and curling in behind her.

She stills for a second so I whisper, "It's me," which has her body softening.

"You're drunk Chance. You should go back to the spare room as you'll probably regret the whole night in the morning," she whispers.

"I'm cold without you. I don't wanna be cold anymore," I tell her, squeezing her back to my front as I nuzzle my chin into her neck, my whole body relaxing for the first time since she left me.

"I'm sorry Chance," she says, as I drift off.

"I know," I mumble, before I'm back asleep.

Waking up I feel overheated as I squeeze my arms around something. Well someone. Raising my heavy eyes I lift my head, gazing at the girl in my arms. Lacey. She's fast asleep and I don't want to wake her so I gently peel my arms out from under her. She rolls onto her back, sleeping soundly. I watch her for a minute as it's the first time I've been this close to her, where I could watch her uninterrupted, since she's been back. She looks older but she's still Lacey. There's the freckle I always loved and the chicken pox scar between her eyebrows. Heaving out a breath, I remove myself from the bed and sneak to the spare room, remembering the guys from last night. Theo is awake when I enter.

"There you are. You all good?" he asks.

"Yeah my head's pounding," I tell him.

"I'll catch up with you later. I'm gonna wake Miles and try to get us home before our parents realise we didn't make it home last night," he says, standing and walking over to Miles. Shaking him gently, he wakes him.

"Come on Miles, let's go home."

"Sweet," Miles mumbles, half asleep. We all step out of the room trying to be quiet, as it's early morning judging from the light filtering in behind the curtains. At the front door, we are nearly free and clear before I hear the voice behind me.

"Chance, a word before you go son," my eyes close at the sound of Mr Connelly's voice.

"You guys go," I tell Theo and Miles.

"Thanks for last night sir," Theo says, which Mr Connelly nods at. My friends close the door as they exit and I'm left with Mr Connelly staring at me.

"You want to talk about why you were so drunk last night?" he asks.

"I had a lot on my mind," I tell him honestly, as I push my hands into my pockets.

"I used to drink when I had a lot on my mind too until I lost the most important person in my life," he says, making me drop my head. "I'm lucky I was given a second chance to make things right with her. A piece of advice from an old man who nearly lost it all. Don't waste your second chance with her. She may act like she can handle anything but I think we've both caused her enough heartache. Don't you?" I want to argue she played a part in the breakdown of our friendship too but we can't keep blaming each other as it doesn't help. We can forgive and move forward and hope we can become strong again.

"Yeah I do. I won't hurt her. I promise," I tell him, strong in my conviction.

"That's what I want to hear. Now head home before your mum catches you. Chance?"

"Yeah?"

"There are no answers at the bottom of a bottle son."

I nod before leaving his house and walking the short distance to my own. I push my window open, climb in and hop into bed. I fall asleep again with my best friend on my mind.

LACEY

15TH FEBRUARY
Dear Diary,

Theodore just left my house. I know! He came around when I called him. He owed me one after last night. I'll get back to last night in a minute. I asked Theodore if he had any ideas on what I could do to fix my friendship with Chance. He told me to keep doing what I'm doing and eventually Chance will see he's being a stubborn ass and come around. His words not mine.

I asked him if Chance told him what happened between us but he said no, it's pretty much the one secret Chance has kept from him. He said if he could, he would tell Chance to stop being an idiot and be friends with me already but then he also said because he doesn't know what happened, he doesn't know if I deserve forgiveness or not. Theodore is still the same smart ass kid he used to be so even though he wants me to call him Theo, I think I will kindly have to refuse.

He left my house and said he was headed to Chance's. I'm wondering if I should talk to Chance today before I lose my nerve. I'm a bit scared to make the first move now he's sober as I don't know if he regrets last night or not.

Now back to last night. Chance outed us and told everyone at the party we were best friends. When Theodore rang my house, he told me Chance wouldn't move without me so I had to sneak out to go to Kyle's house. I'm glad I did because I don't think they would have been able to get Chance to budge at all.

Emma was not happy to hear about my history with Chance. She thinks we are lying about it. Dad was not happy about me sneaking out. I think he's trying to stay on my good side, worried I will run back to Mum again so he gave me a warning instead of grounding me. He said next time it happens he'd prefer I wake him and tell him rather than sneaking out and putting myself in danger. I guess I can do that next time. I hope there aren't any more rescue missions in the near future.

I need to clear my head a bit so I might go for a walk and get some fresh air while the afternoon sun is shining. Hopefully the fresh air will help me find the answers to my problems.

Wondering what to do,

Lacey

CHANCE

15TH FEBRUARY

I wake with a killer headache. Luckily for me, Mum doesn't know I snuck out last night or how I ended up at Lacey's. I hope her dad doesn't mention it. It would suck to be grounded right now. Mum left to go grocery shopping and Theo rang to say he's coming round. I'm lying in bed, waiting for him to arrive. I might fall asleep again if he doesn't get here soon.

I hear the faint knocking on the door before it opens and I hear Theo yell, "Chance, I'm here," before he walks in my bedroom door.

"Hey," I say, looking up from where I lie on my bed.

"How you feeling?" he asks, chuckling.

"Head's a killer but apart from that, I'm good."

"Well, you did drink half the vodka bottle. I'm surprised you didn't puke," he tells me, as he sits at the end of my bed.

"Sorry man, was I wasted?" I ask.

"Yeah bro. You wouldn't leave and I can't carry your big ass home by myself."

"Sorry man."

"You already said sorry. You don't need to keep apologising. That's what friends are for."

"I wasn't embarrassing, was I?" I ask.

"Do you remember anything from last night?"

"Bits and pieces. How did we end up at Lacey's by the way?"

"Well my friend, you wouldn't leave the party without 'your best friend'," he says, making air quotes, causing my eyes to widen.

"Nooo."

"Yes," he replies, smiling. "I'm such a great friend, I rang your bestie and she came running. You told everyone she is your best friend and you guys have history. Emma wasn't happy and Luke thinks you're dating but everyone else was plain shocked."

"Ugh," I say, sitting and dropping my face into my hands. "Anything else?"

"Not really. Miles, Lacey and I helped to walk you home but then you were too wasted to climb back in your window so Lacey suggested we take you to her house. Her dad caught us sneaking in and told us to crash there. I think you were in Lacey's room because you disappeared for a bit but I don't know what happened. We walked out this morning which you must remember because her dad caught us again," he tells me.

"Yeah, her dad wanted to give me some advice and make sure I'm not gonna hurt her," I tell him.

"Have you talked to her yet?" he asks.

"Nah not yet. Was she mad she had to come save me last night?"

"Mad?" he scoffs, "It's the happiest I've seen her in a long time. Think she was happy you were calling her your best friend again.

You don't need to worry about her wrath or anything if you're concerned because I'd say it's the complete opposite. She wants her best friend back as much as you do," he tells me. "Stop over-thinking it, Chance. Forgive the girl. It's clear as day you two are miserable without each other. I'm not saying you have to admit your undying love for her but being friends again wouldn't be the worst thing in the world," he tells me.

"Yeah, I think you're right," I mutter.

"What was that? I don't think I heard you," he says, cupping his ear.

"You're right," I yell, causing his smile to grow.

"And don't you forget it," he says, making us both laugh.

"You wanna play some basketball?" I ask, flinging the covers off and getting out of bed.

"I would but you should fix things with your girl. Time to rip the band aid off," he suggests.

"Fine, I'll go talk to her," I tell him.

"Good," he says, patting me on the back. "My work here is done so I'm gonna head home. Let me know if you need anything, otherwise I'll see you Monday. Don't forget I have my cousin's wedding tomorrow so I won't be free to do anything," he tells me.

"Thanks for coming over bud," I tell him, as I walk him out to the front door.

"Laters," he calls, as he walks off in the direction of his house. Closing the front door I walk to the bathroom, deciding to shower and start my day, even though it is already late in the afternoon. I grab some painkillers for my throbbing head and wonder how much of it is from my hangover and how much is from the dread of having to go and fix things with my best friend.

After my shower I'm pulling my shorts on when I happen to catch a glimpse out my window. I pull the curtains further apart to check and sure enough, there's Lacey walking towards our tree. Now's as good a time as any I tell myself. Psyching myself up I rush out the back door, without thinking to put a shirt on. Luckily it's a nice day out. Jogging towards our tree, my bare feet hitting the soft grass, I catch sight of Lacey as she takes a seat against the trunk of the tree so the full green foliage covers her from the heat of the sun. She's got headphones in from her MP3 player so is unaware of my arrival until I'm standing right in front of her.

Her wide eyes stare at me as I gaze at her for a minute before taking a seat next to her. I lean back against the rough tree trunk, my bare back wishing it had a shirt on now. Stretching my legs out in front of me, I don't know what to say. Lacey holds out one of her headphones for me to take, a smile warming my face as it reminds me of what we used to do. Taking it, I push the ear bud into my ear as I hear the lyrics of Blue's song 'If you Come Back'. We sit in silence, side by side, listening to the music playing through the headphones. After the song finishes, another plays and her head softly drops onto my shoulder. I let out a sigh as I lift my arm and wrap it around her shoulder, drawing her closer. We sit there in the same position, not talking for the longest time, as one song ends and another begins and the air cools around us.

Goosebumps sprout along my skin as a breeze swirls around us. Lacey must notice because she lifts her head from my shoulder. I lower my arm, pulling my headphone out of my ear and she does the same. Looking at her, I notice the tears about to pool on her lash line.

"I'm sorry I messed us up Chancey," she whispers, and seeing her hurting as much as I am makes my decision for me. I don't want to be mad and hold a grudge against her anymore. She's been my best friend forever and I don't want to throw our friendship away when she's here and she's trying her best to be my friend again.

Pulling her into my arms I whisper, "I won't say it's okay because what happened hurt me. I wish you'd have talked to me back then instead of running off and leaving me."

"I know. I wasn't thinking straight and then I was so ashamed about what I'd done to our friendship I thought you deserved a better friend than me. I didn't deserve to be able to call you my friend after I treated you so badly," she replies, sniffling into my shoulder.

"Well we can't change the past. We can move on and learn from it. Next time," I say before she cuts me off.

"There won't be a next time," she says.

I let go, holding her shoulders with my hands so I can look into her eyes as I speak, "Next time and there will be a next time, because friends fight and then they make up Lace. We need to talk when we do and not run off. That way we can fix it before we lose each other again."

"I really am sorry. Do you think you can forgive me?" she asks, tilting her head.

"I promised once to give you unlimited chances so you're forgiven. Back to best friends?" I ask, as a smile grows on my face.

"The bestest of friends," she squeals, as she jumps towards me, embracing me tightly. A warm feeling fills my chest as I hold onto her like I've wanted to since I knew she was back. We hold onto each other for a few minutes before we reluctantly let go. She silently holds out a headphone for me, making me smile. She tucks the other in her ear and we both lean against the tree, sitting in silence like we've done a million times before. Listening to a few more songs before we say goodbye for the night.

LACEY

15TH FEBRUARY
Dear Diary,

I couldn't wait until tomorrow to write it so you get two entries from me today. I can't believe it. Chance has forgiven me. He's forgiven me. I thought I'd lost him for good. I'm grateful he's my best friend again. I'm going to be the best friend ever and this is a promise I intend to keep. I won't mess it up like I did last time. He's too important to me.

I came inside from sitting with Chance out by our tree in our old spot for a bit. We listened to music like old times. My heart is so happy.

Feeling grateful,
Lacey

CHAPTER 31

CHANCE

21ST FEBRUARY

It's been one hell of a week. I have my best friend back but sometimes it feels like old times as if nothing happened and then other times we are awkward around each other. Mainly it's when there's a touch or a lingering look involved. I can't help it, I still have feelings for the girl. We never got to explore our feelings and after loving her the way I do for so long it's hard to keep them under control now we are back on good terms.

We handed in our English assignments of our letters to our younger selves. Lacey wanted me to read hers before she handed it in so I suggested we read each other's letters. It opened my eyes and let me know how she felt about what went on between us. I hope she felt the same about my letter. Funny how we both wrote to our younger selves in regards to decisions involving the other person. Sitting in English I can't wait for the weekend. We have spent the week fielding questions from all of our friends. They can't believe we kept it a secret and pretended like we didn't know each other. Kyle finally clicked when I explained Lacey was the black haired girl from his party I saved. He was a bit drunk then so it was hard to picture her as the black haired girl when her hair is now an orange colour from when she tried to strip the black out.

Emma has been asking the most questions. She corners us when we are on our own and drills us relentlessly, trying to poke holes in our stories. She asked me if I've ever thought about Lacey in a girlfriend way and I denied it but I think the bright red of my face might have given my real feelings away. She hasn't tried to get back with me this week so I'm hoping she's finally ready to move on if nothing else. Having Lacey back, I see what I felt for Emma doesn't even compare to what I feel for Lacey. Glancing at Lacey I can't help but run a strand of her orange hair through my fingers, causing her to look at me.

"How about we fix your hair tonight?" I ask, while the teacher's back is turned.

Her eyes brighten as she asks, "What do you have in mind?"

"We could ask Mum to help? She colours her hair all the time," I tell her.

"You don't like the orange on me?" she asks, a hint of a smile poking through.

"I miss the old Lacey with the poofy hair if I'm being honest," I tell her, my smile growing.

"You think you're so funny," she says, as she tickles my side quickly before dropping her hand when the teacher turns around.

"At least you brush it now," I tease, which has her cheeks puffing out, holding back her laugh. She waits until the teacher turns again before she pinches the top of my hand like in last card torture. I remain quiet while I pull my hand away. We carry on like this for the remainder of class, riling the other up.

When the bell goes I say, "Should we head to the supermarket and get something to colour your hair with?"

"Sure, sounds good," she replies, hooking her arms through her backpack.

We make our way towards the gate, meeting Theo at the gym. We've gotten into a new routine this week. Theo and Lacey both meet at my house in the mornings and the three of us walk to school together. We walk home together too, using the gym as our meeting point in the afternoons.

"We're going to the supermarket to get something to fix Lacey's hair, you wanna come?" I ask Theo, as he does his handshake with me.

"Yeah I'm in. It's about time you fixed your hair Lacey, it's been hurting my eyes," Theo teases.

"Oh shut it Theodore," Lacey fires back. They carry on their friendly argument all the way to the supermarket. Standing in the hair product aisle we don't have the slightest clue what to buy.

"I think you should get this one with the highlighting cap in it. If you mess it up, it's not your whole head, it's a few strands and they will be easy to hide. My cousin Hilda bleached her whole head once and my aunty was furious because it started falling out," Theo tells us, which has both of us looking at him in shock. He notices our faces when he stops looking at the back of the dye box he's holding. "What?" he asks.

"Are you trying to scare me?" Lacey quietly screams at him.

"I'm sure you'll be fine," he placates her, patting her back, before looking at me and rolling his eyes. I let out a chuckle causing Lacey to whip her head my way.

"My hair won't fall out, will it?" she asks.

"No, we'll have Mum with us so I'm sure we will be fine. Let's get a couple different ones to see what Mum thinks," I suggest, grabbing the one with the hair cap and also another blonde dye kit promising bleach blonde waves.

"What did you use to get the black out?" I ask, as we walk to the checkout. The lady scans the items and I pull out my cash to pay for them.

"They have a product you can use to strip the colour out of your hair but it left me with this," she says, lifting a piece of her orange hair.

"I'm sure Mum will know what to do," I tell her, as I carry the plastic bag with the dye boxes in it while we walk home.

"I'll see you guys Monday. Hopefully your hair is still intact," Theo calls out, making Lacey poke fingers at him while he walks off in the direction of his house, howling with laughter.

"Let's see if Mum is home," I say, opening my front door, walking in and yelling out for Mum.

"In the kitchen honey," Mum calls out, so we make our way down the hallway.

"Mum, can you help us get Lacey's hair colour back to its original state?" I ask, causing Mum to look at Lacey's hair.

"I don't think it'll be your natural hair colour but I'm sure we can get it a bit blonder at least instead of this orange. It might take some work," she tells us. I show her the two boxes we bought and she umms and ahhs a bit before deciding on the highlighter cap. She tells me to drag a chair into the bathroom for Lacey to sit on, then throws a towel over her shoulders to protect her school uniform. Pulling out the beige looking hair cap she pulls it over Lacey's hair and I can't help but laugh.

"Shush you," Mum says. She grabs the little wooden hook from the box, using it to poke at the holes in the cap and pull strands of hair through. It takes a while but by the end she's satisfied with the amount she's managed to pull through the tiny holes.

"It may not look like much Lacey but it will make a big differ-ence. Next time we can do it again and hopefully pick up more of the orange until eventually it's all gone," she tells us. Reading the instructions and mixing the bleach, I can't help but laugh at Lacey as she looks even worse now with the little streaks of orange hair poking through the cap.

"Stop laughing, this was your idea," she complains, crossing her arms over her chest.

"Sorry Lace. You remind me of those Barbies you had when you were little. Remember, their hair had missing sections where you could see the scalp," I remind her, which makes her burst out laughing at the memory.

"My hair better not fall out or else I will look like those Barbies you have such fond memories of," she says, making us laugh harder.

"Oh you two," Mum chides, hiding her own smile while she applies the bleach to Lacey's hair. Mum quickly covers all the strands with the purple mixture which stinks so bad we have to crack a window to get some fresh air into the room before the fumes make us puke. Mum tells us we need to leave it on for forty five minutes so we listen to music in my room while we wait. When it's time to wash it out, Mum struggles to pull the cap off so tells Lacey she'll wash the bleach off then pull the cap off afterwards.

"Kneel and put your head over the bath honey," Mum instructs Lacey. Lacey kneels and leans over the bath while Mum pulls the shower head from the wall and rinses out the bleach before she washes it with shampoo. Once it's done, she manages to wriggle the cap off, letting the blonde streaks fall against the orange before she washes it again. Her damp hair falls against the towel as she stands.

"We'll have to wait until it dries to see how it looks. If it needs more, we can try again another day," Mum says, as she looks at Lacey in the mirror.

"You wanna have a movie night Lace? We could go check out some new releases and grab some fish and chips if Mum has any money to spare?" I say, causing Mum to laugh.

"Fine. Grab enough for me too," Mum says, walking away as she goes to get her purse.

"I'll run home and get changed out of my uniform then we can go," Lacey says, handing me the towel. Fifteen minutes later we are walking to the video store, Lacey thanking her lucky stars her hair didn't fall out.

"It looks much better already," I tell her.

"You know Chance, I'm still the same Lacey even if my hair is a bit different," she tells me, kicking a stone as we walk.

"I know. I'm sorry if I made a big deal about it. I guess I wanted to rewind and go back to how we were before everything happened and I thought we could do it by changing your hair. I'm sorry," I apologise.

"I wish we could go back too and forget what happened. We should focus on building new memories instead of dwelling on the past."

"I think it's a great idea. Here's to new memories," I say, holding my hand out for a high five which she slaps, laughing. Scanning the video aisle we each pick a new release. I pick *8 Mile* while she picks *Maid in Manhattan* then we order our fish and chips and wait for it before walking home. I grab a blanket from the cupboard and we snuggle under it. Unwrapping our fish and chips from the brown paper, Mum takes her share, leaving the rest on the coffee table for us. We rock, paper, scissors and of course Lacey wins so we watch her movie first.

"Before you guys press play, why don't you run home and tell your dad you're crashing here for the night. Chance can sleep on the couch," Mum says.

"Okay," Lacey says, her glee shining through as she races home at top speed then snuggles back under the blanket again when she returns.

After the two movies are finished, Lacey sleepily walks to my room to crash in my bed. Mum checks on me to make sure I'm on the couch before she heads to bed herself. I wait another half an hour to make sure the coast is clear before I sneak into my room. I know we rekindled our friendship but I can't help but feel the pull of her. She lies cuddled in my blankets on her usual side of the bed. She lifts her head as I creep in, a soft smile on her face is all I can see in the darkness of the room. I crawl onto my side of the bed and get under the covers. Without second guessing it, I press flush up against her back, pulling her into my chest as I wrap my arms around her. I hear her audibly sigh but don't bring attention to it as I feel the same. Falling asleep with a smile on my face, I make a mental note to sneak back to the couch before Mum wakes, which may be hard now I'm settled

LACEY

22ND FEBRUARY
Dear Diary,

Yesterday Chance suggested we fix my hair so we recruited his mum to help us. Now it's dry, it looks pretty good. I don't think I'll risk another bleaching yet as I don't want it falling out. Stupid Theodore has me scared I'll end up bald.

We watched movies last night and ate fish and chips while Chance filled me in on all the gossip about the kids at school from previous years I have missed out on.

Once his mum was asleep, he snuck in and cuddled with me. It was one of the best sleeps I've had in a long time. I know we are getting our friendship back on track but it is hard to hide my feelings I have for him. I don't think I ever stopped loving Chance. Even when I ran away from him, I still loved him. It's probably why it hurt so much because I knew I was breaking both our hearts.

I'll focus on our friendship for now and down the line, hopefully things will fall into place. I can't see my future without Chance in it now. I hope one day he feels the same way and we can give us a proper shot like what should have happened a few years ago before I messed everything up.

I'm off to meet Chance to go get some ice cream so I'll write later. Contemplating life,
Lacey xx

CHAPTER 32

CHANCE

7TH APRIL

Things with Lacey are back to how they used to be. We are back to being best friends and the past is now forgotten. I haven't talked to her about my feelings because I don't want to ruin what we have. I'd rather have her as a friend than nothing at all. She climbs through my window most nights so we can cuddle and sleep together like we did the night we fixed her hair. It's pretty much back to its natural colour with the help of my mum. She has bleached it a few times now and luckily for Lacey it hasn't fallen out.

I have soccer trials for the school team after school today. It's pretty much a given the seniors trying out will make the squad. It's more a formality to see if any of the younger guys are good enough to join our team this year. Lacey said she'd hang around to watch instead of walking home by herself. Theo is still our goalie, the position he's held since third form.

"Why don't you tell her how you feel?" Theo asks again. We have this conversation at least once a week and it's always the same.

"I don't want to wreck our friendship. I lost her once, I don't want to lose her again," I huff out, as we finish changing into our sports gear. Walking to the fields, I catch sight of Lacey lying on the grass with a book open above her. As I get closer, I get a view of the cover and see it's an Animorphs book. I haven't read it yet so I'll have to ask her about it later.

One thing Lacey has gotten from me over the years is my love of reading. Some nights when she climbs in my window, I'll read to her like I did when we were little, which more often than not will send her into a deep sleep. I have to read from where she fell asleep the next night otherwise she gets in a grump because she's missed events. I don't mind, I like having an excuse to cuddle next to her with not a care in the world. Sometimes I wonder if she can see my feelings for her on my face. Theo mentions how I often look at her with lovey dovey eyes, which ends with me punching him in the shoulder while he laughs at me. My heart always picks up speed when she's near and I often think she can hear it or else see it beating out of my chest as it goes so fast at times, especially when she touches my hand or something.

She looks away from her book as she sees us coming. I wave with a huge smile on my face and she returns it with a thumbs up for good luck. We both know it's not needed, making our smiles grow. The trials are over after an hour of running drills and having a game against each other. The coach Mr Jensen tells us he'll have the team list on the gym door tomorrow morning and for us to check it out then. Racing over to where Lacey now stands, endorphins running through my body, I fling her over my shoulder and twirl her around as her laughter rings out.

"Put me down before I puke all over you."

I swing her around a few more times, feeling dizzy myself. I pull her legs towards the ground and hold her around the waist, keeping her feet off the grass. We stare at each other with big smiles on our faces, before I glance at her lips. I notice she does the same, the laughter ceasing as we both realise she's flush against me and if I move forward I could touch her lips.

"Stop messing around you two and let's get home," Theo yells, from the other side of the field, where he's shoving his goalie gloves in his bag, not looking at us. We shake ourselves out of the moment and I drop her on her feet, turning to grab her backpack as I compose myself. Flinging it over my shoulder with my own, I wrap my arm around her shoulder pulling her close as we wait for Theo to join us.

"You guys were looking good out there," she tells us.

"We are hoping to take it out this year. There's one or two young guns who I think would add something to the team but I think it will probably be the same players we've had for the last few years. We work well together."

"Champions. Champions," Theo chants, making us laugh as we head home. The awkwardness of the moment before long forgotten.

LACEY

7TH APRIL

Dear Diary,

I swear Chance was going to kiss me. He looked right at my lips and I watched as his tongue peeked out and licked his own, as if he was subconsciously getting ready to bring them closer to mine. Stupid Theodore interrupted us. I don't know how much longer I can hold these feelings in. It's getting harder every day. Don't get me wrong, I'm so thankful I have my best friend back but sometimes when I climb through his window at night, I wonder what it would be like for us to finally be together as a couple. To finally be able to call him mine.

I already have the girls at school asking me constantly if Chance is my boyfriend. A few of them are convinced we are going out and keeping it to ourselves. I think some of them have crushes on Chance so they stopped flirting with him because they think we are together. I don't blame them because we do act like a couple sometimes but it's how our friendship has always been. I keep holding on to hope one day we will be more than best friends.

I better cut this short as I have a lot of homework tonight.

Hanging on to hope,

Lacey

CHAPTER 33

CHANCE

17TH MAY

Mum finally relented and said I could get a mobile phone. I'm so excited about the news I run over to Lacey's to see if she wants to come with me and Mum to help me pick one out.

"Lacey?" I call, as I walk through her unlocked front door.

"Chance? I thought we were meeting later?" she asks, when I find her lying on her bed, flicking through a *Girlfriend* magazine. Her hair is twisted back in parts with all these colourful, glittery butterfly clips. Girls, I think to myself.

"We were but Mum said she is taking me to get a mobile phone. You wanna come help me pick one out?" I ask.

"Shut up. Really? Yes, I'm coming," she squeals. We've both been wanting our own phones since Theo and a couple of the kids at school have them and they said they can text each other.

"Let's go."

"Daaaadd," Lacey calls out.

"In here," Mr Connelly calls from the lounge, where he sits in front of the TV.

"Dad, Chance is getting a phone and I really want one. Could I get one as an early birthday present?" she pleads, with her hands together as if in prayer.

Her dad watches her, holding in a laugh before sighing, "Okay but it's all you're getting for it. When your birthday comes around, I don't want you complaining about how you didn't get anything for your birthday either."

"Thank you so much Dad," she shrieks, as she jumps into his lap, wrapping her arms tightly around his neck.

"Go and grab my wallet from the room," he says. She races there and back in two seconds flat. Handing him his wallet, he pulls out $150 in cash and hands it to her.

"It's all your birthday money since it's your eighteenth so make sure you get a phone you can afford," he tells her, flapping the money at her before she grabs it between her fingers.

"Love you Dad," she tells him, leaning down and kissing his cheek.

"Let's go, Chance," she says to me. She walks back into her room and slips her pumps on. She grabs her pink highlighter wallet off her bedside table and rips the velcro open. Squishing the notes in, she closes it before pushing the wallet into the back of her flared jeans which hang low on her hips and show off her flat stomach. I can't help but look at the sneaky band of skin peeking out between her jeans and her tank top. She pulls on a puffy jacket, zipping it up and hiding the patch of skin from view.

She tugs on my hand, leading me out of her room as we yell goodbye to her dad and make our way to my mum, who's waiting in the car for us. Driving to the mall Lacey talks about how she wants a sparkly pink phone but if they don't have one, she will bedazzle it so it's nice and sparkly.

"Ugh they don't have any pink ones," she complains, as she looks over all the phones the store has on view.

"I think the orange or yellow one is as good as a pink one if not better," I tell her, pointing out the Alcatel one touch coloured phones.

"Yeah you're right, they do look pretty cool. I'm so excited. Which colour should I get? You pick," she tells me, linking her arm with mine.

"Hmmm, get the yellow," I tell her.

"Okay."

"What one do you want, Chance? Do you want me to get the cashier to grab the yellow one for you honey?" my mum asks us.

"Yes please," Lacey squeaks, as she bounces next to me. A ball of energy.

"I'll grab the blue grey Nokia Mum," I point out, so Mum tells the cashier to get that one too as well as two sim cards. Lacey hands over her cash while Mum pays for mine. We happen to see some funky phone holders shaped like arm chairs so Lacey gets an orange one with her remaining money and Mum buys me a green one. Walking out with our new phones, we can't hide our excitement as we talk the whole car ride home about how cool they are. Rushing to my room when we get home, we open the boxes and quickly read the instructions.

"Ugh, we gotta charge the battery for hours," I complain, pulling out my new phone from the plastic holder. I unwrap the charger and plug it into the socket connecting my phone.

"I'm gonna show Dad and charge mine at home. You wanna do something while we wait?" she asks, heading to my door.

"We could shoot some hoops," I offer.

"Sweet. I'll be back soon," she says, as she takes her haul with her. I sit reading over my phone's instruction booklet, itching to be able to play with it and learn all the functions. The waiting is horrible. Lacey comes back about ten minutes later so I grab my basketball out of the closet and we head outside. It's quite sunny today even though it's getting colder because winter is coming.

"What did your dad think of your phone?" I ask, bouncing the ball on my driveway before taking a shot.

"He said it's super bright," she says, laughing which makes me smile. She chases the ball as I miss and takes her own shot, getting it in.

"Wanna play Donkey?"

"Sure."

I take my shot but miss so Lacey takes her turn. She lines her shot up, making it swish.

"When did you get so good at shooting hoops?" I ask, because the Lacey I knew wasn't coordinated at all.

"The last couple of years I played netball at my old school. I was the goal shoot," she tells me, which has my mouth dropping open.

"You played a sport?" I ask, amazed as I didn't think she had any interest in them. It makes me realise we missed huge chunks of each other's history.

"Yeah. Our team wasn't amazing or anything but it was fun and it helped me make some new friends," she says, as I take another shot and get it in this time.

"What else did you do during the time you were away?" I softly ask, causing her eyes to find mine. Unspoken words pass between us and I wonder if whenever we acknowledge the time we were apart, if there will always be a small amount of pain associated with it.

"Not much. I played netball. I went to parties. I cut my own bangs at one point which Mum was not happy about. I had to pin them back while they grew out because they were horrible," she says, making me laugh.

"When's the baby due?" I ask.

"Next month. I'm quite excited to have a little sister now I've had time to process and get used to the idea," she says, taking a shot.

"Are you gonna visit them?" I ask, as she hasn't gone to see her mum since she got here.

"Mum said the next school holiday after the baby is born she'll get me a plane ticket so I can meet her and spend some time with them."

"That's cool," I say, my heart racing at the fact I would have to spend time apart from her again and even though I know it's for two weeks, it brings back memories of her leaving before.

"Donkey," she yells, as her next shot goes in. "You suck at this game, Chance," she jokes, making me rush her and pick her up around the waist, her back to mine as she holds the basketball. I swing her around, tickling her. My hands slide under her puffy jacket, touching the skin on her stomach I caught sight of earlier. She stills in my arms as a jolt of electricity shocks me. Does she feel it too? Wrapping one arm around her stomach, I place her on the ground, spinning her to face me. Her blue eyes look at me, as we are caught in a trance. Our chests rise and fall as we stare at the other, neither of us moving.

I keep my grip firm on her waist and I'm about to pull her close to me when I hear, "Chance, Lacey, come get something to eat," yelled by my mum, from the back door of my house. Our trance broken, we step back from each other, both turning quickly to go into my house, not mentioning what happened. Eating the sandwiches my mum made in silence, we ignore the moment we had outside.

"Let's check my phone to see if it's charged," I tell Lacey, as I gulp some water, washing down my last mouthful of food. She quickly does the same then we rush to my room.

"It's charged," I tell her, grabbing it off the charger. She races out of the room not saying a thing and I know she's running home to check her own phone. She's back a few minutes later with her phone and its box. We sit silently going through functions on our phone, learning how they work. We save each other's new numbers and then send text messages to each other while we are sitting side by side on my carpet, leaning against my bed.

"Aww cool, mine has a game called *Snake*," I tell her, as I play the game. Watching the snake move around the screen and directing it so it doesn't hit itself. It quickly becomes addictive and Lacey wants a turn. We spend the rest of the day playing on our phones before Lacey heads home for dinner. While lying in bed, I decide to text Lacey.

Chance: *Good night x*

Her reply is instant and my eyes light up when I hear the text notification sound.

Lacey: *Sweet dreams x*

I smile to myself before powering my phone off and turning my lamp off so I can go to sleep.

LACEY

17TH MAY

Dear Diary,

I got a mobile phone today. I can't believe it. Dad let me get one. I know it's for my birthday but still. It's so cool. It's a bright yellow colour which makes me think of sunshine. I would have loved a pink one but I must say the yellow is growing on me.

Chance's phone has this cool snake game on it. I can't wait to play it tomorrow and beat his high score. I'm sure he's been playing it all evening trying to get as high as he can, so I can't beat him.

We had another moment today while we were playing basketball. I'm so sure he would have kissed me if his mum hadn't interrupted. I should bite the bullet and kiss him and see what happens. I'm scared as we are back to a good place and I don't want to wreck it again.

It's so easy when I'm with him. It's as if the world fades away and we are the only people around. If I could have that feeling forever, wouldn't it be worth it? Isn't that what love is supposed to feel like? Like nothing else matters in the world except the two people in the moment? I think it would be amazing to have that type of forever love. The type of love they show in the romance movies I love watching.

Chance texted me to say good night. These phones are the coolest things ever. I'm going to reply then go to sleep.

Sweet dreams,

Lacey

CHAPTER 34

CHANCE

5TH JULY

I'm anxious today as Lacey is leaving. She's not leaving me for good but she's travelling to the South Island to visit her mum. She had her baby sister Rachel a few weeks ago and Lacey is extremely excited to meet her. She hasn't stopped talking about her new sister since the day she was born.

She mentioned her dad was sad after the announcement of her birth but he's come to terms with the fact his ex wife has moved on. Lacey's happy he hasn't turned to drinking but instead is attending more AA meetings to keep on top of things and how he's feeling.

When she talks of her dad now you can hear the pride in her voice. There was a point in time I didn't think she would feel that way about her dad again. I'm glad they've been able to mend their relationship. He is a great man and has been like a father figure to me over the years. He lost himself for a while but is back on track now.

He gave Lacey some money yesterday so she could buy her new sister a present. We went to the mall after school and she dragged me into a baby store where she gushed over how tiny all the clothes were. She picked out a pink outfit, of course it had to be pink. I'm grateful she's got a sister so she can inflict her pink craze onto someone else.

"Chance, Dad is taking me to the airport now. Come say good-bye," I hear Lacey call, when she enters my front door. I kick my feet off the side of the bed, huffing as I traipse down the hallway to meet her. One look at my face and she bursts into laughter.

"Aww Chancey, I'll be back in no time. You have Theodore to keep you company in the meantime," she says, walking back out the door knowing I will follow.

"It's not the same," I sulk, following her steps along the concrete path to her driveway.

"Two weeks will fly by. You'll see," she tells me, turning to face me.

"Are you sure you're coming back?" I ask, eyes on the ground pretending to kick a stone. I watch as her pink sneakers come into view before she wraps her arms around my waist. I move my arms, wrapping them tightly around her shoulders, squishing her into my chest.

"I'll never leave you again. I promise," she says, quietly.

"Pinky promise?" I ask, which has her angling her face to look at me. A bright smile shines at me, taking my breath away.

"Pinky promise," she replies, releasing one arm to hold out her pinky. A smile tugs at my lips as I link my pinky with hers.

"And lock it," I tell her, holding my thumb out, making her smile grow as she presses her thumb to mine.

"Better now?" she whispers, as we both wrap our arms back around the other, staring into each other's eyes.

"Come on Lacey. Let's get a wriggle on," her dad calls, as he lugs her black suitcase to the back of his car.

"Five more minutes Dad?" she asks, without breaking our stare off.

"Sure, if you want to miss your flight we can wait another five minutes," her dad jokes. "It's two weeks, kids. You'll be together again soon," he tells us, as he opens his driver's side door, hops in and waits for Lacey.

"Not soon enough," I say to her.

"You'll be okay without me, won't you?" she asks, worry lining her forehead.

I don't want her worrying about me so I say, "I'll be fine. You enjoy your time with your mum and your sister." Her smile slips back onto her face and it makes me want to tell her my true feelings before she goes.

"Lace?" I say. The beeping of her dad's car horn has us jumping before she rolls her eyes.

"Coming Dad," she yells, turning her head to him then back to me. "I better go Chancey," she says, before she presses her lips quickly to mine. It happens so fast I don't realise she kissed me until she's walking around the side of the car and hopping into the passenger seat. I stand rooted to the spot as they reverse out of the driveway, both waving frantically at me. All I can think about is the fact her lips still give me the tingles and I wonder if she meant to do it or if it was an accident. Damn it's going to be a long two weeks.

LACEY

5TH JULY

Dear Diary,

I'm on the plane heading to meet my sister for the first time. I can't believe I have a little sister. I can't wait to see her and hold her. I hope they like the outfit I picked out for her. It's a teeny pale pink dress which is so cute.

I have something to confess. I kissed Chance. I did it but I'm a coward because I did it at the last second before I left. I had a feeling he was going to say something but my dad interrupted us with his car horn and I had to go. I stole a kiss from Chance before he even realised what I was doing. I needed something to get me through the next two weeks.

I know he's going to miss me but I'm going to miss him too. I've gotten so used to falling asleep in his arms. I haven't told him I struggle to sleep when I'm in my own bed now. I usually toss and turn until I fall asleep because I try not to go to Chance's window every night. I don't want to be a bother.

Hopefully I'll have the guts to tell him how I feel about him when I get back. Let's hope these two weeks don't drag out too long.

We're landing soon so I better go.

Kiss stealer,

Lacey

CHAPTER 35

CHANCE

12TH JULY

Theo has been hounding me all week to go to a party with him tonight. I finally relented and told him I'd go. It was his birthday last month so he's saying this is his night to celebrate his belated birthday. He had a fancy dinner at a restaurant with all his extended family so we didn't do anything for him at the time. We walk to Joel's house with Miles. Joel's a year younger than us and he's having a party because his parents are out of town for the weekend. Theo got wind of it and wanted to go since it's a change from our usual parties at Kyle's place.

"Have you heard from Lacey?" Miles asks, as we walk along taking skulls of the bottle of vodka Theo bought from the alcohol shop since he's of legal age now.

"Yeah we text sometimes. She's quite busy with her mum and sister."

"One more week until she's back man," Miles says, patting me on the back.

"You're such a sad sack Chance. Come on, cheer up. Tell the girl you wanna be her boyfriend already," Theo chimes in, before taking a skull, then coughing from the burn.

"Yeah, I reckon it's about time you told her man. It's obvious you both like each other," Miles says.

"You reckon?"

"You'd have to be blind not to see how you guys look at each other," Miles tells me, cheering me up a bit. I take a skull, loosening up as the liquor warms me on the inside.

Arriving at the party after a half hour walk we are buzzed when we walk through the front door. Kids from both year levels surround us. There's a lot more people here than at our usual parties. We walk through the lounge where a few couples are already making out on the couch, while others dance to the loud music pumping through the speakers. In the kitchen we find Luke and Kyle chatting to a couple of girls from school while Emma sits on the kitchen bench, sipping on a fruity lolly drink. We say hi to everyone and then Emma slides off the bench coming to stand beside me.

"Hey Chance, can I have a quick word?" she asks quietly. Staring at her she doesn't look drunk so I nod. She pulls on my shirt sleeve, leading me towards the hallway where it's quieter.

"What's this about?" I ask, not wanting to sound abrupt but it comes out that way.

"Do you like Lacey?" she blurts.

"What? No," I deny.

She lets out a huge sigh before saying, "You know I reckon you like her and I wanted to say I think you should ask her out."

"Why would you want me to ask her out?" I ask, because since we broke up she's been trying to get back with me.

She takes a gulp from her drink before saying, "I realised something on the last day of the school term. I was watching you, I know a stalker right. I was watching you and you were with Theo talking to him about something and then your face changed. I swear it was like a total one eighty. One minute you had a straight face looking at Theo and then you turned and your face glowed as you smiled at whatever you saw." I raise a brow at her not understanding. "It was Lacey. She was what you were looking at when your face changed. She looked happy to see you too. I know you and I were together and I'll always be sorry for cheating on you but I can honestly say you never once looked at me like you looked at her. It's how I know there's no point trying to get you back when you are clearly in love with someone else," she says. I don't know how to respond so I don't say a word. "It's okay Chance, I wanted to clear the air and say I'm sorry again for how we ended. If you like Lacey then go for it. With the way she looks at you, she definitely feels the same."

"Thanks Emma," I tell her, before giving her a friendly hug then heading back to the guys. I find Theo doing shots with Miles, Luke and Kyle and decline when they offer me one. I want to stay at least semi sober so I can get us home after Theo and Miles helped get me home the last time. I keep an eye on Theo as he has a lot more shots than the others and then he parks himself next to Missy who he begs to give him another chance. She didn't take him back after she caught him dancing with the girl at Kyle's party. I don't think he intentionally meant to hurt her and he hasn't looked at another girl this whole year. I've asked him about Missy a few times but he changes the subject pretty quick.

Missy is listening to him as he drunkenly tries to talk to her. I stand behind the couch mouthing to Missy if she wants me to take him away but she shakes her head with a smile, happy to listen to his drunken rant. I take a seat on an armchair not too far from them to keep an eye on Theo in case he gets out of hand. Miles is still in the kitchen with Kyle and Luke and I think he's nearly ready to head home so it's a waiting game to see when we can tear Theo away from Missy.

I pull out my phone from my front pocket and see I have a text message. I open it and it was sent from Lacey a short while ago.

Lacey: *Are you awake?*

I quickly send a text message of my own.

Chance: *Yeah at a party with Theo. You OK?*

I stare at my phone waiting to see if she replies straight away or if she's fallen asleep as it's after midnight now. I'm about to play *Snake* to pass the time when a text pops through.

Lacey: *Miss you*

Reading her message I sigh, half from the alcohol in my system and half from the fact I miss her. When she's gone it's like my world is dull and empty.

Chance: *I really miss you*

I reply and because I've had a bit to drink I feel brave. It's also a lot easier asking in a text message than in person so I don't have to see her face.

Chance: *Do you regret having sex with me?*

I stare at it for the longest time before taking a big breath, closing my eyes and hitting send. Theo distracts me as his voice increases in volume as he's pleading now with Missy to give him another shot. I nearly miss the text that comes in.

Lacey: *No. I'm glad it was you.*

Lacey: *Do you regret it?*

She sends a second text and I instantly reply.

Chance: *No. I'm glad it was you too.*

Feeling brave, I ask something else.

Chance: *Have you done it with anyone else?*

I tap my foot as I anxiously wait for her answer.

Lacey: *No. Have you?*

Breathing a sigh of relief I reply.

Chance: *No me neither.*

Miles walks into the room once I send my message.

"Should we head out?" I ask, nodding my head towards Theo on the couch.

"Yeah, let's get him home," he agrees, so I take one last look at my phone and see I missed a text message.

Lacey: *Gonna sleep now. Get home safe.*

Chance: *Heading home now. Theo's drunk.*

"Come on mate, let's get you home," I tell Theo, as we walk over to him and Missy.

"How about you give me a ring tomorrow Theo and we'll talk when you're sober," Missy tells Theo, which he agrees to.

"How are you getting home Missy?" I ask, while Miles helps Theo stand. He's not as wobbly on his feet as I thought so at least he should be able to walk unassisted part of the way home.

"Can you guys walk me? It's on the way and not too far," she tells us.

"Yeah come on. We'll get you home safely," Theo tells her, slinging an arm around her. Having her with us means he's guaranteed to leave which is good. Missy's house is a few blocks away from the party and we watch as she removes her shoes then quietly enters her front door, not wanting to wake anyone. Knowing she's inside and safe, we carry on our walk home with Theo telling us about how much he misses her. I didn't realise how much he liked her as he's not one to talk about his feelings. If I'd paid closer attention I would have seen he'd given up talking to other girls in any way other than friendly. No flirting or cheeky smiles with anyone but Missy which is a big change for him.

Miles tells me he will come out of his way to help me walk Theo home but I convince Theo to crash at my house instead since both our parents knew we were at a party tonight. It's only a big deal if we sneak out without permission. He hands me his phone so I can text his brother Anthony and let him know Theo is safe and crashing at mine. We drop Miles off at his house and Theo and I carry on to mine which isn't too much further.

"You gonna get your girl or what?" Theo slurs, as he staggers down the sidewalk.

"Yeah, I think I am," I tell him, which has him patting my back.

"It's about bloody time," he says, making us both laugh.

Making it to my place, I set Theo up on the couch before opening Mum's door and letting her know I'm home and Theo is crashing on the couch. I walk to my room, kick my shoes off and pull my shirt and jeans off, before crawling into bed. Hopping under the covers I remember my phone so I grab my jeans off the floor and get my phone out of the pocket. I check for any messages but there are none. I text Lacey letting her know I got home safely before I power my phone off and close my eyes, filled with optimism everything will work out with us after all.

LACEY

12TH JULY
Dear Diary,

Oh how I miss Chance. Don't get me wrong, I love spending time with Rachel and my mum and Doug but her routine gets repetitive and boring. She sleeps, gets breastfed by Mum, brings the milk back up so needs an outfit change and then goes back to sleep. I'm not sure she even knows I'm here half the time but she is cute to cuddle when she's sleeping. Not so much when she's screaming blue murder because she's hungry.

One more week and then I'll be back with Chance and Dad and I can't wait. I know I've lived here for a few years but I don't think it ever felt like my home. My home has always been where Chance is. I can't wait to get back to it.

I couldn't sleep tonight because I was missing him so much and I've had trouble sleeping here without him. There's no way I'm telling him. I messaged him and he was out at a party. I don't think he was drinking much as his texts didn't sound like he was drunk.

He said he hasn't had sex with anyone else and I can't say his confession didn't make me happy. When we did it, it was for all the wrong reasons. I'm glad we both haven't been with anyone else and I'm hoping he feels the same way as I do about him.

Hopefully when I get back I will be brave enough to tell him. I'm sure he feels the same way, I'm too chicken to ask him. Hopefully I'll find the courage. I have a whole week left to build some up before I see him again.

Better try to sleep as it's after midnight now.

Seeking courage,

Lacey

CHAPTER 36

CHANCE

25TH JULY

It's been a week since Lacey came home from visiting her mum and sister. She hasn't mentioned the kiss she gave me before she left and she hasn't mentioned the text messages from when I was at the party either. I'm doubting myself now. Does she feel the same way about me or not? I've looked for clues all week but it's the same Lacey she's always been. It's not like she has a big neon sign above her head saying 'I have feelings for you.' Although I wish she did because it would make my life so much easier.

It's Friday afternoon now and we've got a talent show for the last two periods of school. Students signed up and have been practising since before the holidays. We all file into the gym, taking seats on the floor with our legs crossed. The teachers don't care where we sit as long as we are in rows of our year group. The young ones are at the front and the students in their final year of school, like us, get to sit right at the back. I find Lacey as all the students push through the double doors, finding a spot to sit. I grab hold of her sleeve, tugging until she looks at me. Locking eyes with me, she steps around a girl until she's beside me then I grab her hand, pulling her along behind me, to find a seat. We manage to find Theo and Miles together so sit with them.

During the talent show we laugh at the comedy act one of the guys from our year performs. I'm amazed at all the students who have great singing voices too. There were a few who were nervous and you could tell they had talent, if only their voices didn't crack while singing. There were also a couple of group dance performances and some single dancers as well. Sitting next to Lacey, I can't help but look over at her every time she laughs. Theo has been telling me every day to tell her how I feel and every time I go to tell her, it's as if my throat closes and I can't get the words out. While I'm lost in my own thoughts, wondering how to tell Lacey, she taps her finger against my knee. I look at her but her eyes remain on the front of the gym where someone is singing.

"Some of these singers remind me of you when you'd have your headphones on and you'd be blasting Mariah Carey and singing at the top of your lungs," she whispers, making herself giggle. I smile at the memories.

"Don't lie. You loved it when I sang to you," I tease, making her laugh harder.

"I didn't want you to feel bad so I pretended to enjoy it," she teases back. While she's laughing, an idea strikes me in the head. Music. It's always been a big component of our friendship. I could tell her how I feel in a song.

The last performer finishes and the music teacher Mrs Darcy comes to the microphone, "That concludes the talent show we had scheduled for today but before I dismiss you I'd like to open the floor to anyone who would like to add a last minute performance. Any takers?" My hands begin to sweat, I feel the pounding in my chest and the voice in my head pushes me so far out of my comfort zone I feel I might puke. Sometimes you gotta go hard or go home.

"I'll make you a deal," I quickly turn to Lacey, who raises her brows at me with a smile on her face.

"What?"

"If I sing you a song, you gotta promise me something," I tell her, rushing to get my words out.

Her brows raise even higher before she stutters, "You're gonna go sing? Are you serious?" her smile growing.

"Deadly serious. You in?" I ask.

"Okay but no crying to me when everyone laughs at your off key singing," she jokes, laughing.

"Pinky promise," I tell her, holding out my pinky which she takes, and then she holds out her thumb.

"And lock," she reminds me, causing my smile to grow.

"I'll sing," I yell out into the crowd, causing Theo and Miles to cheer me on.

"I can't believe you are doing this," Lacey squeals, as she squeezes my knee. I turn to her, watching her face light up and it motivates me to stand, believing the risk I'm taking will pay off. I'm about to step around students and make my way to the front when I feel a pull on my pants leg.

"Chance, you didn't tell me what I promised you," Lacey squeaks, finally realising she made a promise not knowing what it was for. I bend down and bring my face close to hers.

I grasp her jaw softly with my hand, angling it before I whisper in her ear, "You promised to love me forever." I move my face back in front of her, staring into her wide eyes while I gently pinch her chin before letting go and making my way through the crowd. Taking the microphone off Mrs Darcy, I realise because I'm doing this on a whim, I don't have any music prepared so I'm going to have to sing acapella. Let's hope I don't sound too horrible. I've got the love of the only girl I've ever wanted riding on this.

The room quietens, all eyes on me, waiting for me to sing. I take a deep breath and risk it all for my girl, my best friend, hoping she feels the same. I sing the words to the song *I think I'm in Love With You* by Jessica Simpson. A song from our childhood and one of the many I could have chosen from. There will be no mistaking how I feel with these lyrics and that's the point. I need her to finally understand how I feel about her. Singing the lyrics, I'm glad I still remember them. I lock eyes on a shocked Lacey as she sits in the same spot, watching me. The room is silent apart from my cracking voice, sounding through the speakers. At this point I know my voice is making some people cringe but I don't care as my gaze is locked on the person who matters right now. The only person who has ever mattered. I make my way through the crowd of students to Lacey, singing my heart out. I hold my hand out for Lacey to take, pulling her to stand in front of me. Clasping her hand I can feel hers shake within mine as I finish the song, dropping my hand with the microphone by my side.

"You're in love with me?" she asks, as I tuck a stray hair behind her ear.

"I think I've been in love with you since the day we met when you claimed half of my tree for yourself," I tell her, which forces the biggest smile to appear on her face.

"Okay," is all she says. My brows pull together.

"Okay?" I ask.

"Okay, I promise to love you forever," she tells me, my own smile growing. I look beside her and throw the microphone into Theo's lap. I swiftly pick up my girl, bringing my lips to hers, as she wraps her arms around my neck, holding on tight. The tingles shoot through me, as I move my lips against hers and the crowd breaks out in a thunderous cheer. I kiss her for as long as I can and even then it's not enough, before I pull away. Both of us with stupid smiles on our faces.

"I'm gonna hold you to that promise," I tell her, still holding her off the ground.

"You better," she replies, before leaning in and taking my lips between hers once again.

EPILOGUE

CHANCE

MANY YEARS LATER

Sitting under the familiar weeping willow tree I can't help but feel a sense of calm rush over me as I lean my back against the rough bark. This always was my favourite spot. Flipping the last page of the hard covered book, I place it in a pile with the others before grabbing the pretty pink box in my hands. To some it may not look like much but this box is my whole world.

"Hey Papa," I hear the tiny voice call, somewhere above me in the tree branches. Glancing upwards I catch sight of my grand-daughter Celeste straddling one of the many branches, high in the foliage.

"How long have you been there?" I ask, unsure if she passed me or not while I was sitting here.

"A while. I was listening to you talk to Nana," she admits, which has me smiling.

"Come on down, would you? Your mum is probably wondering where you are," I tell her. She rolls her eyes, the splitting image of her nana but she listens and climbs down. Right on cue her mum, my daughter Hope, calls out for her from the back door of my house.

"You better hurry," I tell her. She makes it to the bottom of the tree safely before standing in front of me.

"Do you need help carrying the books inside?" she offers.

"No, it's okay Celeste. Remember they're called diaries," I tell her, smiling at her.

"Yes, diaries. I remember now," she tells me.

"Celeste, come on inside now," Hope calls out again.

"I better go. Bring Nana in soon, it's getting cold," she tells me, before running to her mother.

"I will, I promise," I say, watching as she runs away. "She reminds me so much of you," I say, as I place the pink box on the grass, digging through the diaries to find the one I'm after. Once I find it, I pick up the weathered book with the peeling cover, worn from all the rereads it's had. I flick to the first few pages finding the spot I'm after and reread it.

Dear Diary,

I'm currently sitting in a hospital bed with my dad sitting in the chair next to me. I can't help but admire my new cast. It's a pretty shade of pink (my favourite colour ever) and is the coolest thing I've ever gotten. I have my new friend Chance to thank for it. I think he's super special.

I knew the moment I laid eyes on him, he was special. He's like those treasures you find that you don't want anyone else to have so you bury it in your favourite box where you can keep it safe and no one else will ever find it. When you pull it out of your box and hold it in your hand, you know deep in your bones how special it is and it brings a smile to your face because it's yours. It's the exact feeling I got when I truly saw Chance for the first time and he showed me his scar. He was my treasure. I can't lock him in my favourite box but I can do anything in the world to keep him safe and it's what I'm going to do.

Beyond excited,

Lacey

Picking up the pink wooden box, I hold it tightly in my hands. Closing my eyes, a smile comes to my face before a lone tear slides down my old, wrinkled cheek. I swipe it away feeling the now faded scar on my skin. Lace was right, I do feel it in my bones how special the treasure in my box is. You see Lace, my love, died a few years back after spending a lifetime together. She always thought of me as her treasure but she was the hero of our story. She endured so much and still managed to find a way through my stubbornness to bring us back together. It's why I keep her ashes in this treasure box. I like to come out to our old tree once in a while and relive the memories with her. The good, the bad and the ugly memories. They may not be important in the grand scheme of things but they are important to us. Like we said all those years ago, ours is a friendship so great one day they'll write stories about it. We didn't realise way back when Lacey was writing our stories in the pages of her diaries. A tradition she continued until the end.

"Let's get you inside Lace," I whisper to the precious box in my hands, tucking it under my arm, as I steady myself to stand. I make the familiar trek back to my house as I carefully hold her diaries and my so-called treasure box safely in my hands.

THE END

PLAYLIST FOR CHANCE & LACEY

'All I Want For Christmas is You' by Mariah Carey
'All I Have to Give' by Backstreet Boys
'Fantasy' by Mariah Carey
'Anything' by 3T
'How do I Live' by LeAnn Rimes
'I Want You Back' by N'Sync
'All 4 Love' by Color Me Badd
'I Love Your Smile' by Shanice
'I Can't Make You Love Me' by Bonnie Raitt
'Amazed' by Lonestar
'Dreamlover' by Mariah Carey
'Crazy for This Girl' by Evan and Jaron
'Gone' by N'Sync
'If You Come Back' by Blue
'I Think I'm in Love With You' by Jessica Simpson
'Mysterious Girl' by Peter Andre
'Happiness' by Billy Lawrence
'MMMBop' by Hanson

FEEDBACK

Did you enjoy this book? Would you like to give feedback? Did you know word of mouth is what makes the publishing world go round? It's especially true for an indie author like me.

If you enjoyed reading this book, please feel free to share your opinions or post a review online. We would love to hear from you. Or even better, let your friends know and encourage them to read the book.

Check out my Facebook and Instagram. I love hearing from my readers.

www.facebook/sarahdelanywrites

www.instagram/sarahdelanywrites

If you enjoyed this book, you may enjoy my other books. I have written three others and they make up the TNT Trilogy. They are available on KU (Kindle Unlimited) in ebook form. They are available for purchase on Amazon in ebook and paperback form. You can also purchase them in paperback form from many online bookstores. If money is a problem, you can also borrow them from your local library. Did you know if it's not available in your local library, you can recommend it to the librarian. They are always looking for new books for their patrons. It's a great way to help and support indie authors like me.

ABOUT THE AUTHOR

------Sarah Delany------

Chance & Lacey is Sarah Delany's fourth novel and her first standalone book.

She is one of eight siblings, has a loving partner and is a stay at home mother to four boys and one girl. That's right, since she wrote her last novel she has become a mother again.

The reason she knows the butter trick is because that's exactly what happened to her when she was younger. Sarah is a New Zealander who currently resides in Brisbane, Australia.

www.ingramcontent.com/pod-product-compliance
Lightning Source LLC
Chambersburg PA
CBHW020354120726
47904CB00002B/560